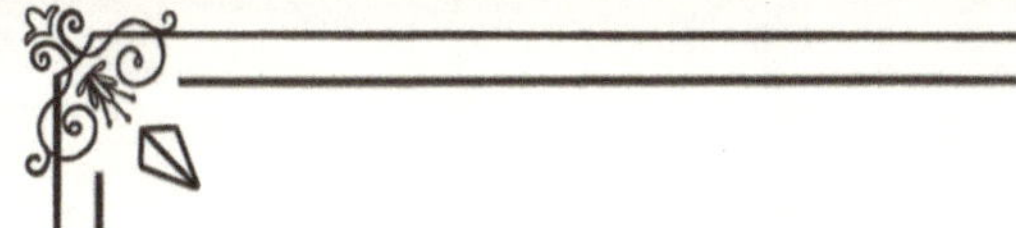

DRAGON SAGA

BOOK FOUR

THE FRACTURED SOUL

NICOLETTE
ANDREWS

Editing by Katie Crum & Charity Chimni
Case Laminate Art by Lauren Richelieu
Dust Jacket Art by Msriza
Exterior Design & Interior Formatting by Charity Chimni
Interior artwork by Nadica Borshkova

First Edition

This book was made possible by the amazing Charity, thank you for working so hard and helping keep me sane!

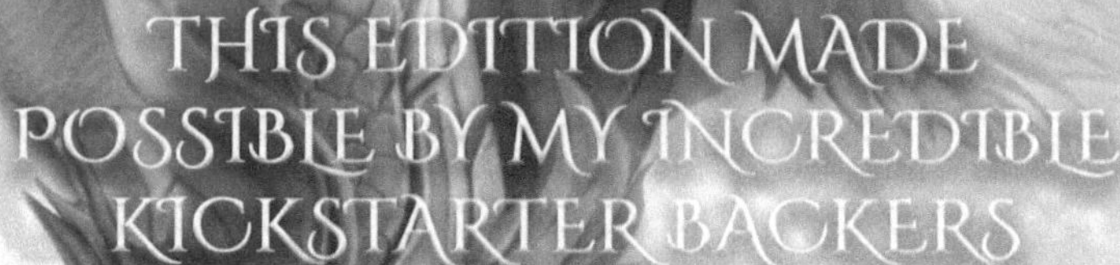

THIS EDITION MADE POSSIBLE BY MY INCREDIBLE KICKSTARTER BACKERS

EXTRA SPECIAL THANKS TO:

ALAINA CARGILL, AMBI CESE, ARIEL S, CAYLA H., CHEYENNE THOMPSON, LAUREN WAYMAN, LISA L, MARIA MEJIA, MARINA HATFIELD, MORGAN RANGIER, RACHEL, RACHEL RASMUSSEN

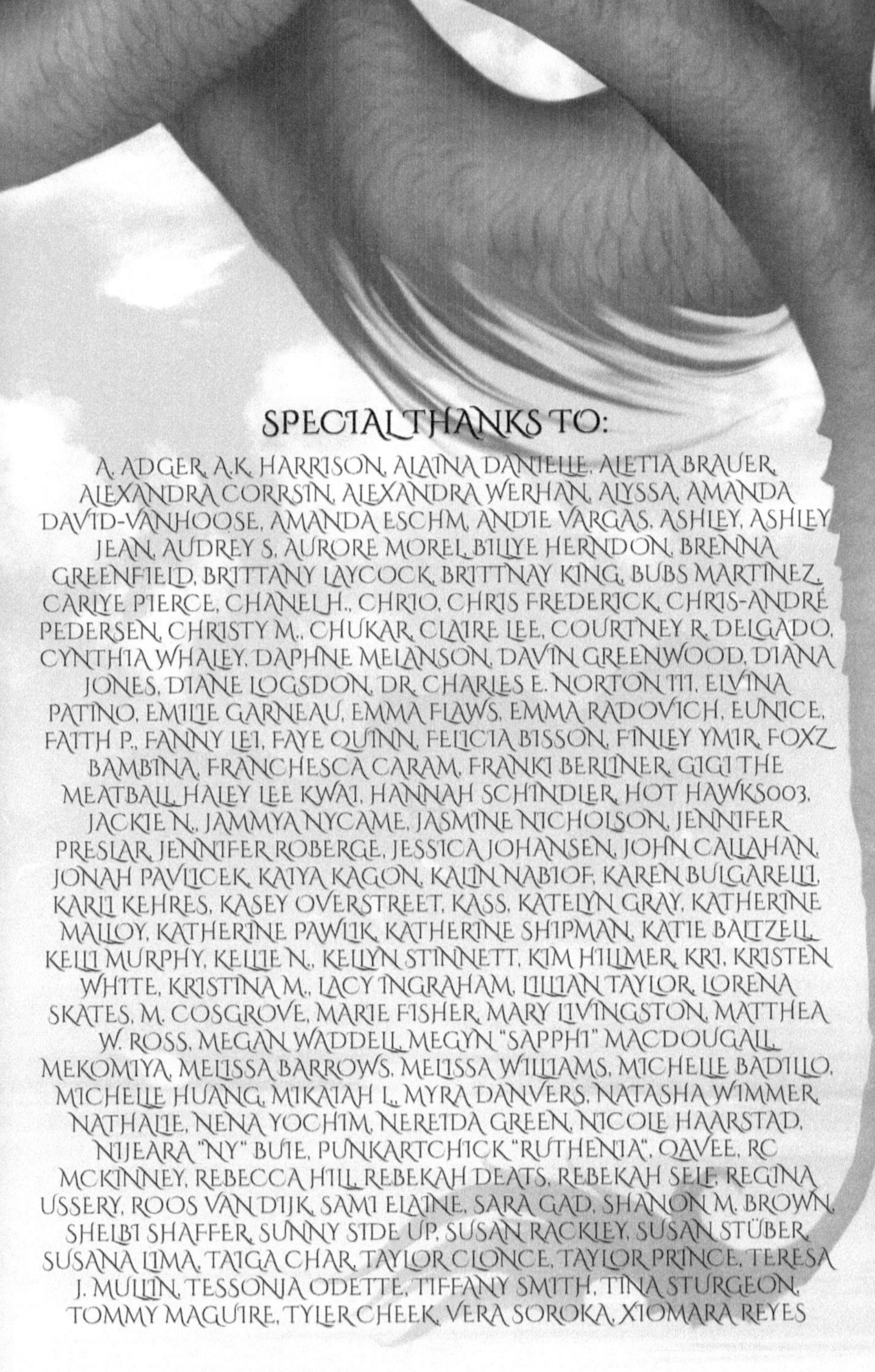

SPECIAL THANKS TO:

A. ADGER, A.K. HARRISON, ALAINA DANIELLE, ALETIA BRAUER, ALEXANDRA CORRSIN, ALEXANDRA WERHAN, ALYSSA, AMANDA DAVID-VANHOOSE, AMANDA ESCHM, ANDIE VARGAS, ASHLEY, ASHLEY JEAN, AUDREY S. AURORE MOREL, BILLYE HERNDON, BRENNA GREENFIELD, BRITTANY LAYCOCK, BRITTNAY KING, BUBS MARTINEZ, CARLYE PIERCE, CHANEL H., CHRIO, CHRIS FREDERICK, CHRIS-ANDRÉ PEDERSEN, CHRISTY M., CHUKAR, CLAIRE LEE, COURTNEY R. DELGADO, CYNTHIA WHALEY, DAPHNE MELANSON, DAVIN GREENWOOD, DIANA JONES, DIANE LOGSDON, DR. CHARLES E. NORTON III, ELVINA PATINO, EMILIE GARNEAU, EMMA FLAWS, EMMA RADOVICH, EUNICE, FAITH P., FANNY LEI, FAYE QUINN, FELICIA BISSON, FINLEY YMIR, FOXZ BAMBINA, FRANCHESCA CARAM, FRANKI BERLINER, GIGI THE MEATBALL, HALEY LEE KWAI, HANNAH SCHINDLER, HOT HAWKS003, JACKIE N., JAMMYA NYCAME, JASMINE NICHOLSON, JENNIFER PRESLAR, JENNIFER ROBERGE, JESSICA JOHANSEN, JOHN CALLAHAN, JONAH PAVLICEK, KATYA KAGON, KALIN NABIOF, KAREN BULGARELLI, KARLI KEHRES, KASEY OVERSTREET, KASS, KATELYN GRAY, KATHERINE MALLOY, KATHERINE PAWLIK, KATHERINE SHIPMAN, KATIE BALTZELL, KELLI MURPHY, KELLIE N., KELLYN STINNETT, KIM HILLMER, KRI, KRISTEN WHITE, KRISTINA M., LACY INGRAHAM, LILLIAN TAYLOR, LORENA SKATES, M. COSGROVE, MARIE FISHER, MARY LIVINGSTON, MATTHEA W. ROSS, MEGAN WADDELL, MEGYN "SAPPHT" MACDOUGALL, MEKOMIYA, MELISSA BARROWS, MELISSA WILLIAMS, MICHELLE BADILLO, MICHELLE HUANG, MIKAIAH L., MYRA DANVERS, NATASHA WIMMER, NATHALIE, NENA YOCHIM, NEREIDA GREEN, NICOLE HAARSTAD, NIJEARA "NY" BUIE, PUNKARTCHICK "RUTHENIA", QAVEE, RC MCKINNEY, REBECCA HILL, REBEKAH DEATS, REBEKAH SELF, REGINA USSERY, ROOS VAN DIJK, SAMI ELAINE, SARA GAD, SHANON M. BROWN, SHELBI SHAFFER, SUNNY SIDE UP, SUSAN RACKLEY, SUSAN STÜBER, SUSANA LIMA, TAIGA CHAR, TAYLOR CLONCE, TAYLOR PRINCE, TERESA J. MULLIN, TESSONJA ODETTE, TIFFANY SMITH, TINA STURGEON, TOMMY MAGUIRE, TYLER CHEEK, VERA SOROKA, XIOMARA REYES

Lord of the Sea's Palace
Namahane Village
Hidden Temple
Mt. Kiriyama
Aokigahara Forest
Mt. Iwaki
Temple of Mt. Iwaki
Kaedemori Clan House
Mountain God's Shrine
Tengu Mountain
White Palace
Sun Temple
Osaka
Kaito's Palace

ONE

Suzume's body ached down to her bones. Dragging leaden feet, she staggered down the hall. A frigid wind blew off the ocean, and a chill crept up her spine. With winter closing in, the days had gotten shorter, and lately, she'd been rising before the sun. An ungodly hour to be precise. What was more shocking was the fact that she did it willingly. Even she was surprised with herself. In the past, she would have only left the comfort of her futon this early kicking and screaming. The constant twinges in her shoulders and ever-present exhaustion would have been ample reason to sleep in.

Cracking opening her heavy-lidded eyes, she flicked her wrist and cloaked herself in ambient heat created by her spiritual power. Bless Ryuu for teaching her the warming trick, it made dawn practice that much more bearable. Seeing improvement in her abilities drove her. Her control over her power wasn't perfect, not yet, but each day she was getting closer. And knowing that made long days of practice worth it. But the warmth of her flame did make her sleepier, and she ambled down the hall in a daze.

"Watch it!" A jorōgumo, hung upside down in the hall, her black hair dangling close enough to tickle Suzume's nose.

Suzume jumped backward and drew her staff. It had been careless to let her guard down, even for a second. Kaito's palace was crawling with hostile yokai. And jorōgumo, half-woman, and half-spider yokai were notoriously vicious. Her top half was that of a woman, with the eight legs of a spider coming from her back.

"Don't try anything, or I will burn you to ash," Suzume said, pointing her staff toward the jorōgumo. She was wide awake now.

"Don't you point that thing at me," hissed the jorōgumo, "you're the one who nearly burned all my work with your carelessness." She gestured toward the glistening threads of her web crisscrossing the hall.

"Are you sure you're supposed to be making webs here?" Suzume asked, taunting her was probably a bad idea, but she wouldn't let the jorōgumo intimidate her.

The jorōgumo opened her mouth, revealing pincers behind her human mouth.

"My mistake," Suzume replied, sheathing her staff once more. On second thought, perhaps it was best to back away slowly. She'd had run-ins with spider-yokai before, and that was enough for her. She scurried away, before the jorōgumo took it in her head to wrap Suzume in that web.

Half asleep as she had been, she'd forgotten for a moment where she was, and what dangers lurked in these halls. While Suzume had trained and perfected her control over her power, Kaito and his subjects had been restoring his palace and his kingdom. Every day more and more yokai arrived, pleading their allegiance to Kaito. It still felt unreal, as if she had stepped into an alternate world, similar to the one she had grown up in but wholly inhabited by yokai.

Outside the halls of the inner palace, she ran past a group of yokai repairing a roof. A gashadokuro, a three-story tall living skeleton handed materials to a group of itachi, weasel yokai, on the rooftop. The gashadokuro turned empty cavernous eye sockets in her direction. Suzume looked away and quickened her pace. But the rattle of its bones followed her footsteps. Ever since it had arrived at the palace, it had given her the creeps; you never knew if he was looking at you or not, but you could always hear him coming. But as creepy as it was, the itachi were far worse. Given the chance, they were likely to trip her or change her tea for seawater. It was fortunate they were busy with repairs, or she might have become the target of one of their pranks.

She weaved her way through the crowded courtyard, past a tsubere otoshi, a floating disembodied head, who balanced wooden planks, and yokai with giant puffed cheeks who blew fire onto forges while another blue muscled yokai hammered metal with a hammer bigger than Suzume's skull.

Making eye contact with yokai was inviting a fight, and so she kept her head down as she walked. But being this close to so many yokai set her teeth on edge and her skin crawling. Before Ryuu had taught her how to suppress her spiritual power at will, she would have been sparking uncontrollably.

Even trying to keep a low profile, eyes followed her. When Kaito had declared Suzume as his woman and under his protection, rather than shield her, he'd put a target on her back. At first, it didn't bother her too much. From the moment she'd discovered her power, she had been a target for yokai aggression. Besides growing up in the White Palace, she'd always lived her life looking over her shoulder. Kaito's seaside palace wasn't much different. His courtiers were just much hairier and had sharper claws.

A hitotsume in silk robes, stood along her path, talking to a group of yokai. She quickened her step and bobbed beneath his swinging arms to sneak past him. Weeks ago, she had memorized her path to the training ground, down to the steps it took to get there. Just fifteen more... fourteen... thirteen...

A wall of silk stepped into her path. Just great. The hitotsume's singular eye bulged in the center of his lumpy skull as he glared down at her. "Where do you think you're going, human?" the hitotsume growled.

Whenever a yokai said human, it always sounded like a curse. Well, the feeling was mutual, she didn't like the yokai any more than they liked her.

"I'm in no mood, please step aside," Suzume said through gritted teeth. Ryuu couldn't scold her for starting trouble, she'd said please. And besides, there were several much more sharp insults she'd rather fling at the mountain of yokai standing in front of her. But as Ryuu liked to remind her, frequently, that only made things worse.

She attempted to side step-him, only to have him block her way again. "What if I don't? Are you going to go running to The Dragon?" As the hitotsume leaned in toward her, the scent of his rotten fish breath wafted over.

Suzume crinkled her nose. Even Ryuu should understand, the hitotsume had left her no choice. She drew her staff, and thrust the end into his fleshy gut. He groaned, grasping at his belly, as she twirled her staff and slammed the end onto the ground.

"I don't need The Dragon to fight my battles," Suzume said and strode past him.

Two more yokai blocked her path, a squat blue-skinned yokai with long yellow claws, and a second who looked nearly human but for the curled horns, pointed ears, and cat-like eyes.

It had been a mistake to attack them. The yokai loved to fight, almost as much as they hated humans.

"I'm really not in the mood," she said as she clenched her staff tighter. She'd gotten stronger, but with a crowd of yokai gathering ready to turn on her, she didn't feel good about her odds.

"You don't belong here, why don't you just leave, if you know what's good for you," said the one-eyed yokai.

As part of her training, Ryuu had tried to teach her not only how to fight, but when not to. This was one of those times, she was going to have to. She just needed to even the odds. Suzume spun her staff in front of her; flames flickered off the ends, creating an arch. Whirling in place, she cast her spiritual energy outward, creating a flaming barrier between her and the yokai.

"I think I'll stay." She placed her hands on her hips, giving the yokai a defiant stare. "You're outmatched, why not leave before I take it in my head to burn you to a crisp?"

The yokai onlookers took a step back away from the flames.

"Is that all you got?" The hitotsume said, as he stepped through the flames toward her. "You think a few sparks are going to stop me. I was born of flames." The hitotsume inhaled and then exhaled it toward her.

With a swipe of her staff, she dissipated the flames sending them flying into the atmosphere. She was fairly fireproof, but who knew what sort of toxic fumes were in the hitotsume's breath.

Him being non-flammable was unexpected, but not something she hadn't seen before.

"So you want to play that game," Suzume smirked. She had gotten up early to train, after all, this was a perfect chance to use the song she'd been dying to try.

One hand outstretched to the brightening sky, and her staff planted on the ground. Suzume focused her energy on calling from the elements. The energy coursed through her veins, setting them ablaze like molten lava. And the words to the song of suffering were on the tip of her tongue, she only needed to gather a little more.

"That's enough of that," Kaito grasped her outstretched hand, placing himself between her and the hitotsume.

The ice of his grip, crept along her skin, cooling the flames that had been building there. With a touch, he dissipated the energy she'd been gathering, it burst from her like smoke.

"I don't need your help," She hissed at him.

"No, but he does, you weren't really planning on killing one of my subjects were you?" He leaned in so close that his lips brushing against her ear. The hairs on the back of her neck stood on end, and her stomach fluttered.

It was too close, too intimate. The yokai already didn't respect her, and saw her as Kaito's favored pet. He was only making things worse. She'd tried to keep him out of any disagreement she had with his subjects. In fact, she'd been avoiding him as much as possible for weeks. She didn't want to be seen as gaining all her power through him. She wanted to be his equal. She lurched backward, ripping her hand away from him.

His smile didn't falter. Then to the yokai, he said, "I thought I've made it clear, the humans in my palace are under my protection." His voice thundered as he spoke, and those yokai milling about looked away.

"She's not just a human, she's a priestess and a danger to us all." The hitotsume puffed up his chest as he faced Kaito.

"And you're fortunate I arrived in time before she turned you to ash. This time, I'll let you off with a warning."

Suzume's heart stuttered in her chest. Had Kaito just praised her? Albeit indirectly. It wasn't like him. Was this sincere? Kaito turned his back on the hitotsume. There was a smile on Kaito's face, and she couldn't help but smile in return while her stomach did backflips. This was why she couldn't be near him. What was she thinking, this was Kaito!

"You've let that woman soften you, The Dragon you were before would never—" The hitotsume called.

Kaito turned to the side, and shot a spear of ice at the hitotsume. It grazed the one-eyed yokai's shoulder before shattering on the ground.

The surrounding yokai gasped and muttered amongst themselves.

"You missed." The hitotsume stood up taller.

"I didn't miss, if I wanted, you'd be dead where you stand. Test me further, and I'll see your hide stretched out on this courtyard," Kaito said, coldly.

A chill ran down Suzume's spine, even her blanket of fiery heat couldn't keep out. The orange sky of sunrise turned gray as clouds rolled in. Kaito's arms were in shimmering pearlescent scales, his hands tipped in claws, as he partially shifted into his dragon form. The air crackled with Kaito's energy, it was fortunate she'd learned to block it out, or he would have flattened her to the floor with his spiritual pressure. As it was, she felt it building in her ears.

The hitotsume grasped his bleeding shoulder, before scooping his head in a bow and scurried away. How she envied Kaito for that. To be able to command that sort of presence and bring a crowd to your bidding with just a glare.

"Shall I escort you to the training grounds?" Kaito said, turning to her with a smile and an arm extended toward the practice yard. The scales and claws were gone, and the sky was lightening once again, the clouds disappearing as quickly as they'd rolled in.

"I don't need an escort," Suzume said before ducking past his arm and heading toward the training grounds. She was going to have to train harder if she were going to be seen at Kaito's equal.

The remaining yokai were no longer watching with wary expressions. Kaito's compliment was quickly forgotten, as his strength and power eclipsed her own. Empty words praising her ability wouldn't turn the yokai's feelings for her. To them, she was nothing but Kaito's pet.

"Well, I need to protect my subjects from you." He kept pace with her.

"He deserved it, he picked a fight with me first," she replied, as she lengthened her stride, in an attempt to get away.

"That's how yokai are, don't you know that by now?"

She was used to his taunting, and knew better than to rise to his bait.

"I am well aware." The training grounds were in sight now. At the edge of the sandy pit, Ryuu, Kaito's son, and her teacher awaited. Along with him were Souta, the wind of Kazue's soul, and Hikaru, the earth of Kazue's soul. Together they'd been learning to resonate and strengthen their combined power in order to face Hisato, but all that was missing was the last piece of Kazue's soul, the water of her soul. They'd been searching for months but had not been able to find them.

"You're avoiding me," Kaito said, his voice dipping lower as he leaned in close.

A shiver snaked up her spine, and she stumbled. Kaito caught her from falling by grasping her arm, and she glanced up at him on instinct. It was true she'd done everything she could to stay away from him. Kaito claimed he wanted to honestly pursue her, that his feelings were real. But there was no time for romance, not when she still needed to get stronger. Not when Hisato was out there gathering an army, not while he had her family in his clutches, and the last piece she needed to defeat him eluded her.

She pulled away from him. "I've been busy."

He took a step closer, and her heart raced, a smile curled his lips. "Even after all this time, you're still frightened of me?"

A blush burned on her skin as she thought of the night they'd first met, when he'd held her close, his icy skin pebbling hers, and the threat of power just beneath that handsome mask. But she wasn't that naive, spoiled princess anymore.

"You don't frighten me." She jutted her chin forward, and he took another step forward.

He was so close she could run her fingers down his muscular chest. But she dared not, not with an audience, perhaps not ever. The temptation was real, but giving into him was like admitting defeat, admitting that she would amount to nothing more than being his property. His pet in a gilded cage.

Staying close to Ryuu made avoiding Kaito easier. Neither man wanted anything to do with the other, and they both seemed happy to pretend the other didn't exist.

"Then stop running from me." The tips of his fingers grazed her cheek. Their sort of kiss flashed through her mind. The memory was enough to make her knees weak. He had kissed her out of necessity, to share his power with her to stop Hisato. But it hadn't stopped haunting her since, wondering what it would be like to kiss him for real. No other man had quite infuriated or enticed her the way Kaito did.

"Suzume, we're waiting for you." Ryuu approached with a somber expression.

Suzume jumped away from Kaito as if she'd been struck by lightning. What was she thinking?

Kaito tore his gaze away from Suzume, and furrowed his brows at Ryuu. The two men squared off. Though they were father and son, there was no affection between them. Before Ryuu had been born, Kaito had been sealed in stone by Ryuu's mother, Kazue. And from the time they'd met, interactions had been chilly.

"I believe you are interrupting us," Kaito said icily, arms crossed over his chest.

"She needs to train." Ryuu stepped closer, mirroring Kaito's body language. At a glance, you would never suspect they were father and son. Nothing of Kaito's features were reflected in Ryuu. But their mutual jealousy and stubbornness exposed their blood ties.

"Don't you have things to do, you should get going." She turned to leave, and Kaito caught her wrist. Sparks raced up her arm, damn her body for exposing her true feelings.

"I cleared my afternoon for you, come meet me later, I have a surprise."

Her heart raced in her chest, there was something in his gaze that made her both terrified and excited. What could it possibly be? She should tell him no, but he'd piqued her interest.

"Alright."

He let go of her hand, and she jogged away before he could detain her further.

Ryuu joined her, jogging at her side. "Is he the reason you're running late this morning?" Ryuu said with a quirked brow.

She shrugged. "No, there was a small altercation, nothing important."

They reached Hikaru and Souta, who greeted her with quick bows, which she returned reflexively. Ryuu stood behind her, arms crossed over his chest. "I told you they're never going to accept you if you keep fighting them."

"Well, that's fine with me, cause I have no problem with them hating me."

Ryuu heaved a long-suffering sigh. At times he felt more like a father with his nagging than a teacher.

"What were you two talking about?" Ryuu murmured, his gaze flickering toward Kaito.

Her face heated with embarrassment. "Nothing, really."

Ryuu gave her a disbelieving grumble.

Kaito hadn't left as she expected but leaned against a nearby wall watching her. After months of avoiding him, her resolve was starting to crumble. He'd said he would make her come to him, and as much as she tried to fight it, she couldn't deny the draw she felt. The least she could do was see what his surprise was, it couldn't hurt, could it?

TWO

Kaito leaned against the armory building, his eyes trained on Suzume. When they'd first met, she'd been arrogant and stubborn. The first thing he had seen when he'd woken from centuries of sleep had been her. Shoulders squared as she confidently challenged him. But even then, he could see it was nothing but words and wind. Now every movement she made, even while talking with that bastard, Ryuu, was done with a head held high. She was no longer propped up by false confidence but with certainty. She threw her head back in laughter and playfully slapped at that bastard's arm. It took all his self-control not to march over there and shove them apart. What did Ryuu want from her anyway? Begrudgingly, he'd allowed him to stay in his palace. But every moment he was around, it was like a knife twist reminding him of Kazue and her betrayal that gave that bastard life.

Ryuu and Suzume broke away from the group, and entered the sand sparring ring. He'd made sure that this place was repaired first. When she'd first come to the palace, Suzume's power was growing but still needed mastery. Now, as she bowed to that bastard and took her place across from him, he could see her skill. On occasion, he'd broken away in secret to watch Suzume practice. And though he hated that bastard, he must admit he was doing an excellent job at teaching Suzume.

He leaned forward trying, to get a better view as the two opponents circled one another. Her form was good; her footwork still weak but improving. Perhaps it was time they sparred again; it had been months since they'd done so. Suzume thrust toward Ryuu, who blocked her, followed by a parry. Suzume stumbled a bit, and Kaito took a step forward. But before Ryuu could bring down a blow on her back, she had recovered and was on the offensive again. There was a fire in her gaze that was never there before, and he must admit it had a certain allure. The wood of their staffs clacked together as Kaito inched closer and closer to the edge of the ring. Ryuu's staff struck Suzume, and she stumbled backward.

"You've got this!" Kaito shouted to Suzume.

She glanced over her shoulder toward him. And in that moment when she looked away, that bastard used it as a chance to strike. His staff caught her around the ankles, and she fell to the ground, the butt of his staff pressed to her neck.

"You need to focus more," that bastard said with a menacing gaze.

Kaito strode over toward them, and shoved that bastard's staff aside.

"Don't you think you're being too harsh."

"Don't you think you're interfering too much?"

Kaito balled his hand into a fist, what he wouldn't give to punch that bastard in his smug face.

"You're interrupting my practice," Suzume said, placing herself between Ryuu and Kaito, her arms crossed over her chest.

He clenched his teeth to hold back an argument, she was too stubborn and too blind to his kind gesture, just as she had been with the hitotsume. He knew she didn't need him to fight her battles, but he wanted to defend her and protect her from the dangers of his world. But how quickly she jumped to his defense crawled under his skin and continued to pick at his insides like carrion. Couldn't she see he was doing this for her?

"My mistake," he said, taking a step back and out of the ring.

Suzume turned her back to him, and faced that bastard instead. "We should get back to work."

Fists clenched, Kaito slunk back to the fringes of the sparring ground. But he wasn't going to let this go quite so easily. And instead, he stalked the perimeter of the sparring ring, eyes trained on Ryuu. Who, much to his agitation, refused to acknowledge him. When Suzume would glance in Kaito's direction, he'd give her a sharp rap. The same sort of knock Kaito would have given one of his subordinates if they weren't paying attention.

He'd given her space, because he thought that was what she needed. Suzume didn't like to be told what to do. And at times, he found her stubbornness charming. But the glacial pace at which their relationship had been progressing, was starting to wear upon him. He'd held himself back, thinking with time and patience she would come to him. But as he had given her space and focused on restoring the palace to its former glory, this bastard had used the opportunity to get his claws into Suzume, monopolizing her time and turning her against him. That would end today, he was done waiting.

After an agonizing eternity of pacing and waiting, her training was over. A rosy glow graced her cheeks, and sweat plastered tendrils of her hair to her forehead. That bastard reached up and stroked Suzume's head. His hand lingering on her crown, and she looked up at him and smiled! A smile that should have been reserved for Kaito. That was enough. Kaito strode across the yard toward them. How dare that bastard casually touch her, and why didn't she knock his hand away? She didn't have feelings for that bastard, did she?

Kaito grabbed that bastard by the arm and yanked him away from Suzume. The bastard met his gaze. Kazue's eyes. It was Kazue's dark eyes staring out of that bastard's face. At times it was easier to pretend, but there was no denying it; this was her son. The bastard shook free of Kaito's grip.

"Practice is over, now she's mine," Kaito said to Ryuu as he grabbed Suzume by the shoulder, pulling her closer to him.

She wriggled in his grip, tugging herself free. "I've only just finished, can't you give me a minute to catch my breath at least?"

"She doesn't belong to anyone," Ryuu said with a threatening edge to his tone.

That bastard. Maybe he'd given him too much leeway, made too many concessions to him for Suzume's benefit. Perhaps it was time he taught him a lesson.

"I hope you didn't presume to challenge me." Kaito bared his teeth at the bastard.

"When I do, you'll know." He stood up straighter, trying to make himself look more intimidating. It would be easy enough to destroy him; as a half-breed, he wouldn't have even a tenth of his strength. Kaito smirked to think of the look of humiliation on the bastard's face when he brought him to his knees.

"You two can fight it out, I'm going." Suzume flapped her hand as she slipped past him.

He was lucky Suzume walked away. The bastard's lesson would have to wait for another day. With one last glare at the bastard, Kaito followed after Suzume, jogging to catch up with her.

Threading his fingers with hers, she glanced up at him, eyes wide but didn't protest or pull away.

"Come, I have something to show you."

They strode through the courtyard, and the yokai parted before them. Some bowed, others reached out to touch the hem of his sleeve. Everywhere they went, the whispers followed, Kaito held his head high. He reveled in their attention not just for himself, but for Suzume as well. Never before had a yokai publicly taken a human as their lover. In the past, it had happened in secret. The children of such unions reviled and ostracized. That was why Kazue had betrayed him after all. Perhaps if he had not kept Kazue in secret, tried to undermine her power, things would have been different.

He shoved those thoughts away. Kazue was gone, and he wouldn't make the same mistakes again. Some among his subjects disagreed with his choice of partner, but all of them could agree Suzume was powerful and worthy to stand at his side. While he had slept, the world had changed, humans ruled, and if the yokai were to survive, they would need to adapt. And Kaito would lead the charge into this new era.

"Is the surprise humiliating me in front of all the yokai by parading me around like your pet dog?" Suzume asked, her gaze flickered furtively to the yokai that crowded the halls.

"There is nothing to be embarrassed about, you are my woman, the envy of every other woman in my kingdom."

She snorted, but he ignored her. It had taken time and planning, but after today she would have no reason to not walk with her head held high.

Past the crowds, they entered into the inner ring of the palace. Where only his innermost circle of trusted advisors could enter. It was quieter here, and outside the prying eyes of the court, Suzume exhaled. Just beyond the first row of buildings, their first surprise awaited. Kaito tugged Suzume along, bringing her to the inner courtyard garden. As they approached, the perfume of sakura blossoms filled the air.

Suzume gasped, letting go of his hand to approach the blooming tree. "How can they bloom in winter?" She reached for a low hanging branch, her delicate hands red and chapped.

"I asked Hikaru for a favor, he used his mastery of plants to coax this tree to bloom," Kaito said plucking a blossom and putting it in her hair.

She stroked the petals of the flower, as she stared mouth agape in wonderment at the tree. "It's beautiful, this was the surprise you wanted to show me?" She turned toward him. Her expression one he'd never seen before, it was softer than usual, unguarded and beautiful. It took all his self-control to not kiss her right then and there, but this was only the first part of his surprise.

"I heard they were your favorite."

She turned back toward the sakura tree, but he caught the flush of color on her cheeks though she tried to hide it. "You didn't have to do this..."

"That's not all," he grabbed her hand again, leading her up the steps.

"There's more?" she asked, her voice rising with excitement.

"Turn around and close your eyes."

A single brow rose. "Are you playing a trick on me?"

"I promise, it's not a trick." He spun her around and covered her eyes with one hand. "No peeking."

She wriggled in his grip, her body shimming with excitement, and with his free hand, he slid the door open. Then carefully led her into the room beyond. When the master carpenters had arrived, he'd set them to the task of building this room to adjoin his own. It boasted a large sleeping platform draped in hanging curtains to give privacy, a sitting area large enough for entertaining, a balcony overlooking the ocean and a door which connected this room with his own, allowing them the freedom to meet without risking being seen by the prying eyes of the court. In the center of the room, silken kimono and jewelry had been laid out as well.

"What is it, the suspense is killing me?" Suzume squirmed in his grasp.

Kaito led her to the center of the room. "Ready?"

She nodded her head vigorously. "Just let me open them already."

Kaito chuckled before removing his hand and stepping back so he could see her expression as she took it all in.

Suzume skimmed the room with her eyes, her smile fading as she did. Was it not enough? Should he have given her more silk and jewels?

"What is this?" Suzume asked.

"I had this room made for you," Kaito said, gesturing around the room.

Arms wrapped her upper half, her gaze traveled around the room, they rested on the silk and jewels. She took a few steps toward them, and stooped down to pick up a jeweled hairpin. A single bell dangled off the end of it and delicately chimed as she picked it up. Without a word, she set it down, picked up the silken kimono with the pattern of cherry blossoms on a dark purple background, and frowned.

"Do you like it?" Why wasn't she saying anything, she'd been in awe of the cherry blossoms, and he thought she would be ecstatic over the gifts.

"Why did you give me these things?" she asked quietly.

"Do I need a reason?" He stepped closer and wrapped an arm around her, but as he tried to pull her close, she slipped out of his grasp, and she walked over toward the door, which connected the two rooms.

"Where does this room lead to?" She asked. He couldn't get a proper read of her expression. She should be excited, shouldn't she?

"It connects our two rooms," he purred and stepped closer to her, but as he did, she put up her hand.

"Before when you said I was your woman, what did that mean?"

"What are you talking about?" He tried to tame the irritation in his voice.

"Just answer the question." Her gaze flickered over him.

"I think you know what I meant by that; I've been patient, haven't I?" He stalked closer to her, and she backed away until her back was against the wall. She tilted her head back to look at him. He pinned her to the wall as he leaned against it over her. "You've been playing hard to get, but I'm done playing, Suzume, I want you."

He dipped his head down to capture her lips in a kiss.

"What am I to you, a consort, your concubine?" she asked as his lips ghosted over hers, there was a catch in her voice.

"You are whatever I say you are."

She shoved him hard and caught him by surprise as he stumbled backward.

"You can't buy my affection with presents, and I won't be anyone's concubine. Ever." Suzume turned on her heel, storming out of the room.

Buy her? What was she saying? Kaito chased after her. "Suzume, come back here!" he growled.

But she ignored him, retreating into her room across the courtyard where she slammed the door shut.

He could chase after her, force her to explain herself, but there was no use. It wouldn't make a difference. He roared in frustration, and retreating into the room, he upending the chest of jewels and silk, the items scattered around the room, and it did little to soothe his temper. Even Kazue, who'd resisted him on their first encounters, had not been this infuriatingly stubborn. When would she stop running away from him?

There was a knock at the door, and Kaito spun around prepared to rip the head off whoever it was that dared to speak to him.

Shin, an okami and his best friend, leaned against the door-frame. "Did I come at a bad time?" he asked with a hardly repressed smirk.

"Don't get me started," Kaito snapped.

"Then I wasn't mistaken in that I just saw Suzume storm out in what looked like indignation." Shin's smirk only infuriated him further. When he had first returned to swear himself into Kaito's service after freeing himself from his old master, Kaito had been relieved to have him back. But right now, he was questioning whether or not to murder him.

"She's impossible. I bought her every gift she could have wanted, jewels, silk, I had this room remodeled just for her. But does she thank me for any of it? No!" Kaito paced around the room, and tried very hard to resist the urge to kick and tear the entire room apart.

Shin picked a silk kimono, running it over his clawed hand. "You're really using these old tired tricks on her?"

"What would you have done differently?"

Shin shrugged a shoulder. "Presents were never my style, I have other ways of seducing a woman."

"Don't let Akane hear you talking like that," Kaito said, half-heartedly. But Shin had nothing to worry about him and his mate, Akane, their bond was strong.

"I imagine it wasn't the presents that sent her running off in a huff," Shin said.

"That's the thing, I don't know why she insists on running from me. Everything was going exactly as I planned, and then she asked me what I thought she was. Shouldn't it be obvious?" Kaito growled low in his throat.

Before, when he'd been the ruler of all Akatsuki, he'd have any woman falling at his feet. Chasing wasn't necessary; they came to him. Could she have feelings for that bastard, Ryuu, had he read her wrong and she wasn't interested in him?

"What did you tell her?"

"Tell her what?" Kaito asked, running a palm over her face.

"When she asked what she was to you?"

"I don't remember, we were just talking, and she mentioned being my concubine..."

Shin shook his head and tutted. "You told her she wasn't a concubine, didn't you?"

"No... why would I? I've had countless lovers and concubines, all of them were eager for the role. Even her mother is the concubine of the human emperor..."

And then it hit him like a ton of stones, the reason Suzume had been so angry wasn't because she didn't want to be with him. It was the term consort. The jewels, the silk, even this room, it was all hollow with a title. This wasn't about gifts, this was about a title, if he were going to make her his, he would have to make her his empress.

THREE

Suzume's feet pounded on the sand. Her breathing ragged. Just a bit further. Just a little faster. The ocean roared as the waves crashed over one another, before reaching toward the shoreline, dragging sand and shells under the endless churning cycle. Suzume timed her breaths, as she put one foot in front of another. She needed to focus her thoughts on just her breaths, her stride, the swing of her arms. Don't think about the silk, or the jewels. Sea spray splashed across her face. Don't think about that door that connected those two rooms.

Jogging backward in front of her, Tsuki said, "Care to tell us what happened that's got you all fired up?"

Suzume shook her head, huffing for air. Her mind kept circling back to that door.

One of her earliest memories of Mother waiting. She watched the door every night. Even as a child, it had caught Suzume's attention. It was just a door made of paper and wood like any other and yet Mother was fixated upon it. She had joined her,

"

sitting quietly by her side, watching that door waiting for it to do anything.

Before her brother, the emperor came often through that door. And when he did, Mother was full of smiles and laughter. Those were happy days when the emperor brought her sweets and saw her off to bed with her nurse. Then after her brother was born and they moved to the small palace, the door was different, but Mother watched it just the same. The emperor's visits became less frequent, but her mother's waiting never ceased. Nightly visits became, weekly, then monthly. As the visits became more infrequent, gifts came before the emperor did. She still remembered the first one, a hairpin with a jade flower. When a year had gone by without a visit, a bolt of silk arrived. Mother put in her jade flower hairpin and waited for him. The visit was brief, the emperor never stayed long. A year turned into years, the gifts stopped coming, and so did he. Mother never stopped waiting. That was what it meant to be a second wife, a consort.

It was a life Suzume swore she would never have. When men sent her gifts, she always refused; they thought she was being coy. But a gift always came with strings attached. Mother had her parties, false friends who sought her favor, but when they were all gone, she was still left waiting for the emperor. Even when he had forgotten all about her, she still belonged to him. Because no matter what power her mother grasped for herself, no matter how many allies or money of her own, she would only ever be his caged bird living in a gilded cage.

Lungs burning, eyes watering from the salt in the air, and energy flagging, Suzume slowed to a stop. She leaned forward, taking gasping breaths of cold air. Her constant shadows, Naoki and Tsuki stood over her. Naoki bound to her by Kazue's heart, which Suzume had absorbed, and Tsuki and his sister Akira trapped in one body and cursed to guard the staff Suzume held. All of them were prisoners of their fate. She couldn't go anywhere without them following. And though Suzume had run away from Kaito once, she had returned thinking he saw her as an equal, that they were a team. But perhaps it had all been her own delusion, and she was as foolish as Mother, who kept waiting on the emperor. She'd let her feelings for Kaito cloud her judgment, but if she accepted his gifts, then she'd never escape the gilded cage. Left forever in the shadows as he ruled over the yokai.

"This isn't like you to try quite this hard at strength training," Akira said, she used her brother's face to speak, not bothering to take control of the body they shared.

"What... I... always... try... this... hard..." Suzume panted out between breaths.

Tsuki smirked. "Well, if you're feeling ambitious, why don't you try racing me?"

He'd likely offered because he wanted her to admit defeat. But tired as she was, she wasn't going to back down from a challenge, not one from a yokai.

"Where to?" She stood up and tried to steady her breathing.

"What about that islet?" He gestured to a long strip of sand jutting out into the ocean.

It wasn't too far. She could make it that far, at least.

"Sure."

They both got into position, Suzume steadied her breath as

much as she could. But she was still winded from the first run. It didn't matter, she just had to get to the finish line.

"Count of three." Tsuki held up his fingers, curled one downwards "...one... two...three—" As soon as the word left his lips, he was off, and his form shrunk along the horizon. Suzume's aching legs, already tired from a morning of exercise, burned with exertion as she struggled to catch up. More than anything, she wanted to lay down in the sand and never get up again.

It would be easier to give up. To admit the superior nature of yokai over humans. Why keep fighting for more? Why not just be happy to live in luxury? With Kaito's protection, she wouldn't have to worry about attacks. He could guard her from everything, he was strong enough to do that. She could live a life of leisure.

But she wanted more.

No. She wasn't just satisfied with hitting the finish, she had to win. Even if it killed her, she was going to get stronger. She would prove to Kaito and everyone that she was more than just a concubine. She wouldn't become her mother. She wouldn't spend her days waiting for a powerful man to give her gifts, she didn't need Kaito to protect her.

The sand shifted beneath her feet as she increased her speed. Inch by inch, she closed the gap between her and Tsuki. As she got closer, Tsuki glanced over his shoulder.

"Catch me if you can," he taunted.

But it only spurned her further. Just a little more. Just a little faster. The pain in her body faded away as a strange euphoria overcame her. She was closing in.

Now she was at his shoulder. A few more steps. The islet was right there. Shells along the shores glittered in the noonday sun. She could do this, just one last burst of speed to finish it. She surged forward, surpassing Tsuki a few seconds before reaching the islet where she collapsed into the sand.

The warm sand clung to her sweat-drenched skin as she stared up at the cloudless sky. Her heart throbbed in her ears, and she couldn't keep the smile from her face.

"Good race," Tsuki said as he fell onto the ground beside her.

While Suzume gasped for breaths, his breathing was normal, he hadn't even broken a sweat.

Suzume sighed heavily. "You let me win, didn't you?"

Tsuki chuckled, "You wanted it more."

Of course, he had. Even when she pushed herself nearly to exhaustion, there was no way for her to win unless it was handed to her. A human, no matter how hard she tried, was always going to be inferior to a yokai. She clenched a fistful of sand in her hand and sat up. The ocean stretched out until it met the horizon. Maybe if she could run to where the sky touched the sun, she'd finally be equal to a yokai. But not today, and perhaps never.

Naoki had joined them and hovered nearby, his gaze continually scanning the horizon. Until Hisato was defeated, she would always be in danger, among the yokai or even out here, on this desolate beach. That was her life, there was no pretending otherwise. And as much as she didn't want to be caged, that was probably the safest place to be. But that didn't mean she had to like it.

"Ready to talk about what's bothering you?" Akira had taken control of her body she shared with Tsuki, and unlike her brother who'd sprawled on the sand, she knelt gracefully beside Suzume and brushed sand from her kimono.

"Not really," Suzume replied as she let the sand run through her fingers.

"Suit yourself," Akira said and looked out across the ocean, the breeze caught strands of her long ebony hair, and they fluttered across her face.

Suzume closed her eyes as the ocean breeze rolled over her. If only it could carry away her unwanted feelings. When he had complimented her strength in front of the yokai and given her the sakura tree, her heart had fluttered. She should have known it was all leading to the one thing all men sought from her.

She jumped up to her feet, and cupping her hands around her mouth, she shouted. "You're an idiot!"

"I'm assuming you're referring to Kaito?" Akira asked in a disinterested tone.

Damn him. Why did he make her constantly question herself and his intentions? Sometimes it seemed like he was being sincere, and other times, she felt like she was swept up in some giant joke. When he confessed, she'd held herself from replying because she feared the moment she spoke her feelings aloud it; would all come to an end. The kind gestures, his tender looks... But holding this in, it felt like it was shredding apart her insides, maybe she should open up to Akira, if only to get it off her chest...

A jolt of electricity shot down Suzume's spine, and her head shot up. She'd felt this sensation before, a piece of Kazue's soul was nearby. She scanned the beach, it could very well be Souta or Hikaru come to find her because she'd been gone too long. But she saw them every day and never felt like this, only when she'd first met them.

"Naoki, are Souta or Hikaru close by?" Suzume asked.

His spiritual sense was stronger than hers, as was his ability to differentiate different spiritual energies from a distance. Something was calling to her, without a voice and without a sound. The pieces of Kazue's soul longed to be reunited, and the part of her that was Kazue was reaching out for that last missing piece. As if by instinct, Suzume's gaze was drawn down the shore, past the driftwood and seaweed, which littered the sand. Naoki's dark gaze was trained on the horizon, back toward the castle in the opposite direction of where the call was coming from. This had to be the missing piece, she'd found it at last.

"I cannot sense them nearby, but I feel it as well," Naoki said.

"Did you sense something?" Akira asked as she stood, her expression eager.

For Akira and Tsuki, finding the missing piece of Kazue's soul could mean being free of her curse at last. Hikaru, Souta, and her had tried to separate them, but it was no use. The only way they would regain their individual bodies was if all the pieces of Kazue's soul were reunited, and they were at their full power.

"I can feel it, the last soul piece is nearby, it's calling to me," Suzume took a step in the direction of the call.

"We should go and find them!" Tsuki said, using his sister's face.

"It might be a trap," Naoki said. "It would be wise to go back for reinforcements."

They'd been searching for months for the last soul piece without success. Naoki was right, it was likely this was a trap set by Hisato. But if it weren't, she might lose her only chance to find the missing piece. Besides, going back meant asking Kaito for help, and she didn't need him just to check.

"There's no time. Let's investigate first, and if need be, we'll go back for backup," Suzume declared before running in the direction the soul piece was calling her to.

Thick gray plumes of smoke rose up in the sky from the direction she was headed. Its source was blocked by a small rise along the shore. But as she rounded the corner, a scream pierced the air. Was it the soul piece? She picked up her pace.

Villagers ran toward them, and behind them, plumes of smoke choked the air, and flames engulfed their huts. The soul fragment called out to her, coaxing her to find them; they were close by. But she couldn't just abandon this village to find the soul piece.

"We have to help them," Suzume said to Naoki and Tsuki.

"But what about the soul piece?" Tsuki asked.

"They'll have to wait." Before Tsuki could respond, Suzume rushed toward the village.

The heat of the flames slowed her down as she approached, and she threw her arms up to shield her face as she got closer. Squinting into the blaze, she scanned for villagers or anyone who'd been trapped by the flames. From behind a scorched hut, a creature stepped out. The bottom half of it made of glowing coals stacked one on another, connected by a torso of blistered and red human flesh. Half of its face was human, but on the other side, the skin had been peeled away, revealing more burning coals. It had to be one of Hisato's hybrids. Perhaps this was a trap after all.

The song of destruction Ryuu had taught her was on her lips, she raised her hand to draw power from the flames around her. As the power swelled within her, she charged at the hybrid. And with her staff pointed at the hybrid, she unleashed the power of her song. But when the force of her song rolled over him, as if it were nothing but smoke. And it continued barreling toward her.

Suzume hesitated a second too long to swing and defend herself. The hybrid grabbed the end of her staff, and it caught on fire as it tried to pull it from her grasp. She thrust forward, sliding the staff in its grip and caught the coal side of its head, shattering it, like breaking apart embers. It screamed and stumbled backward, clutching at the broken side of its face.

If it were impervious to her song. She'd have to find another way to stop it. Tsuki was nowhere to be seen, and Naoki was preoccupied with fighting three other hybrids. She was on her own. Not far from the village was a dock. Being that this hybrid was made of coal, perhaps water could hurt it? And if she could coax it out over to the water, she could knock it into the ocean and extinguish it.

"Come here, you fiery abomination." Suzume taunted as she ran for the dock. The monster growled, a sound like rocks rolling over one another as it chased her. As she approached the dock, she felt the tug of the missing soul piece once again. They were very close. She stopped and searched the villagers who had gathered on a nearby hill, huddled together as their village burned. One among them had to be the missing piece. But which one?

A flaming fist reached for her, and Suzume stumbled, tripping on the uneven boards of the dock. The hybrid was closing in, and Suzume backed away, getting closer and closer to the edge of the dock. The hybrid hadn't come alone, two more hybrids, their bodies blistered and burned, followed close behind. There was no running around them and knocking one in. If she jumped into the water to escape, she'd drown.

The back of her foot found the edge of the dock. And the hybrid grasped her by her shoulder. Its touch burned, and she cried out. Swinging her staff wildly, she struck the hybrid, but it only squeezed her harder. Its flames came closer and closer to her, and she strained to keep her face away from the fire.

A whooshing sound filled her ears. And water dripped on her face. The hybrid looked up, and she followed his gaze. A wave three times her height crested over them and the dock. She had mere seconds to brace herself before it came crashing down on them. The water boomed, and Suzume was off the bridge and into the ocean. The water churned around her, and in the darkness, she couldn't tell up from down. She flapped her arms ineffectually, trying to find the surface. But the waves tossed her back and forth like a child's plaything. There was nothing she could do but hold her breath and pray.

A hand reached for her, grabbing her by the wrist and pulled her from the depths. As she broke the water's surface, Suzume sputtered and gasped for air. Naoki held her around her waist, as he swam them both toward the shore. When they reached the sand, Suzume knelt on all fours gasping for breath.

Had that wave not come when it did, she would have been killed by the hybrid, she was certain of it. The tug of the missing piece of Kazue's soul was gone, but Suzume was certain it had to be them, the water of Kazue's soul had saved her life, but where had they gone?

Four

Tsuki's blade sliced through the flesh of the hybrid. Black ichor sprayed from the wound and splattered on his face. Without pausing to wipe it away, he leaped through the flames, racing between the burning huts of the village. The occasional battles they'd encountered since Suzume had found them at the shrine, had not quenched his thirst for blood. The thrill of battle was upon him once more. He was one with the swing of his blade, the pounding of his heart, and the cries of his fallen opponents. The hybrid whose arm he had parted from his body, roared and came charging for him, black blood oozing from the stump left behind.

Either it was too stupid or too enraged to notice. It swung at him with a fisherman's spear. It might as well have happened in slow motion, there was little challenge in hacking its hand off and letting it fall to the ground. It jabbed its bloody appendage at him spraying Tsuki and the flames.

"You're making a terrible mess," Akira said through their shared bond.

The drum beat of blood lust thundered in his ears, and he didn't bother to respond.

Thick, foul-smelling smoke rose up around them as it charged for him like a mindless animal. The hybrid monster lumbered toward him, passing through flames which caught the ragged shreds of its clothes, it did not so much as flinch. Fighting it wasn't a challenge, nor was it exciting if it didn't react. With an upward thrust of his blade, he embedded his sword in the soft giving flesh of its gut. Thick congealed black blood ran down Tsuki's arm, soaking his sleeve as the hybrid continued to thrash. It waved its hand-less arm at him, until its heart pumped out the last of its life blood. With a slow stagger, it crashed onto the ground. Tsuki knelt down, wiping the edge of his blade on what remained of the burned and tattered clothes of the hybrid. How terribly anticlimactic that had been.

"Can you stay focused, we don't have time to fight these things," Akira scolded him through their mental link.

"Can you sense them?" Tsuki asked Akira.

"There's a lot of noise, but I can feel them; the last soul piece is close by."

They didn't have their father Naoki's affinity for sensing spiritual power. But he trusted Akira's instincts. When they were free of each other at last, there would be time for him to slake his thirst. Besides, these fumbling atrocities weren't even worth the effort.

The fire around them grew higher and the radiant heat warmed his face. He'd been so absorbed in the fight, he hadn't realized how big the blaze had gotten. The roof of a nearby hut collapsed, and from within, someone screamed. The poor humans hadn't deserved to die, but that was the cruel reality of humanity. Even if there were a way to save them, he wouldn't have bothered. There were only two things that mattered, finding the missing piece of Kazue's soul and protecting Suzume long enough for her and the others to separate Akira and him.

The screaming stopped, and smoke choked the air. Time to go. They might be immortal, but burns would still be painful to heal, and he didn't want to mar his handsome face. As Tsuki passed the burning remains of a hut, it started to shift. A beam lifted off the ground, revealing the scorched back of a villager. How had a mere villager survived the flames and a caved-in roof? As they rose to their full height, it exposed their burnt skin, which glowed like coals in a fire. The flesh on his arm had split open, and long clawed fingers burst from fingertips. Now that was something he'd never seen before.

"What is that?" Akira asked; he could feel her disgust through their bond.

"Does it matter? They all fall to my sword in the end," Tsuki said as he drew his blade.

The fumbling monstrosity rose from the flames and took a few staggering steps toward him, clutched in the disfigured hand was a fishing spear.

It was all so obvious now. These pathetic creatures used to be the villagers. It swung its spear at Tsuki, which he dodged. He would have mercy and make its death swift. With a single swipe of his sword, he beheaded the monster. Its head rolled along the ground, wide, surprised eyes stared up at the smoke-filled sky, while the body slumped forward, the black and red blood staining the ground.

"Whose making these things?" Tsuki asked.

"It doesn't concern us. We need to find the missing piece," Akira replied.

She was right, as she always was. Tsuki found his way out of the burning village and onto the beach, which was covered in ash and stray pieces embers. Where the shore met the sea, Suzume stood on the end of a dock as three hybrids closed in upon her, and behind her, the ocean rose up to unnatural heights.

"It's her, I can feel Kazue's energy!" Akira shouted in his mind.

The wave crashed down upon Suzume and the hybrids, sweeping them off the dock. He had to save her, she was a terrible swimmer. But Naoki was already there diving into the water to save her.

"Don't worry about Suzume, Father will protect her. We need to find the soul piece before it escapes again."

"Where are they?" Tsuki asked as he scanned the beach, and the rise just beyond. At the top of the hill, a group of humans had clustered together. None particularly stood out, but someone had to have made the waves rise up that way. It couldn't have been a coincidence.

"Close, maybe just over that rise, but they're getting away. We must hurry." Tsuki didn't need to be told twice, and he raced up the hill past the group of humans who felt the breeze as he zoomed past them, but saw not a hint of them. Humans could not see them unless they wished it, and rarely did he care to. As he crested the hill, he spotted a woman in a priestess haori and hakama running for the forest which bordered the beach. As she looked behind her, their eyes locked. She turned and ran faster toward the forest.

"That's her!" Akira said.

Picking up speed, he bolted down the hill catching up to her with ease and grabbed her by her bicep. She spun around to face him. The face was that of a stranger, but the eyes peering into his were all too familiar. She did not struggle or try to break free, and instead, a faint smile curled her lips, and he was transported back to that day all those centuries ago. Back then, he thought he'd caught easy prey, when in reality, it was he who'd fallen into her trap.

"It looks like you've caught me, Tsuki." The voice was wrong, but the words were the same. The past and the present had collided and become one.

On reflex, his grip slackened, but Akira used his hand and grasped her tightly before she could slip away. If she hadn't taken charge, he might have stumbled backward to escape her. It wasn't possible, Kazue had split her soul apart. She was effectively dead, and yet it was her, back from the dead.

"Don't let her rattle you," Akira chided.

"But how does she know my name?"

"It doesn't matter. We have her now, and it's time to bring her back to the others."

"You know my name, that's surprising. I guess we can skip introductions then, and you'll come with me," Tsuki said as he tugged her along. She gave no resistance and walked calmly beside him. Which was only that much more suspicious.

"I know much more than your name." She canted her head to the side. "You and Akira were Akatsuki's deadliest assassins. You with your blade and Akira with her charms. The two of you drained the spiritual power of your targets and sold it to desperate yokai hungry for power."

It had been centuries since then, but it was possible their reputation had preceded them. Tsuki squeezed her arm tighter. She was trying to get under his skin, but he wouldn't let her.

"You think you're clever? There wasn't a yokai alive five hundred years ago who didn't fear us. Everyone knew we had skills no one else had."

"But did they know who you saved a portion of that power for?"

Tsuki froze mid-step. No one knew about that apart from Akira, Tsuki, and Kazue...

"It was a lucky guess," Akira said but with less certainty. He could feel it. Was it possible a soul piece had memories the others didn't?

"A lucky guess, or you remember more than the others."

"I remember everything. You were ordered to kill me by a yokai by the name of Hiramoro. He wanted my power for his own. But in the end, I absorbed him, like all the rest." She smiled faintly, the innocent smile that had lured him in when they first met. He'd underestimated Kazue, not realizing what danger lurked beneath that sweet exterior.

It was possible she had some of Kazue's memories; the others had a few, though none detailed as this. She was more cunning than he gave her credit for.

"Impressive, perhaps when we get back to the palace, you can tell us more about what you remember from the old days."

The soul piece threw her head back and laughed. The sound made the hairs on the back of his neck stand on end, and he reached for the hilt of his sword with his free hand and gripped her tighter with the other.

"You haven't changed a bit, have you? You'd make the same mistakes all over again, that cost you your mother." Her eyes flash a sky blue as she smiled.

Tsuki drew his blade and pressed it to her throat. He should have killed her that day, the moment he met her.

"Careful. We need her, remember?" Akira warned.

Tsuki took a deep breath and let the anger fade from him. "Do not test my patience; vengeance has a way of honing a blade," Tsuki said, meeting her gaze.

"You're no less arrogant than you were back then, Tsuki. Haven't you realized you've already walked right into my trap."

"She's put up a barrier!" Akira said.

Tsuki scored her neck with his blade, and bright crimson blood welled up running down her neck. "Perhaps I have learned a thing or two. I've learned not to let my guard down for an innocent face."

Once more, she didn't struggle against him, or try to break free. And why would she? They were within her spiritual barrier. "I thought with a new life, we could start over." She grasped his wrist that held her blade and pressed it harder against her own neck.

"Is she insane?" Tsuki asked Akira through their shared bond.

He tried to pull the blade back, but she held it close.

"I do not fear death, but you need me alive."

"Don't do anything hasty," Akira said. *"She knows we need her, let's see what she has to say."*

"What is it you want from us?" Tsuki asked, and dropped his blade to his side. She had called his bluff, he couldn't kill her. Though his hands itched to do so.

"I want you to help me reunite the pieces of my soul." Not Kazue's soul. Her. What arrogance was this for a fragment to think she owned the pieces of Kazue?

"That's what we want to do, Suzume and the others have been looking for you. We don't need to fight…"

She shook her head. "No, I mean all, including Hisato. We all belong together, the five of us."

He should have known Hisato was behind this. No wonder they'd spent ages looking for the missing piece only to come up empty-handed, he had beat them to her.

"If they are reunited, we can be freed at last," Akira said.

"Are you insane? We trusted her once and look where it got us," Tsuki replied.

"I'm afraid I can't do that," Tsuki said, before Akira could try and do something reckless. This last piece was too like Kazue for comfort.

She sighed heavily. "I was hoping we could do this the easy way."

Her song pierced the air, and the notes vibrated all around him before it struck him like a blunt object, propelling him backward. He landed on his feet, but just barely and wobbled for a moment as his head spun. She'd caught him once with that trick, but she wouldn't catch him a second time.

"I didn't want to do that." She shook her head solemnly.

Tsuki smirked as he gripped his blade tighter. "And I don't want to have to do this." Kazue might have defeated him, but this woman only had one-quarter of her power, he would defeat her with ease. He rushed toward her.

A funnel of water shot at him, drawn from a jug she kept at her hip.

"Watch out!" Akira's warning came a second too late.

The force of the water pinned him to the ground, as he thrashed and kicked in an attempt to muscle his way back onto his feet. Past the thunder of water in his ears, the dissonant sounds shook inside his skull and made his skin crawl. It only grew stronger, intensifying and manifesting in a ringing in his ears and a buzzing in his head. Wave after wave of blinding pain rolled through his body, it felt as if his body were being torn apart limb by limb.

Then without warning, the water was gone, and so was the worst of the pain. But the ringing of his ears faded much more slowly. Tsuki sat up, clutching his aching head as he saw double. A figure stood over them. They were saying something, but he couldn't quite make out what it was.

"Are we hurt?" The voice was Akira's and his own overlapping each other. The flesh of his arm bubbled and writhed, as his fingers grew long then receded. Who was in control of their body? It wasn't Tsuki, but he couldn't feel Akira nor could he make sense of the jumbled images in his mind or the clashing of voices fighting for control. The lines between them had blurred to where they were indistinguishable; there was no Tsuki, and there was no Akira, there was only them. They grasped at their face, clawed at their nose, their mouth, their ears, which were all unfamiliar and half-formed bastardizations of their individual selves.

"Why can I not hear our voices?" They tried reaching out to find the divide that marked their individual personalities. But it wasn't there, it was only them. Two voices ringing together, panicked, angry, and afraid.

Kazue stood over them, a smile curling her lips.

"What have you done to us?" Their voice was a cross between one or the other.

"You have a choice, help me or become of one mind and one body."

"Anything, just stop the pain!" Their throat was raw, their entire body throbbing from the constant shifting.

She pressed her thumb to their forehead, a warm trickling feeling spread throughout their body, and in a few moments, they were back to normal.

"Akira, Tsuki! Where are you?" Suzume shouted over the rise.

Kazue glanced in her direction then back to them. "Tell her nothing of what happened today. I will summon you again soon."

Her barrier fell, and she bolted for the forest before disappearing from sight. Whatever she had done to them, it had completely drained them of energy, and Akira, who had taken control of their body once more knelt on the ground gasping for breath.

"*What did she do to us?*" Tsuki asked. It had felt like when Kazue sealed them together, only much worse.

"I do not know. A fragment of Kazue's soul should not have this sort of power on her own. It doesn't make sense."

Suzume crested the hill, with Naoki beside her. Her clothes were soaked and clung to her skin, and her hair was hanging in wet strings around her face. She hurried down the hill toward them.

Akira stood as she approached, wiping the dust from her kimono.

"We say nothing to Suzume, understand?" Akira told him.

"Are you sure that's a good idea? We've been looking for so long, perhaps together we can find her before she gets away."

"No. We've already underestimated her once. We won't do it again. Can't you feel it, the dissonance remains, even now."

Not telling Suzume felt wrong. All that stood in the way of defeating Hisato was getting the remaining soul piece on their side. In the hands of Hisato, she was already too powerful. Their connection was weakened; even now, he felt something inside them that wasn't there before, a darkness that might consume them both if they didn't obey.

FIVE

There was someone in Ryuu's quarters. He reached for his blade, Tetsuyama, which hummed, eager to be free of the sheath which contained its energy. With a steady hand, he slid his door open, and then let it drop. His neko spy lounged on the tatami, his back to him. The neko's blue flame forked tail twitched back and forth as he speared morsels of fish with his claw. Without turning to greet him, the neko popped a morsel into his mouth.

"I see you've helped yourself to my dinner," Ryuu said dryly.

"You should have found your father sooner, the food here is much better than at the shrine." He polished off the last of the fish and moved onto the bowl of miso soup next to it, tilting it back and drinking it all in one long gulp.

Father. It was impossible to see The Dragon as a paternal figure. Sire felt more appropriate, The Dragon had not done much more than provide his seed. The fearsome Dragon of legend, who'd conquered and ruled over Akatsuki, was a surprisingly jealous and arrogant fool. In his innocent and lonely youth, Ryuu had hungered to eclipse his sire, to prove his worth. It was fortunate he'd long ago abandoned such naive dreams, or he might have been disappointed.

The neko slurped the soup as he watched Ryuu from the corner of his yellow cat-eye. Though the neko was bound to serve him. He was never quite servile and delighted in any chance to annoy Ryuu. At first it had gotten under his skin, in that first century he'd tried to break the neko. But as time went on, he learned that respect could not be forced. And so they remained bound together for eternity in this vaguely antagonist servant and master relationship. At least he was a competent spy.

"Since you're back, I'm assuming that means you've found more information for me?" Ryuu asked as he picked up the jug of sake from the tray. Empty. Of course, it was. He set it back down again with a subdued sigh.

Smacking his lips, the neko set down the empty bowl. "I have, but there wasn't much to find."

"What did you find?" Ryuu asked

The neko fanned out his hand and examined his nails. "A shrine in the center of a valley. I descended into it and was overcome by a blinding fog. I stumbled around for a while, and when I came out of it, I was miles away. I made additional attempts, but the results were all the same. The closest I got was following some human carrying supplies, but once he passed through the torii arches in the pass, I could follow him no further. As far as I can tell, there are multiple layers of barriers around it. As a yokai, I couldn't get close enough to confirm anything, but they don't put that many obstacles around some rural shrine without a reason." His whiskers twitched as his cat ears swiveled toward the door.

Ryuu drummed his fingers on his knees. A hidden shrine in a valley under numerous protective seals. As the neko could not get closer, it was clearly of human design. It could be nothing but more likely it was hiding something, perhaps this is where Izume and her father had hidden away the last piece of Kazue's soul after they'd stolen it from him.

"Were you expecting company?" The neko asked seconds before the knock at the door.

"You could have warned me sooner," Ryuu said.

The neko shrugged as Ryuu headed for the door and picked up Tetsuyama on the way. Though he was among allies, old habits were hard to break. A half-breed like him was resented for simply existing. And given his uneasy place in The Dragon's court, he would take all precautions.

One hand on the hilt of Tetsuyama, Ryuu slid the door open. Suzume awaited him, her hair was damp, and her haori singed, and yet she smiled brightly. A smile which was too much like her mother, Izume's.

"What happened to you?" Ryuu asked, as he stepped aside to let her in.

"I've found them, the last soul piece!" she said as she rushed inside, leaving wet sandy footprints on the tatami.

At last, the pieces of Kazue's soul were reunited. But this was only the beginning; with the soul united, they would need to learn to resonate before they could hope to defeat Hisato. "Where are they? I am eager to meet them."

Suzume frowned. "Well, there's a slight problem... they kind of ran away."

"Then you haven't really found them?" The neko asked, raising a single whiskered brow.

"I have, they're close by, I can feel it." Suzume placed a hand over her heart. It pulled at her burned clothes and exposed the blistered flesh of her shoulder. She'd been injured, and yet she was smiling, excited even. How she had changed...

There was more to this story, and he would rather not have an audience. Ryuuu caught the neko's gaze and jerked his head toward the door, indicating he should leave.

"I know when I'm not needed." The neko rose up with an exaggerated stretch, before sauntering toward the door, his forked tail swishing as he walked.

"Please, sit," Ryuu said to Suzume as he extended his arm, Ryuu gestured toward the cushions beside empty dinner plates.

Suzume took a seat on one of the cushions and drummed her fingers on her thigh, as she stared at the door. "We shouldn't be wasting time, she might be getting away as we speak."

"You've been injured, seeing to your wounds should come before anything else." Ryuu went to fetch the medical kit he kept just in case. Once he found it on the top of a nearby trunk, he brought it over to Suzume. "Let's see that shoulder burn."

Suzume pulled up her burnt haori closer to her neck. "They'll heal. I only agreed to come back to the palace, because Naoki is worried chasing her might be a trap."

Ryuu sat back and crossed his arms over his chest. He knew that glimmer in her eyes, it was too much like her mother, Izume. When she set her mind on something, nothing would deter her.

"He's right not to let you rush in. What if you had been more seriously injured? You're safer here within these walls, while we make a plan. Now let me treat your burn."

She sighed heavily, pulling down collar of her haori to expose her burned shoulder. It was an angry red. "You sound like Kaito, if it were up to the two of you I would be locked inside forever."

A scoff escaped his lips without meaning. Just like The Dragon? She couldn't really mean that. Kaito might be his sire, but they were nothing alike. He dabbed the salve on her burn a little harder than he intended, and Suzume hissed.

"We've spent months searching for the missing piece of Kazue's soul, doesn't it seem odd that she arrives now, right under our noses?" He said as he wrapped her burn.

It could not have been mere coincidence that the soul piece arrived now, just as the neko returned with news of the hidden shrine. The two must be connected.

"But what if she's been trying to find us as well? Today when the hybrids attacked me, she raised a wave to save me from them." Suzume pulled back up hoari.

"Or she could have been trying to drown you," Ryuu replied, while packing away the salve and bandages.

"If you're trying to tell me to be patient and just wait, I've done that, for months. I can't sit still any longer, not while Hisato has my family." Suzume threw her arms up, and the glass in front of her wobbled dangerously until he caught it in time and moved it away from her flailing appendages.

To someone who'd lived as long as him, a few months were the blink of an eye. But for Suzume, it might feel like an eternity. The memories of the restless youth he'd once been bubbled up to the surface. If he told her about the hidden shrine, her hunger for adventure could put her in more danger than she already was. At times he envied her innocence, having never truly experienced danger and loss as he had. She had the confidence of youth. If only she could remain this innocent forever.

"This could just as likely be a trap set by Hisato. He has used pieces of Kazue's soul to trick you before."

"This won't end until all the soul pieces are united. I'm done waiting, either you join me or I go alone." She jumped to her feet and made her way to the door.

Just the thought of her rushing in, straight into a likely trap, made his chest tight. He'd lost too many over the centuries, he wouldn't lose her too.

"Don't go," Ryuu said with a sigh.

Her hand was reaching for the door when she turned and scowled at him. In that moment, she was very much like Izume. How many times had they argued, only for her to storm out and him to chase after her? Izume had him wrapped around her little finger in those days, and without realizing it, Suzume had done the same.

He ran a hand over his face. What was he doing?

"Even Kaito has stopped treating me like a child, why can't you?"

Would it be inappropriate to confess he saw her as a child? Young and foolhardy. In her, he saw a reflection of himself at her age, ready to take on the world, unaware of the dangers that lay before him. And being that she was Izume's daughter who he had sworn to protect from the moment of her birth, he was even more obligated to keep her safe. And unlike the parents who had abandoned him, he wanted to protect her from all the world's dangers.

"I apologize, you are right, your strength has improved immensely in the past few months. And I should give you more credit to your abilities," he said.

"But?" She narrowed her eyes at him.

"Just today, I received information about a hidden shrine in a valley not far from here, it could be that is where the last piece of Kazue's soul is hidden," Ryuu said hesitantly.

"We know exactly where to find them, what are we waiting for?"

Ryuu approached her and put his hand on top of her head. "I acknowledge your powers have improved. But if this is a trap Hisato has set, then it puts more than you in danger, but us all. We cannot let him capture you."

She heaved a sigh. "Then what do you suggest?"

It was a hollow triumph. He couldn't avoid investigating the shrine now, nor would he put Suzume in danger. Which left only one option. He would have to go there himself.

"I will go and find out what secrets the shrine hides. And if I find the last soul piece there, I will bring them back."

Suzume scowled at the ground. She didn't like it, but it was what was best for her. Just then there was a knock on the door. Ryuu and Suzume shared a look, and he reached for Tetsuyama once again, but when he opened the door, Rin was there to greet him with a smile.

"Oh, you're both here, good. Kaito has called for a council meeting, he says he has an important announcement to make." Her smile was strained.

Bad omens came in threes. What was it that The Dragon was planning?

SIX

As Kaito entered the audience hall. Streams of golden sunlight filtered through sliding doors, and a salty breeze blew onto freshly painted red arches that towered over the assembled yokai as they rolled back, like the waves from the shoreline for him to pass through. This was what he had been missing, a sea of adoring subjects.

Many of the old clans had returned, as he caught a glimpse of familiar faces in the crowd, he smiled and nodded, receiving solemn nods in return. This was who he was meant to be. And after centuries of suffering, his kingdom was restored. A yamawaro, a hairy one-eyed yokai, wearing nothing but a loin cloth bowed deeply before him.

"Master, we of the yamawaro clan are at your service." His coarse hair stuck out in all directions as his forehead nearly touched the ground, his clansmen followed in his footsteps.

This wasn't the representative of the yamawaro he remembered. As he glanced around the room, seeking out familiar faces, strangers stared back at him. The palace might be restored, but the old court was gone. Allies had fallen in his absence, and friends had yet to return.

"You shall be rewarded for your loyalty," Kaito said, before striding away. If he weren't careful, they'd all start groveling, and then it would be hours before he got to his announcement.

At the front of the room, his closest generals and advisers awaited him. Hana and the other dragons who'd once followed his brother, Jirou, bowed at his approach. When Kaito had come to reclaim his kingdom, he had found Jirou playing pretender. And when Jirou betrayed him and tried to kill Suzume, he had no choice but to kill him. Jirou might be gone, but his specter continued to haunt him. At times he thought he caught a glimpse of Jirou, among the other dragons or in the halls. Kaito had killed many times before, but this death among all others lingered. Like a wound that would not heal. And perhaps never would.

Even though the dragons had followed his brother, they were loyal to Kaito now and had earned their place as his elite guards. Beside them were Rin and Shin, his oldest and most trusted friends, along with Naoki and the leader of the Oni whose father had once been Kaito's general. They all bowed as he approached, Shin, in particular, giving Kaito a wolfish grin. With his trusted general at his side, and his subjects before him, all he needed was his empress to rule beside him.

He took his place on the dais facing his subjects. Their hungry eyes stared up at him, they wanted peace. Centuries of fighting had left his once peaceful kingdom divided. As their ruler, it was his duty to restore peace. Hisato had sown discord among them all for too long, and the only way to unite Akatsuki and stop Hisato was to make peace with the humans. They would resist; it was in yokai nature to hate humans. But he would make them see, if there could be love between a human and a yokai, then couldn't there be peace among their two kinds?

Kaito scanned the crowd, but Suzume was nowhere to be seen. Was she really still angry? He'd stayed away from her, even when Naoki had reported the attack on the nearby human village. Even after he had learned Suzume had nearly drowned. He hoped she would come to him, so they could plan their next move, but the chilly silence between them only grew. Everyone was ordered to come to hear his announcement, he couldn't declare her his bride without her here. Kaito motioned for Rin.

"What is it?" she asked in a hushed tone.

"Where is Suzume?"

Her fox ears tilted backward as she looked around the room. "I told her she couldn't miss this, just like you said." Her bushy tail flicked back and forth. "She didn't seem happy about it. Are you sure we need her here just for a council meeting?"

"Yes, it is crucial that she is here."

Rin sighed heavily. Before stepping away from the dais.

For now, he would proceed as planned. If anyone could coax Suzume here, it was her. "I am happy to see many new and familiar faces here in my hall," Kaito said, his voice echoing around the room. "I see we have the uwan, shojo, and yambiko clans here."

Each representative stepped forward, bowing their heads as they were acknowledged. It helped to fluff a few egos before getting into the meat of the matter. They were of lesser power, and before he'd been sealed, he would never have bothered paying them any lip service. But clawing his way back to his former glory was not without sacrifice. And he wanted them all in a good mood before he revealed his plans.

"There is still much work to be done," Kaito said, his voice booming over the crowd. "These are trying times, indeed. For centuries our kind have been at war with one another. But it's time we put our differences aside and join hand in hand as one kingdom once more. The feuding between clans will come to an end, and we shall rise to a new era of peace."

The yokai cheered, their voices a mix of roars, squawks, stamping feet, and growls. Kaito basked in their admiration for a few moments before holding up a hand to silence them.

"There are still many more of us missing, where are the tengu, the kirin, the baku, and the reiki?" Kaito looked across the crowd. None of those who were gathered would look him straight in the eye. While many had returned, some had never come back. None hurt him more than the tengu. Before Kazue had sealed him away, the tengu had been his strongest supporters. The Elder's oldest son, Morikazu, had been his general. And yet months had passed, and multiple attempts to reach them had come back unanswered.

Shin stepped forward. "Great Dragon," he said loud enough for his voice to carry.

"Yes, Shin." Kaito gestured with his hand for him to continue. At the back of the room, Rin led in Suzume, whose head was down and her arms crossed over her chest. Good, everything was going according to plan, then. Only as Rin made her way around the edges of the room to return to the front, Suzume remained at the back of the crowd, with that bastard, Ryuu. They were mere inches between them, their shoulders almost brushing as he leaned down much too close to whisper in her ear. Kaito balled his hand into a fist as Suzume's lips curled in a smile. What was that bastard saying to her?

"What do you think of this plan, Great Dragon?" Shin prompted. With his back to the crowd, they could not see the furrowed brows on his face. He'd been so distracted by Suzume's entry he'd lost track of what he was saying.

"I trust your judgment Shin, it shall be done as you say," Kaito replied.

"Then, as I suggest, Hana to the kirin, and the oni to the reiki, and I shall go to the baku, while Rin goes to the tengu."

Beside him, Rin yelped before clamping a hand over her mouth. Her ears flat against her head as she glared at Shin, who smirked back at her.

"It is decided then," Kaito said, his eyes still on Suzume. She was avoiding looking at him. Instead, her head was tilted, so she faced Ryuu. She must be doing this to drive him mad.

Rin cleared her throat. "Once the clans have rejoined us..." Rin prompted him in a whisper.

He'd been so distracted by Suzume flirting with that bastard, that he'd nearly forgotten. The crowd stared up at him, awaiting his announcement.

"With the clans' alliance, we will nearly be a unified Akatsuki once more. But one piece remains," Kaito said and paused letting the tension build. Suzume tossed her hair over her shoulder, laughing at something Ryuu said. He needed to end this and now. "To truly bring peace to Akatsuki, we must end eons of war with the humans, and I plan to do so by marrying the human emperor's daughter, Suzume."

There was a collective gasp around the room, followed by the heightened whispers of the onlookers. Heads swiveled around as many bodies fidgeted among the crowd. Suzume's gaze snapped up toward him at last, her eyes were blown wide. Beside her, that bastard crossed his arms over his chest, brow furrowed.

"You must be joking," the oni leader shouted.

Kaito glared in his direction. "I am quite serious."

The oni flattened his lips together, his hand reaching for the hilt of his blade.

"This madness, you would marry a human?" asked another yokai.

"I have declared it before, and I will say it again, Suzume is my woman, and through our love and union, we shall unite our two kinds."

The ebb of voices rose as one, where no single one could be distinguished from the rest. A yokai at the back of the room pointed out Suzume. And they started to close in around her. Suzume reached for her staff, and Ryuu stepped forward, thrusting out his arm to protect Suzume.

"Calm yourselves!" Kaito roared, but his command was lost in the voices rising up in anger. Unable to calm them with a word, Kaito jumped down from the dais, pushing the crowd. A press of bodies closed the space between them, and he lost sight of Suzume. They closed in around him, claws, hooves, and hands grasped for his sleeves, his face and his shoulder. Twisted, angry faces shoved and pushed, trying to get into his face.

"We cannot accept a human."

"How could you betray your own kind!"

"Kill the human!"

"Out of my way!" he growled, as he shoved them aside.

The Dragon's guards, Shin and Rin, encircled him, pushing back the crowd and giving him space to move forward. He'd known they wouldn't approve, but he never expected quite so volatile a reaction. Shin led the way, cutting a path through the crowd, leading him out of the hall, more and more yokai poured out chasing after him, their shouts reaching a fever pitch. But where was Suzume? He had to make sure she was safe.

"Where is Suzume?" Kaito asked Shin.

"I'm more worried about you getting torn to shreds," Shin said with a shake of his head. "What were you thinking?"

Kaito didn't respond, instead focusing his energy trying to find her in the crowd. But there were too many yokai, too much noise. They pushed through the mob, and made their way to the inner palace, where none but his inner circle could enter. The guards blocking the entryway, stopped the crowd, and in the courtyard beyond Suzume stood with hands on hips, Naoki, Tsuki, and Ryuu on guard.

As he approached, her head popped up, and she stomped toward him. "Are you trying to get me killed?" She pointed a finger at his chest.

Flames flickered around her body as her temper rose. Normally he would have found it charming, but right now, his only concern was her safety. He grasped her, pulling her into his embrace.

"I'm so glad you're not hurt."

She shoved him back. "No thanks to you."

"What were you thinking declaring you'd marry a human?" That bastard Ryuu said, inserting himself into their conversation.

Kaito met that bastard's gaze, a growl rumbled in his throat. "It doesn't concern you."

Ryuu grabbed Suzume's shoulder, pulling her closer to him. "Suzume's safety is my concern. And if you cared for her, you wouldn't have done something so reckless."

"You forget your place," Kaito snarled, taking a step closer to Ryuu and jabbing his chest with his index finger. He never should have let this bastard stay; he'd known from the moment they met he was trouble.

Suzume inserted herself between them, hands on either of their chests. "I don't need either of you to protect me." Then pointing at Kaito, she said, "But you must want me dead. Don't you realize those yokai all hate me more than before now? How could you suggest we get married?" Her voice rose, she was flustered.

He grasped Suzume's wrist. "Let's talk, alone..."

Before she could protest, he dragged her into the room he prepared for her, which remained empty since their fight. Someone had cleaned up since he tore it all apart.

When they were alone at last, she yanked her arm free, and stood back, her legs apart, and her hands balled into fists as if she were preparing to spar with him.

"I'm done playing games with you, do you want to sleep with

me or do you want me dead? I can't keep up with this back and forth anymore," Suzume snapped.

Kaito blinked a few times as her words sunk in. Hadn't he made himself and his desires clear? "Isn't it obvious, I plan on marrying you," he said in a teasing tone.

She swung her hand back, presumably to slap him but he caught it before that. It was so small and fragile, and belied her inner strength, that fire, and tenacity which had drawn him to her. The perfect balance to his ice. It had taken their fight for him to realize just how perfect she would be ruling at his side.

"This isn't funny." Flames flickered in her dark gaze, and she tried to pull free, but he held on tighter.

Pulling her close, he snaked one arm around her waist. He'd wanted to do this for so long, to feel her melt into him. But instead, her hands were pressed against his chest as she arched backward, doing her best to pull away from him. She really didn't believe him when he said he wanted to marry her? Did she not think his feelings were sincere, either?

"It's not a joke, I want to make you my empress," he said in a more solemn tone.

Her mouth fell open, as her eyes grew wide. He knew how much she craved power, she was ambitious. Being a human among yokai wasn't easy, he knew that. But Suzume had proven herself more than capable of standing against them. She'd defeated the hybrids attacking the village without fear. That sort of strength was what he needed in his partner. Didn't she see that?

She shook her head. "It has to be, because the yokai will never accept me to rule over them."

The yokai had never questioned his decree before. When he'd hidden Kazue away, it had been to protect her from his enemies, not because he feared rebellion from his people. They feared change, but they would come around, he would make them see the benefits of a human alliance.

"Since when did you need anyone else's approval? You will make them love you." He dipped down, his lips nearly brushing against hers. But she turned her head away.

"How do I know you mean it, that this isn't a trick." She crossed her arms over her chest, watching him warily.

"Are my words not enough for you?" he asked, trying to fight back the agitation that threatened to bubble up. What else did he need to do to prove his feelings for her?

"You've tricked me before, when we first met—"

"From the moment I met you, I was drawn to you. I tried to fight my feelings for you, but no matter how I ran from them, I couldn't escape them. The only times I lied to you was when I said I didn't want you." There, he'd said it.

She bit her lip, avoiding his gaze. He reached for her hand, threading their fingers together, she didn't pull away this time. At least that was progress. Though he wanted to pull her into his embrace, they might need to take things slow.

"I don't even know how I feel yet. Marriage feels too sudden," she said to the ground.

"You were willing to marry that general," Kaito said.

"That was different," she said softly, her lips parted ever so gently.

"How so?" He leaned in closer, their faces were inches apart.

"I knew how I felt about him."

"You loved him?"

She laughed, the faintest smile at the corner of her lips lingered. "Not at all. And that's what made it easy."

He tugged her a little closer. She didn't pull away, but she wouldn't look at him either. It was small progress, he could be glad for that at least. Cautiously, he turned her hand palm up and caressed the newly forming calluses there. "Your life is your own, and now the decision is yours, I will not force you." Though he would very much like for her to hurry up and stop torturing him with this endless waiting.

She tilted her head back, exposing the column of her throat, as she met his gaze. He wanted to kiss his way up it, to express with his touch just how much she was driving him mad. But she was wary, uncertain, and he wouldn't ruin this moment, or let her run away again.

It was tempting to force a confession from her, to make her confront her feelings for him. But he knew her well enough to know that would give him the opposite of what he wanted.

He cupped her cheek, his thumb grazing her lip. "I promise not to rush you. I will let you come to me. But I am an impatient man, don't keep me waiting forever."

She melted in his grip, and it took all his willpower not to kiss her. He stepped back.

"I'll await your decision."

Seven

ocus. Akira just had to focus. The time between night and day was the balancing edge of her and Tsuki's dual existence. Breathe in and out, in and out. She must let everything else fade away, but for the air that filled her lungs, the cool caress of the waves against her bare feet, the grit of sand between her toes, and the lingering rays of sun kissing her face.

The rhythm of her heartbeat synced up with the pounding of the waves. Closing her eyes, she dove down into the space between, the world of the physical and the world of the spiritual. Seeing with her mind's eyes, she sought out the twin rivers of energy of her and Tsuki's souls. They burned bright in the darkness of the spiritual realm. One midnight blue and one the golden sun of a noonday. All living things had their own river, the life blood of the soul. They were unique in that their spiritual river was doubled, two nearly identical rivers that ran parallel within them. Centuries had passed since Kazue had bound their souls together this way. And though Akira had tried countless times to untangle them, they remained two in one. Until now.

The rivers' edges had overflowed their banks, and the space in between had become a muddy mire, filled with thick, sluggish ooze. This must be the source of the dissonance, or perhaps a symptom of the water of Kazue's soul's song. Reaching out toward the black ooze, she dipped her hand into it. The ooze pulled her down to the elbow and where her fingertips brushed against something round and smooth. A stone? Her fingers fumbled to grasp it, until at last, she took hold of it. As she did, she heard a whisper. No. A hiss.

The stone dragged her down below the surface. Darkness enveloped her, trapped her inside an empty void of nothing, where she endlessly tumbled, free-falling while the air was squeezed from her lungs, warmth leached from her skin, and all sense of touch erased from her memory. Akira opened her mouth to scream only to have it filled thick black sludge. She was drowning. No, they were drowning, because somehow, impossibly, Tsuki was here beside her even in the spiritual realm. But she could not feel where he began, and she ended. The lines were smeared beyond comprehension. Who was Akira, and who was Tsuki? Everything was a jumble of fear and rage. And then it stopped.

There was nothing, just a yawning emptiness of bleak eternity.

Akira's eyes flew open, and she gasped. Panting for breath, she fell to her knees in the sand. The sun had started to sink below the horizon, the twilight in-between had passed. The tide was rising, and it soaked her knees as she tried to catch her breath.

"Did you find anything?" Tsuki asked. He had not felt it as she had. Not like the first time. But whatever it was that water of

Kazue's soul had left in them was waiting, biding its time growing. She felt it eating away from the inside out, like a canker that would slowly kill them. How much longer before it consumed them both?

"Darkness. The dissonance is getting stronger, just as she said it would. I tried to remove it, but it pulled me under." Akira stood and wiped the sand from her kimono. Tsuki expected her to protect them; as his older sister, it was her job to keep them alive. They'd come too far to lose everything now. Damn that woman. She knew too much and was too powerful for a mere fragment.

"I think it's time we ask the others for help," Tsuki said. She could feel his fear through their bond.

All these centuries together, and he was so rarely afraid. Nothing scared her reckless brother. His uncertainty was seeping through and putting her on edge as well. This was worse than what Kazue had done to them. If this continued they would lose themselves entirely. Though she shared his fears, enlisting the help of others was out of the question. None of them could be trusted to not use their condition against them.

"No, I will find a way to remove the darkness. I just need more time," Akira said.

"Just like we were able to separate?"

How dare he throw her failure back in her face. When it was his arrogance that had trapped them both. If only he hadn't underestimated her power on first meeting, or believed her lies. Both then and now, she was the one left cleaning up his messes. He'd grown too attached to Suzume and the others, and put too much faith in their ability. If this fragment had this much power, then perhaps she was strong enough to separate them at last.

"I can feel your anger. Now more than ever, we need to be united," Tsuki said.

And he was right. They'd squabbled enough in those early centuries. It left them weak and more entangled. As if they were a rabbit in a snare, they'd been slowly choking themselves to death. With time and patience, they learned to create harmony between them. Their goals must be aligned, one mind, and one purpose. Now it was time to just make a plan and move forward.

"You're right. I know your fears, brother, because I share them. We cannot ask the others for help. Not yet, not until we understand what has been done to us."

Naoki, her father, materialized beside her. And Akira jerked backward, pressing her hand to her chest. Distracted as she'd been, she had not seen him approach. A miscalculation. She despised surprises almost as much as she hated to reveal she'd been surprised. His ability to cloak his spiritual energy and move without a sound often caught her off guard, but under different circumstances, she would not have reacted.

"Father," Akira bowed her head to him.

"The Dragon has ordered us to guard Suzume," Father said.

As usual, their interactions were transactional. There was no affection in the man. What Mother had seen in him, she would never know.

"Is that so?" A small part of her wanted to rebel. She was not beholden to The Dragon, and she resented him trying to order her and Tsuki. If her interests were not aligned, she would have done just that. But as it were, they still needed to keep Suzume safe. Until they were free of Kazue's curse, she wasn't letting go of her last hope of freedom.

Father's dark gaze was fixed on her. Though she couldn't feel his spiritual probes, she had the distinct feeling he was assessing them. Did he feel the darkness growing inside them? If he did, would he tell the others?

"Maybe he knows how to fix this," Tsuki said.

"We don't need his help."

Where had he been while Mother withered away trapped on that mountain top? Where was he as they fought every day to keep her from fading away. Where was he when Kazue had trapped them inside one body. Father only knew how to serve. His loyalty was to Kazue and now to Suzume, who had Kazue's heart. He would be of no help to them.

"The yokai are restless," Naoki replied.

"What's new," Tsuki said without bothering to take control of their body.

"He declared he will marry her," Father said with the slightest downward quirk of his mouth. He would never speak his true feelings aloud, but she recognized his disappointment.

Had The Dragon gone mad? He would make Suzume his wife? She shook her head. Fool dragon. She should have kept them apart when she had the chance. Now their fates were too entangled to separate them again. Kazue's downfall had been The Dragon, and here Suzume was repeating her predecessor's mistakes. Maybe Akira was the fool for continuing to cling to the idea that Suzume and the other fragments could separate them.

"We better do as The Dragon bids then." She gave Father an insincere smile and followed him back to the palace.

"What now? We don't have time to watch her day and night and remove this dissonance," Tsuki said.

"I know," Akira said, and her fingers twitched, if only she could strangle the life out of that damned idiot of a dragon.

"We can't do this alone. Let's ask Father for help," Tsuki said as he tried to take control of their body.

For the first time in centuries, she held onto control of the body they shared. Tsuki was reckless, rushing in to do things without thinking.

"What are you doing?" Tsuki growled.

"Stopping you. We will not rush in without a plan again. That's what got us into this in the first place."

"You would damn us both while you think."

"Don't."

Akira clenched her fists as her skin bubbled and rolled while Tsuki wrestled against her, a black haze filled her vision. Naoki turned and looked at them with a slight frown. He was coming toward them, he would realize that they'd been corrupted. Would he try and subdue them, or cure them? It didn't matter. She wouldn't continue being someone else's puppet.

"Bring me the staff," A voice whispered through their connection. It wasn't Tsuki. A cold chill rushed over her body. This voice was familiar. It was the darkness within them.

"Bring it to me, I command you."

Her footsteps marched forward outside of her control. It was the last thing she remembered before everything went black.

SUZUME'S VACANT ROOM GREETED HER. THE COALS IN THE BRAZIER HAD burned low and cast feeble light on the walls and little else. She trudged across the tatami, passing by her ice-cold dinner. She had no stomach for it and tossed her staff on the edge of her futon, before flinging herself down. After everything that had happened today, she should be exhausted, but her buzzing mind wouldn't allow her to rest. The sound of the ocean rumbled outside the open doors, which led onto her balcony. Flipping over onto her back, she stared up at the dark abyss above her bed. The memory of Kaito's touch, his lips ghosting over hers heated her face. She flopped over and buried her head in the blankets. Was he insane? Truly? One minute he was showering her in gifts like a common courtesan, the next thing he was declaring her his future empress.

And worse, she hadn't rejected him. She said she would think about it. She must be even more insane. The yokai hated her. And it wasn't as if a marital alliance was even possible. Father hated yokai. He'd declared war on them! During her time back at the White Palace, she felt as if she'd reconnected with him. But somehow, she doubted that affection would extend to her marrying a dragon. And this was Kaito she was talking about, who delighted in tormenting her. Whose sort of kiss she couldn't get out of her head. Maybe she was losing it.

She kicked her blankets, rolling over and knocking into her staff, which skidded across the floor. How was it that whenever she was alone with Kaito, she melted into idiotic goo? This was why she had avoided him. She'd tried to distract herself from traitorous thoughts of him, the ridiculous idea of being with him... that way... She wasn't even sure about how she felt, and he was talking about marriage.

She forced a laugh as she sprung up to pace the room. It was out of the question. The humans wouldn't accept it. The yokai wouldn't accept it. She should have turned him down straight away. Kaito had painted an even bigger target on her back. How was she going to train? They would tear her apart the moment she tried to leave the courtyard. She would have to stay in the inner ring of the palace, maybe forever...

Had that been his plan all along? When she denied him the first time, he found another way to cage her? Her face was flushed, and her throat was tight. The walls of her room were closing in around her. She rushed toward the door and out into the courtyard beyond. Once she was outside, she took a large, gulping breath. Clutching her chest as she leaned against a column.

She had to leave, get out of the palace. Maybe jump on a fishing boat and head for the mainland. Somewhere neither Kaito or Hisato could ever find her. Or maybe she could catch up with Ryuu, beg him to take her with him to find the last piece of Kazue's soul. Before she could second guess herself, she turned back to her room, she had to get her staff and go, before Kaito came looking for her. Before she did something else she'd regret.

Wind rustled through the trees, like the whisper of silk, and a chill ran up her spine. A piece of her soul was calling out to its partner. It drew Suzume's gaze to the sakura tree. Souta, the wind of Kazue's soul, stood under the cascade of petals. Had he been there the whole time?

"Can't sleep?" Souta asked without turning to look at her.

She stood up a little straighter. Though she had spent a lot of time with Souta in the training yard, she didn't want him seeing her agonizing over how she felt about Kaito.

"Something like that." If Souta knew she was trying to run, would he notify Kaito, or would he aid her? He was loyal to Ryuu, and Ryuu had told her to wait here for him. So it was likely he wouldn't help her leave. Most of the time, when she and Souta sparred, he beat her. If she tried to fight him, she would lose. She'd have to head back to her room and wait until he went to bed, then she would escape.

He nodded his head as if she had said something deeply profound. He rested a wrinkled palm on the trunk of the sakura tree. "I've seen much in my long life, but I've never seen a sakura bloom in winter."

"Yeah, it's really strange. I should probably be heading to bed, training in the morning, and all..." She gestured back toward her room and started backing away.

"Running away?" Souta said, canting his head to the side as he regarded her with dark eyes.

How had he known? Was he bluffing, or was it written on her face?

"No, it's like you said, I couldn't sleep."

"Ah. My mistake. I guess you've tried running away from him before, and that didn't quite work out, did it?" He turned his back to her and folded his hands behind his back as he regarded the cherry blossom.

She chuckled, but it sounded fake even to her.

"Yeah. I guess not—"

"You must have answered his proposal then?" He turned to her fully now, pinning her with his unreadable dark gaze.

The old man had the uncanny ability to see right through her. Not that she would admit that to him. Souta was also the last person she thought she'd be talking about her feelings with. But the words were caught in the back of her throat; maybe if she just expelled them, she could breathe easier.

"I told him I would think about it." There she'd said it.

"Hmm," Souta replied and held up his hand, catching a falling blossom.

That was it?

"If you don't have any more questions for me, I think I'll—"

"Mortality is a lot like these cherry blossoms. The blooms are transient; even under their normal conditions, they were fleeting. But bloomed in the winter, their beauty expires much too fast."

She contemplated throttling him, were they writing poetry or discussing her running away? She wasn't sure anymore. Petals drifted down and carpeted the ground. The perfume of cherry blossoms filled her nose. For an immortal like Kaito, she was like these flower petals. Something to cherish in that moment but temporary. Once more, she found herself sympathizing with Kazue. No wonder she had sought immortality. Just thinking of aging, and dying while Kaito stayed ever the same made her insides squirm.

"Are you saying I shouldn't marry Kaito?" she asked.

He tipped his hand, letting the petal fall once more. "I am saying that happiness, like these blossoms, can be fleeting. It is better to appreciate it while you have it, rather than worry about when it will be gone."

She shook her head as she rolled her eyes. Leave it to Souta to start spewing philosophy. "But the outcome doesn't change. Even past happiness cannot erase future despair."

He put his hand on her shoulder in a grandfatherly gesture, "How can you be certain if you've never let yourself be happy?"

Her mouth dropped open, and he smiled. With a quick pat, he turned and walked away whistling under his breath. For most of her life, she had always been seeking out future happiness. When she was married to the right man, when she had the power she craved, she thought she would be happy. But had she ever stopped to try and be happy with what she had in that moment? She wasn't sure.

A crash came from nearby, and Suzume swiveled to see where it had come from.

Tsuki strode toward her, or was it Akira. It was hard to see them clearly in the dark.

"You scared the life out me what are you—" She swallowed her words.

He had stepped out of the shadows and moonlight glinted off the edge of their blade as they looked at her with eyes like dark bottomless pits.

"What's wrong with your—" before she could even finish her sentence, he swung his sword at her head.

Suzume ducked to avoid the sweep of Tsuki's blade. As she backed away, he stalked closer. This wasn't Tsuki; it was as if something had possessed him. She reached for her staff and grasped nothing. Tsuki thrust his blade at her, and she dodged by rolling on the ground. She sprung up and clenched her fist as she called for her flame. Tsuki charged her, swinging his blade in a wide arc, forcing her to retreat behind the nearby sakura tree. Sparks lit along her fingertips, but it was nowhere near the blaze she needed to defend herself. The power was there, right beneath the surface. She could feel it broiling inside her, desperate for a release, but try as she might it wouldn't come to her summons. Tsuki hacked at the trunk of the sakura inches from her face, and she bolted back for the veranda.

"I don't want to hurt you, Tsuki," she shouted as he gave chase to her.

A meager flame filled her palm, flickered, and died. Why was her power failing her now? After months of practice, she could summon it without a problem. Maybe she needed her staff, to better channel her power. If she could just subdue Tsuki, they could figure out what had taken hold of him. Her chamber wasn't far away, and Tsuki was closing in as he slashed everything in his path to get to her. She threw open her door and stumbled inside. Her staff, where was it. Earlier she had thrown it down on her bed.

Suzume tossed aside her blanket and upended the futon, but it wasn't there. Fear lodged in her throat.

A crash rattled through the room, and she spun as Tsuki burst through the shattered remains of her chamber door.

On the floor between them was her staff, she must have overlooked it. Tsuki loomed in the doorway, an aberration of himself. His eyes were black and without pupils, and the features a peculiar mix of Akira and Tsuki, her round cheeks, and his angular jawline. Akira's lips but Tsuki's brows. It was as if someone had mixed them together. He stalked closer, and she pounced on her staff. But Tsuki was quicker to it and plucked it off the ground holding it above her head.

"Looking for this?" he taunted, in a grotesque mimicry of Tsuki's typical teasing. His voice echoed as if two people were talking at once.

"I don't know what happened to you, but let's talk this out," Suzume held up her hands in surrender as he slowly moved toward her, sword in one hand and her staff in the other.

A sinister smile crossed his expression; it curled up the corners of his mouth in a bizarre fashion, that was vaguely familiar. The hairs on her neck stood on end; she knew this smile. It was Hisato's.

"What have you done to them, Hisato?" Suzume said, as she backed up, he inched closer. There was nowhere for her to go, but the balcony, and beyond that was a long drop into the ocean. Even if she could swim, the fall to the water below might just kill her. One hand behind her back, she tried to summon her flames to no avail. It was as if someone had put a damper upon them, she couldn't call for it as easily. If only Souta and Hikaru were here, their resonance might be enough.

"We are not Hisato," their voices echoed together as if two voices were speaking at once.

"You're not Akira or Tsuki, either."

"No." Their smile faded for a moment. The skin bubbled and twitched as if something was alive and crawling beneath their skin. They grasped their skull and growled. The white was returning to their eyes, and just for a moment, she thought she saw Akira.

She lurched forward and grasped for the staff. Her fingers barely grazed it before they were yanking it out of her grip. Suzume fell forward onto her knees, and pivoted to face them.

They shook their head, and the pupiless eyes returned. They tilted their head to Suzume, in a mocking bow, they escaped out the door to the balcony. Suzume chased after them, but it was too late. They jumped over the railing and plunged into the crashing waves below. Grasping the edge of the railing, she scoured the white-capped waves crashing upon the rocks below. Thankfully she didn't spot their shattered body on those jagged rocks. She held her breath, and in a few heartbeats, their head popped up between swells, her staff clutched in one hand they swam for the shore.

She had to catch them before they got too far away. As she burst out of her room, she was greeted by Naoki and Kaito

"Are you hurt." Kaito rushed over to her, grasping her by the shoulder, he scanned her up and down.

Even now, when Tsuki and Akira were being controlled by Hisato, his touch made her stomach do backflips. She shook away the thought and removed Kaito's hand from her shoulder.

"I'm fine, it's Tsuki and Akira that are the problem. They've been possessed. "

"Did they try to hurt you, I'll rip their throats out." Kaito bared his teeth and scanned the area as if they would materialize before him.

"It has to be Hisato, there's no other explanation." But how had he reached them, they were always in the palace or by her side. Unless that day, when the hybrids had attacked, they'd run into Hisato. If they had, why hadn't they said anything? They knew he could take control of people...

"I will capture them," Naoki said.

"I'm coming to, it was my staff they took." She looked to Kaito, jutting out her chin, challenging him to try and stop her. Her flame might have abandoned her, but she wasn't going to stand by while her friends were in danger. He might think she was a teacup that would easily shatter, but she would prove to him otherwise.

"We'll need to move quickly if we want to capture them before they get away," Kaito said and strode toward the exit.

Suzume's mouth fell open. Was Kaito possessed as well?

"Coming?" he asked with a quirked brow and the ghost of a smile.

She cleared her throat. "Yes."

"Get on my back, we'll move faster if I carry you," Kaito squatted down for her to climb on. She hesitated for a moment. It was her impulse to argue with him, but he was right. They would move faster if he carried her, Tsuki and Akira had already gotten a big head start.

Reaching out a cautious hand, she wrapped her arms around his neck.

"Hold on tight," Kaito said.

And she clung on tighter, her chest pressed against his back. Every inch where their skin touched felt as if it were aflame, and her face flushed. Either Kaito didn't notice the rapid beat of her heart, or he was kind enough to not point it out. Kaito vaulted upward onto the roof of the nearest building. Naoki followed close behind them as they raced over the tops of the palace. And when they reached the courtyard, Suzume held her breath as he flew over the edge. Suzume yelped and clung tighter to Kaito.

"Don't worry, I won't let you fall," he said with a laugh.

"You better not, I still don't know how to swim."

"I would never let you go." His voice rumbled through her, and her blush deepened. He couldn't have meant it like that, could he?

But Kaito was doing a lot of things that surprised her lately. They sailed over the waves and landed on the beach beyond.

"We're going to go even faster now," Kaito warned her seconds before he dashed along the shore, kicking up sand in his wake.

Down the coast, Tsuki and Akira had swum to shore and were heading for the forest, which bordered the shoreline. If they made it, they would lose them among the trees.

"Head them off," Kaito instructed Naoki.

Naoki nodded before splitting off from them on a direct trajectory with Tsuki and Akira. Though they had a head start, Naoki's speed surpassed theirs. Before they could reach the forest, Naoki cut them off, his swords drawn. Tsuki, too drew Suzume's staff and his own blade as he charged at Naoki.

Kaito slowed a distance from them, letting Suzume off his back. This was where he would tell her to hide and wait for him and Naoki to handle everything. She clenched her hand into a fist, preparing her retort.

"You go to the right, I'll go left, and we'll pin them between the three of us," Kaito said to her.

She blinked at him a few times. Had she heard him correctly?

"You go it?" he confirmed, meeting her gaze. There was no playful smirk or tease in his tone. He was being sincere, he wanted her to fight beside him, as his equal.

She nodded her head, she was too shocked to form words. Then did that mean when he complimented her in front of the yokai, or declared her as his future wife was he really sincere?

Swords clanged, and Suzume shook her head. Now was not the time for dissecting her relationship with Kaito. Tsuki and Akira needed her. Face burning, she ran into position.

"You cannot hope to defeat us. Together our spiritual energy is much greater than yours, guardian," they said in that uncanny echoing tone.

Naoki did not bother to respond, instead swung his blades in a shimmering blur, forcing them onto their back foot. They circled one another trading blows one after another, as Suzume and Kaito closed in on either side. Her flame was there just beneath the surface, waiting to be unleashed. She only had to grasp it. But as she clenched and unclenched her fist, it would not heed her command. She strained and grunted, only earning a few fizzling sparks.

Naoki stumbled backward, falling onto the ground, and Tsuki crowed in triumph. It was a sound like the howl of the wolf that rattled her down to her bones. Tsuki swung toward her, leaving Naoki unmoving on the ground. How was it possible? Naoki and Tsuki had sparred countless times, and not once had Tsuki defeated Naoki.

Tsuki closed in on her, the plan had changed. From behind Tsuki, Kaito nodded. She needed to only distract him long enough for Kaito to sneak up and immobilize him.

"Don't come any closer." Suzume held up her hand, and a few meager embers fell from her palm.

"Don't waste your effort, you won't be able to summon the flame," they said, a dark miasma spewed from their hands and encircled the staff.

What was that? Had whatever Hisato done to them, made them stronger?

"Tsuki, Akira, I know you're in there, you don't have to do this," Suzume said. Kaito was getting closer, just a few seconds more...

Tsuki threw his head back in laughter. "You pretend to be our friend, but we were merely tools to you. Hisato has freed us, given us the power we crave."

"No." She knew Tsuki and Akira were her friends, they wouldn't betray her this way.

Kaito surged forward, his claws extended ready to attack. But as he closed in, Tsuki threw out his arm, and a shimmering black barrier enclosed them. Suzume's eyes were wide as they closed in on her, but as she turned to run, another blast of energy took her off her feet and threw her across the sand.

She rolled over, spitting out sand, as Tsuki closed in.

No. This was Hisato's trick, she refused to believe otherwise. She just had to call up the song of binding. The words were on the tip of her tongue, but as she tried to summon the words, they tangled inside her, as if an invisible hand was choking her. The power was within her, the staff was nothing but a tool. She didn't need it to defeat them. She was getting stronger. She just needed to concentrate. She tried to summon up the energy, the flame, but nothing came. Tsuki stalked over to her.

She crawled backward and away.

"You're nothing without the staff, without us. And we will never be your slaves again."

She tried to crawl away but collided with an invisible barrier. Tsuki held her staff up, dark miasma was pouring out from it as he brought it down toward her.

Suzume closed her eyes and threw her arms out, preparing for the strike. But it never came.

She opened her eyes, and Naoki had hold of the staff. His hair had come undone from his usual top knot and fell in his face. A trickle of blood ran down from a gash on his forehead. The dark mist that covered the staff, burned and blistered his palms.

"Enough," he growled.

Tsuki only smirked. "We've made our choice. You cannot stop us now, Hisato has made us too powerful."

They pushed against one another, pushing Naoki's heels into the sand. Then Tsuki tilted his head to the side, as if hearing a silent call. The smile on his face disappeared.

"Fate has spared you, for today. But we will meet again soon and get our revenge." He shoved Naoki backward before leaping into the air and rushing for the trees and out of sight. Suzume wanted to chase after them, but before she could get more than a few feet. Kaito caught her wrist and held her back. She spun around to face him.

"Don't hold me back, they took my staff." Her breath was heaving, her head spinning. Tsuki and Akira had chosen Hisato? How? It felt like a bad dream, one that she would wake from any moment.

"You did everything you could, but going after them now would be suicide," he said, there was a strange look in his gaze, and she thought she knew what it was. It was the feeling of betrayal, they'd lost their friends to Hisato.

AKIRA WOKE WITH A FOUL TASTE IN HER MOUTH. HER HEAD POUNDED as if she'd drank an eons-old sake. Sitting up, she blinked and squinted into the moonlight. Even the dim light made her head throb. Closing her eyes, she massaged her temple. Her hair was wet and coated in sand, as were her clothes. What she could take in through her blurred vision of her surroundings was an unfamiliar beach, a cove surrounded by cliffs on all sides. How had they gotten here? Where was here?

"Why does everything hurt?" Tsuki asked through their bond.

She stood up on wobbling legs. *"Did you get drunk again? I don't remember you drinking..."* The last she remembered was trying to remove the dissonance in their souls and then...

"You're awake then?" said the Water of Kazue's soul.

Moonlight played tricks on the eyes, because the water of Kazue's soul for a moment had looked just like Kazue. But as she blinked a few times, she returned to this young woman, with a smiling face and ancient eyes. She'd ordered them to do something... It was all a fuzzy blur. And they'd come here. Why?

"Thank you for bringing me the staff." She held up the staff, ribbons of blue aura ran up and down it. The staff had accepted her as its mistress. It shouldn't be possible, only Kazue could hold the staff. The only reason Suzume could wield it was because she had Kazue's heart. Whatever the reason for it, they were bound to serve whoever held the staff. Which meant she was their new mistress.

Panic spiked through her veins. She refused, Suzume, though lacking in skill, had never hurt them. This fragment had already proved her willingness to get what she wanted by any means necessary. They needed a plan, a way to escape before she forced them to do even more heinous deeds. She imagined Suzume had not given up the staff willingly.

The water of Kazue's soul smiled again. It was a patronizing sort of smile. As if she saw them as children, or perhaps her pets.

"You can feel it, can't you. The darkness, his darkness, it corrupts, changes, unless it is welcomed. I didn't want to use force on you, I hoped you would come willingly."

Hisato's darkness. That was what it was, it should have been obvious. Her unusual amount of strength, it all made sense now. But now that she knew she could find a way to work around it.

"Are you hoping to use the staff to lure out Suzume? She won't come alone, The Dragon and the others will help her," Akira said.

"Keep her distracted, and at the last moment, I'll take control and strike, catch her by surprise," Tsuki said through their bond. It was one of those times she was glad for his recklessness.

"I wouldn't do what you're plotting together. I can hear your thoughts, and I will be able to anticipate any move you make."

A cold chill went down her spine as she looked wide-eyed at the water of Kazue's soul. Even Kazue didn't have this sort of power when she was living.

"You keep thinking of me as the water of Kazue's soul. I'm not a mere fragment. I am Kazue, I have been reborn."

Nine

A cold wind blew off the snowy mountain top and sent a chill down Rin's spine. It had been centuries since Rin stepped foot on the tengu mountain. Not since before the fall of The Dragon, when she'd been nothing more than a mere messenger. Now she arrived as his emissary. After Akira and Tsuki's betrayal, she'd been hesitant to leave. But The Dragon had insisted that they carried on as usual. He was counting on her and Hikaru, after all. It would have been filled with pride if her first mission had been anywhere but here. Damn Shin, back only a few weeks and already causing problems. If she were fortunate, she could see the Tengu Elder, without the need for any awkward encounters.

A flurry of snow obscured the path ahead, and Hikaru pulled the collar of his coat closer to his neck. Clouds of vapor escaped as he huffed a breath while trudging through the snow. Being half-human, he felt the cold more keenly than she did. And the trek up the mountain had been more arduous. The tengu she remembered were known for their hospitality, and very soon, they would be by a warm fire, with a hot bowl of soup to fill their empty bellies. In the meantime, they'd have to make do with shared body warmth. Rin wrapped her arm and bushy tail around Hikaru, and he unfurled his hands to put an arm around her waist, bringing her side flush with his. Movement was slower, but she preferred it this way. It seemed so rare that they had moments alone like this.

"Not too cold, are you?" Rin asked as she nuzzled her face against his neck.

"Why would I be when I have you to keep me warm?" he replied with an amused chuckle.

They continued onward. Fog snaked through the trees that dotted the mountainside. Through it, the blurred shapes of a building began to take shape. The tengu castle was made up of multiple stories, that pierced the clouds like the peak of the mountain it sat upon. The highest tower loomed over scattered buildings spread across the sprawling compound. Gray curved rooftops were nearly buried in snow, making it difficult to tell them apart from the snowcapped peaks of the mountain. A large stone wall surrounded the perimeter, it had been built eons ago during the early days when yokai had often warred with one another. Even during times of peace, they had maintained their defenses and were famed for being impregnable.

"We're nearly there," Rin said, and they both quickened their pace. The sooner they got the tengu onto The Dragon's side, the sooner they would have true peace in Akatsuki. Though she had her doubts about the Dragon's plan to unite humans and yokai in marriage. But she wanted to believe in his vision of a reunited Akatsuki. Only then could she and Hikaru return to the quiet life they once had.

A shadow passed by on the snow, followed by another and another. The wind picked up, blowing Rin's auburn hair into her face. Pushing it out of her eyes, she craned her neck, as several sets of dark wings swooped down toward them. She resisted her animal urge to transform into her true Kitsune form to better defend herself. She had come here in peace, and she didn't want to give the wrong signals. Even though they were welcoming to allies, the tengu was a warrior clan. And if she were to take her true form, they might interpret it as a threat.

It was strange that they had sent out this many tengu to meet them, and seeing as the formation in which they flew and their weapons strapped to their hips, she very much doubted this was a welcoming party. Since the fall of The Dragon, the rumors were that they had retreated from the affairs of yokai. Keeping to themselves, all previous attempts at contact had been rebuffed. But what warranted such a hostile greeting? One by one the tengu landed in front of her, their dark black wings spread out behind them as they encircled her and Hikaru with their swords drawn and pointed at them.

"Who are you and why have you dared journey on tengu lands." The speaker wore a white mask with an elongated nose, and his voice echoed when he spoke.

"We come here in peace, I am Rin, emissary of the Great Dragon and friend of the Tengu Elder. We've come with a gift." She held out a parcel wrapped in silk. Resources at the palace were scarce, but Kaito had somehow managed to gather together expensive jewelry and silks to give as a gift for the Tengu Elder.

"Your gifts mean nothing, the Elder will see no visitors, and outsiders are not welcome on the tengu mountain," the leader said, and the tengu at the back of the circle stepped away, making it clear there was only one path they could travel and that was back down the mountain.

Though he tried to hide it, Hikaru's teeth were chattering, and a return trip might prove too difficult with the sun going down and the night growing colder.

"We are no outsiders, but friends. The Elder of the tengu's own son, Morikazu, sat upon The Dragon's council. We have been allies for centuries. Surely you can at least allow us a moment to warm ourselves before we journey back home." She stepped forward, the present on her outstretched palms.

"Everyone knows, the great Dragon was defeated centuries ago." He slashed his sword through the air and knocked her gift from her hands, where it fell into the snow.

She took a step back, and Hikaru's icy hand squeezed hers. This made no sense, the tengu were always such generous and welcoming people before. What had changed in the time since the fall of the Dragon? Whatever had made them so cold, it wouldn't stop her. She hoped she could avoid seeing him again, but there was no choice now.

"Bring me, Morikazu," she said, her voice echoed back at her with the howling wind off the mountain.

Because they wore masks, it was impossible to read their reactions. But the tengu's wings twitched, fidgeting back and forth. Only their leader stood unmoving, the wind catching strands of his ebony hair.

"Who are you to be making such demands of our prince?" he said, his voice booming and echoed off the mountain.

Hikaru frowned, and Rin shook her head slightly, hoping he wouldn't ask questions. She should have told him before they set out, but she wasn't sure how to approach the topic. She never imagined she and Morikazu would ever see each other again. And the tengu clan was so large, she hoped that she'd be able to visit without running into him. But it was too late now.

"Go to Morikazu and tell him the Kitsune, Rin is asking for him. If he does not wish to speak to me, then I will take whatever punishment you deem necessary."

"Are you sure this is wise?" Hikaru asked.

She couldn't look him in the eye. If she weren't absolutely desperate, she wouldn't have dared, but they needed the tengu on Kaito's side and to get Hikaru out of the cold. This was her only hope of getting inside. If Morikazu would answer her summons, that was. Their final parting had not been the most amicable one.

"Trust me." She forced a smile.

"Wait here." The leader flapped his wings and took flight back toward the compound. While the remaining tengu closed ranks around her and Hikaru, removing their last path to freedom.

"Whose Morikazu?" Hikaru whispered in her ear.

She bit her bottom lip. She would tell him but not here surrounded by the tengu warriors, what if one of them overheard and rumors spread? The tengu might be elite warriors, but they were also the worst of gossips.

Rin waved her hand in dismissal. "An old friend." She forced a smile, but Hikaru narrowed his eyes at her.

Minutes passed, and darkness crept in as the sun went down unseen behind the clouds. Hikaru's shivering got worse, and they huddled together to keep warm. The tengu warriors seemed unaffected by the cold, however, they stood as still as statues. And the only movement was the occasional flutter of their black feathers in the wind. What if Morikazu didn't come? What if he were still mad at her all these centuries later. If she had made a miscalculation, then it would have doomed both her and Hikaru.

A dark figure emerged from the innermost ring of the castle, which rose above the others. Rin squinted through the clouds and darkness, which obscured her vision. Whoever it was unfurled their wings and launched into the sky, quickly followed by two more tengu. The trio rose high up into the air, before making a sharp descent downward in a near freefall straight for them. Hikaru grasped Rin's shoulder, trying to pull her away, but at the last moment, they opened their wings and glided just over their heads to land in the snow before them.

The tengu in the center of the group, stood a head taller than his companions. Unlike the guards who'd come to greet them, he wore no mask to disguise his handsome face, which looked as if it had been chiseled from stone, nor did he tie back his long, thick black hair which fell in ebony waves over his shoulder. He strode toward them, and the tengu guards stepped back as he approached.

"Then, Atsukore was telling the truth, it really is you, Rin," Morikazu said in a booming voice that echoed back at him from the mountain tops.

"It's good to see you too, Mori," she said with a solemn tilt of her head.

Mori closed the distance between them and gathered her up into his arms, taking her off her feet, he spun her around in a circle. "I always knew you would come back to me!" he roared with laughter.

The world was nothing but a blur of white and gray, and her head spun. "Mori, put me down, I'm getting dizzy!" Rin protested with a laugh.

Chuckling, he set her back on her feet and rested his large hands on her shoulders. "It's good to see you. And you are looking as radiant as ever. I would ask why you didn't send a message letting me knowing you were coming, but." He shrugged his shoulders and nodded his head back to the castle. "Where have you been for the last five hundred years? I heard the most awful rumor that you married, but I always knew we would be reunited again someday."

Rin very tactfully removed his hands from her shoulders and grasped Hikaru's hand, pulling him closer as she cleared her throat. "It's good to see you too, Mori. Can I introduce you to my husband, Hikaru?"

"An old friend, huh?" Hikaru teased.

There was no more pretending, she supposed. "We were lovers once, long ago."

"This vixen broke my heart!" Mori laughed again. "And now she has returned to wound me further by introducing me to her husband." He clutched his chest as if wounded.

"Jealous?" Rin leaned into Hikaru's shoulder.

"Only a little." He kissed her cheek.

Mori shook his head. "It really is lovely to meet you. I am Morikazu, general of the tengu army, and Eldest son of Yoshinobu." He bowed so deeply to Hikaru, who returned it with an equally deep bow. When Mori stood up again, his expression was open but serious. "I must apologize for leaving you out in the cold so long, it took some convincing to get the Elder to allow you into the compound."

"I appreciate your efforts," Rin said.

Mori waved his hand dismissively. "You know I would do anything for you, Rin. It's the Elder who is slow to act."

The tengu formed two lines on either side of them as Mori led the way up to the tengu compound.

"Why is it that you had to have the Elder's approval to let us in?" That had never been the practice before.

Mori looked over his shoulder at the tengu guards flanking them and shook his head slightly. "We have not let anyone into the compound in a very long time. You should be proud, this is a rare treat." He winked at her.

Rin shook her head. Centuries had passed, but Mori was the same as he ever was. Getting inside the tengu palace was the first step. Getting to talk to the Elder was another matter entirely.

As they approached the gates, Mori made a signal with his hands, and the massive gates were pushed open, allowing them into the inner courtyard of the outermost ring of the tengu palace. Tengu stood along sky-high walkways, watching as they entered. Young tengu pointed at them as they clung to the hem of their mother's hakama. Warriors watched them pass with curious gazes.

"Would we be able to meet with the Elder?" Rin asked.

Mori barked a laugh. "Perhaps if you were to bring back Tomohiko, but short of that, I don't think he'll let anyone near him."

"Tomohiko…" Rin frowned. "Your youngest brother? What happened to him?"

Mori's shoulders tensed, and his pace quickened. "This way," he said, leading them to a nearby building.

She must have struck a nerve, Mori was never good at hiding his feelings from her. The Tengu Elder had eight sons; the oldest was Mori, and his youngest, Tomohiko, she had only met on a handful of occasions. After the fall of the Dragon, many had died in the ensuing infighting and chaos. Perhaps Tomohiko had been one of those casualties? That would explain why the Tengu Elder had shut out the rest of the world, to grieve. As well as the Tengu Elder's resistance to seeing her.

Inside, a meal had been set out on trays on the tatami mats in the main room, and in an adjoining room, a plush futon had been prepared. Tengu servants knelt as they entered greeting them with a deep bow. This was more like the tengu hospitality she remembered.

"I've gotten permission for you to stay one night, but come morning, you'll have to leave," Mori said. He was looking anywhere but at Rin, very unlike him.

The tengu servants filled out, and the last one closed the door behind them. Mori stayed one ear cocked toward the door and a frown on his face.

"We appreciate your hospitality," Rin said. Taking a seat before the feast which had been presented for them. Roasted venison, and mountain vegetables along with steaming bowls of rice and herbaceous soups.

"It is my pleasure, consider it a late wedding gift to both of you," Mori said as he rubbed his arm and stared at the door.

"Are you sure you cannot return with us to The Dragon's palace?" Rin prompted. He was holding something back from her, and she for one wasn't leaving until she found out what it was.

"Believe me, Rin, I would if I could, but the old bird has forbidden it." He paced back and forth, raising and lowering his wings.

"Pity. I would do almost anything to have you back, just like the old days." She took a sip of her tea, while Hikaru covered up his laugh with a cough.

"Do you mean it?" Mori's eyes lit up, as did his wings perk upward.

Rin shrugged. "But like you said, the Elder won't let anyone leave the tengu mountain."

Mori knelt down on the ground and scooted closer to them. Then in a whisper, he said, "That's the problem; my father won't let anyone leave since Tomohiko was taken hostage by the yuki onna. I've been begging him for centuries to send our army to retrieve him. They've kept him alive, we know that for certain. But I cannot rescue him alone. But I know having Tomohiko back would ease his cold heart, and allow me and the others to leave the mountain again."

Rin set her teacup down. This was exactly the opportunity they needed. If they could rescue the Tomohiko, that would be just the chance they needed to win the favor of the tengu. She looked at Hikaru, trying to communicate without words. He nodded his head, and she smiled.

"What if Hikaru and I were to rescue Tomohiko?"

Mori grasped her hands, holding them tight. "You would do that, for me?"

Rin pulled her hands free. "I would do it, if you could help us convince the Elder to form an alliance with The Dragon."

Mori's gaze slid to Hikaru, and he cleared his throat. "Of course, I cannot make any guarantees, but I do believe bringing Tomohiko back could greatly tip the odds in your favor." A smile curled his lips. One she remembered she had found so charming long ago. Hikaru grabbed her hand, threading their fingers together. Perhaps he was a bit more jealous than he would let her know. But it didn't matter; she only had eyes for him. And no matter the cost, she would see to it that they returned to the life they once had.

TEN

Kaito's claws skimmed the clouds. For two days, he and his soldiers had scoured miles of shoreline and forest with nothing to show for it. He spread out invisible tendrils of his spiritual energy, searching out Akira and Tsuki. All he could sense were animals, lesser yokai, the occasional human, and his own soldiers. Their betrayal stung. He wouldn't have called them friends, but they were allies, or so he thought. It was in yokai nature to think of one's self-interest first. And this sort of treachery was not uncommon. His mistake had been assuming their shared goals were enough to prevent it.

He had even trusted them with protecting Suzume... If they had harmed her, he would not rest until he'd torn their bowels out and strangled them with it. Though he could reason their duplicity, what he could not understand is how they had vanished so effectively. They weren't strong enough to disguise their spiritual energy, not from him. And more puzzling was how much more powerful they had become, more so than even Suzume had become when Hisato took control over her. It was as if they'd become a vessel for something else...

Kaito flew lower, skimming over treetops; on the off chance getting closer to the ground would reveal those traitors. A wolf howled. Shin's signal. Maybe he and his mate, Akane, had found something. Kaito dove beneath the canopy of skeletal branches. Two massive white wolves with golden eyes awaited him. Kaito landed and transformed into his human form in one seamless motion.

"Did you find something?" Kaito asked.

Shin and Akane transformed into their human forms as well.

"Nothing for Tsuki and Akira, I'm afraid," Shin said.

"We did find a couple of spies, though," Akane said.

Spies? Was Hisato planning on making a move already? The hybrids might have been just the beginning.

"Take me to them."

Akane turned, her wolf tail twitched back and forth as she led him a little way into the forest to an outcropping of rocks. A group of soldiers was gathered, and at their feet two kijo, their hair was tangled with branches and their clothes nothing more than mere rags. Kijo were notoriously solitary, living all over Akatsuki in remote locations. In his long life, he could not think of a time he'd seen two together. This was unexpected, indeed. They growled at him as he approached like a pair of feral cats.

"Kijo spies, now I have seen it all," Kaito said.

The kijo to the right spat and Kaito stepped backward to avoid it landing on his foot. How dare they, before he had been sealed in stone, none would have even dared do such a thing. In fact, their head would have been separated from their shoulders within moments. But he wanted to know what they were doing here and why there were two of them.

"You're bold to spit upon your captors; perhaps I should carve up your mouth to teach you a lesson," Kaito said icily.

"Raise one hand to strike my sister, and you will lose that hand," said the second kijo.

Sisters. Now, this was interesting indeed. He didn't even know their kind had siblings. They transformed human women, twisted by their own wicked deeds in their human lives and reborn hideous and deformed.

"How did you find them?" Kaito asked Shin.

"They gave us a lovely chase. One attacked, and the other popped up further away. At first, we thought we were dealing with a single kijo, until Akane caught this one." He nodded to the kijo who'd spat at him.

Were they working for Hisato? A pair of kijo felt out of character for Hisato, who was a master of tricks and illusions. But then again, he might have sent them just to distract him keep him off the trail of something else.

"You are fortunate, I am in a rush. Tell me who sent you, and I will spare your miserable lives."

"Why would we tell anything to a pretender like you," said the kijo who'd spat, as she bared her crooked yellow teeth at him.

"You're right, I don't need both of you alive to answer me. Kill her," Kaito said to a soldier, who drew his blade and pressed it to the kijo's throat.

"Don't you dare harm her!" Seethed the second kijo, as she struggled in her bindings, trying to get closer to her sister. A soldier grabbed her shoulder and held her back.

"Tell me who sent you, or I will have him spill your sister's blood," Kaito said.

The kijo stared at him with red eyes narrowed, and he stared back unblinking.

She bowed her head. "He didn't give us his name or show us his face, but he paid us to keep your soldiers, and you distracted."

"What are you distracting us from?"

"I don't know," the kijo replied with a snarl.

"Kill her," Kaito said to the soldiers.

The second kijo leaned toward him. "I'm telling the truth. It was a powerful being, a lesser kami, perhaps. He offered us energy in exchange for our services. Please don't kill her."

Kaito held up his hand to halt the soldier who withdrew the blade. She wasn't lying, it seemed. Something still felt off. Would Hisato have paid a couple kijo just to take them off the trail of Tsuki and Akira? It seemed excessive when he could create portals to transport them anywhere in Akatsuki.

"I spare you today, but should you ever step foot on my lands again, you will not leave them alive. Understand?"

Both kijo nodded their heads in understanding.

"See they leave, and don't come back," he said to the soldiers before striding away.

Shin and Akane fell into step beside them. "You're going to let them go? Before you would have gutted them where they stand."

He'd grown tired of the bloodshed. The yokai were so few now, if he killed everyone who displeased him, there would be none left in another century. Besides, they were weak. Whoever had bribed them had done so with the promise of spiritual energy. They were no threat to him or his kingdom. Let them live and return to whatever hole they'd crawled out of.

"I want you to follow them, see where they go," Kaito said.

"Ah, that's more like The Dragon, I know." Shin chuckled.

"I need to know what this diversion was for," Kaito said.

"We wasted half a day chasing them down, maybe they were to help Akira and Tsuki escape," Akane said.

"No. It had to be something else. Akira and Tsuki aren't that important."

"What if they were part of the distraction as well. What if they were trying to draw you away from the palace?" Akane said.

Kaito froze mid-step.

"If that's the case, we should head—" Shin hadn't even finished his sentence before Kaito was launching himself into the air. Suzume was still at the palace. Hisato didn't want Akira and Tsuki, he wanted Suzume. This entire chase had been designed to leave her unprotected.

Sweat beaded on Suzume's forehead, and her jaw ached from clenching it. She glared at her open palm, envisioning the fire, the flicker of flames, the familiar warmth. Why was this so hard? Just days before, creating a fireball had been as easy as breathing. The fire was there just beneath the surface, a raging inferno waiting to be unleashed. But it was as if something was blocking the power from her. For days she'd been trying to unleash it, only for it to remain elusively outside her reach.

Suzume growled in frustration as she let her hand swing lamely down to her side. Dark gray clouds gathered in the sky, threatening rain.

"Why can't I do it?" she shouted, her voice drowned out by the crashing of waves outside the palace walls.

"You can, you just have to let go," Souta said.

He had been repeating that same phrase over and over, like a chant that would unlock her power. If only Ryuu were here. She almost missed his nagging, at least under his tutelage she made real progress. But he was miles away by now, searching for the last fragment. He was doing something useful. Meanwhile, she couldn't create even a spark, and all Souta could tell her was to 'let go.'

"I've told you, I'm not holding onto anything! What are you asking me to let go of exactly?" She held up her empty hands, turning them over to show him.

"What you hold onto is not in the physical realm, but the anger you are harboring in your heart. For the power to flow, it must be free of all obstacles. You must forgive those who've wronged you." Souta said it like it was as simple as emptying a bucket.

"Forgive." She scoffed. "How can I forgive them, they betrayed me!" She paced around the training grounds, kicking sand in the sparring ring.

Souta watched with a serene expression on his wrinkled face. How was he so calm? This was a disaster. She'd lost her staff and with it the ability to use her power. All because of Akira and Tsuki. She thought they were different. She thought they were her friends. This is why it was better not to let anyone in. Friendship was a dream, something people wanted to believe was real, but in the end, people only wanted you for how much they could get from you. And once they were done, they disposed of you. Suzume kicked over a stand of training staffs and wooden weapons. They fell over with a satisfying clatter.

"Life is chaos, things do not always go as you expect, or how you want. When you go to face Hisato, do you think he will let you fight him in ideal conditions? You must learn to work around the distractions—" Souta said.

"How can I even think about facing Hisato without my staff!" She spun on Souta, her face flushed with anger. "There won't be a battle if I can't use my power. What if I have to learn how to use it all over again. How long will that take? A month? Six? A year or more?" She was breathing hard, her nails dug into her palm.

Souta rested his hand on her shoulder. "You have not lost your power, once the shock wears off—"

She knocked his hand aside. "It's been days, and I still can't summon even a simple flicker. Without the staff, I'm nothing."

She reached for where the staff was usually strapped to her back, only to be reminded again it was gone. Countless times over the past few days, she'd reached for it without thinking.

Saying it out loud made it that much more real. But it was true. Before she'd found Kazue's staff, she was nothing but a walking bonfire. The staff helped channel her energy and helped her control it. Without it, she couldn't summon the flame at will, and it felt as if she'd lost a limb.

"The staff is merely a tool, you will see that with time. How about we meditate to finish today's lesson?"

Suzume ground her teeth. Meditation, that was Souta's answer for everything. It hadn't worked the last dozen times they'd tried, and she wasn't sure what difference it would make this time. But instead of arguing with him, she sat down on the ground. Maybe this time, it would calm her nerves at least.

"Close your eyes," Souta instructed.

She did as she was told. This was stupid. Why was she even wasting her time?

"Listen to the sound of the ocean and breathe in with the rhythm of the waves. In and out..."

The waves crashed, and seagulls cried overhead. She felt like the rocks on the shore, constantly buffeted, over and over, slowly being chipped away until there was nothing left. No, don't think about it. She had to clear her mind...

"Feel the wind as it moves through your hair."

When Kaito had carried her on his back, it had been both thrilling and terrifying. He had treated her as an equal. But she had failed, and nearly gotten herself killed. While Kaito was out searching for Tsuki and Akira, she was locked inside his gilded cage. He hadn't even bothered to ask if she wanted to search, he'd just left her behind. Would there ever be another chance?

"Now open the channels of your energy, let it flow..." Souta's voice washed over her.

What if she never recovered her power? What if she remained helpless, dependent on others, but unable to trust anyone? The thought burst through, raging along her body like a wildfire. No. She wouldn't be caged.

"You've got the flame, now control it," Souta said firmly.

The fire kept on burning, surrounding her, expanding outward with a destructive hunger. She wanted to burn the entire palace to the ground. She wanted to find Akira and Tsuki and make them pay for their betrayal. A tempest wind blew away her fire, and her eyes flew open. Souta had used his spiritual energy to extinguish her fire.

"Why did you do that. I thought I was supposed to make fire."

"Not that, not fueled by rage."

"I think I've had enough for one day." Why was she wasting her time, nothing she did was good enough anyway? The ends of her hair were sparking as were the tips of her fingertips. As before she'd learned to control it, the flame had a mind of its own. Though she should try and calm it, and heed Souta's words about rage-fueled flame, she let it burn. It heated her skin and stoked embers in her gut.

Naoki, who'd been guarding the entrance to the sparring ground, fell into step beside her. Even he didn't serve her by choice. He was bound to her by Kazue's heart, that she had accidentally absorbed. If not, he might have turned on her as well. Nothing around her belonged to her, even the fire that was burning her up from the inside out was Kazue's, she was nothing but the vessel.

The flames danced along her skin once more, kindled by her growing anger. Yokai moved out of the way as she approached, she supposed the only good thing about losing control was everyone was afraid of her. And wasn't there power in fear, maybe she couldn't control it, but the wild, raw energy of the flame had its own influence.

She was nearly across the courtyard, when hitotsume from the other day stepped into her path. He'd chosen the wrong day to mess with her.

"The Dragon isn't here to protect you this time, human." The hitotsume smiled, revealing his pointed teeth. A crowd of yokai surrounded her and the hitotsume. Had they planned this ambush?

She reached for her staff. Only to grimace as she grasped only air. If only he wasn't fireproof, she would have loved to burn him to cinders. Ryuu wasn't here to scold her, and Kaito wasn't here to stop her.

"I'm not going to give you a chance to escape this time."

The hitotsume threw back his head and laughed. "I've been watching you, and I know you can't control your powers, not without your little stick."

Suzume scanned the yokai around her, Naoki was at the back of the crowd struggling against a pair of Oni who was trying to keep him back. She didn't need long, she rushed the hitotsume and landed a flaming punch in his single eye. He howled and stumbled backward, clutching his eye, tears streaming down from it. She might not have control of her power, but Ryuu had put her through her paces learning hand to hand combat.

She swept her leg, to kick his legs out from under him, but the hitotsume caught her arm and twisted it behind her. She cried out as she tried to break free of his grip. Her flames rose higher as red filled her vision.

"Try and beg for your life, I'd love to hear it," he said against her ear.

Suzume grit her teeth. She would kill him with her bare hands if she had to. Another lightning bolt of pain shot through her. He was about to rip her arm out of the socket. Fire engulfed them both as she felt it wash over her like a tide. She thought she'd learned to suppress Kazue, but she'd let her anger get the better of her, given into the primal flame too much. Suzume threw her head back and screamed as flames burst from her lips, and Kazue took control.

Eleven

Smoke rose up on the horizon as Kaito flew closer to the Seaside palace. His worst fears were confirmed. The palace was under attack. Visibility had been reduced, and he couldn't see where they were being attacked from. Spreading out his spiritual energy, he searched for Hisato or his hybrids and instead found only Suzume's raw spiritual power, amplified tenfold. She'd lost control to Kazue again. This must have been Hisato's plan all along, to get her isolated and force her to unleash Kazue.

Embers flew into the air off the burning roofs. Screams echoed as yokai fled away from the collapsing buildings. He never should have left her alone, but he had been so fixated on finding Akira and Tsuki he thought she would be safe back at the palace. If something happened to her, he would never forgive himself.

In the courtyard, an inferno blazed, and at its center, Suzume projected flames at the yokai who rushed her. As a wave of fire shot toward them, they leaped backward, shielding their faces.

Kaito landed at the edge of the blaze, the heat too intense to look into directly, and he was forced to take a step back or be set on fire. As he did, his foot kicked the charred corpse of a yokai, their features indistinguishable but for their single eye in the center of their head. The hitotsume...

Fire yokai closed in on Suzume, braving the blaze with weapons drawn.

"Do not harm her, stand down," Kaito roared at his subjects, to protect himself from the blaze he surrounded himself in his own icy barrier, which melted as quickly as he made it while he crept closer to Suzume.

The fire yokai hesitated to obey his command; their eyes bounced from Suzume, who threw fireballs at Souta, who redirected them onto the ocean with his wind.

"Lay a hand upon her, and you will lose that hand," Kaito growled.

They set their weapons down and instead fled from the palace. Suzume's fire was spreading; in no time, the entire palace would be destroyed. Kaito pushed forward, the flames closed in all around him, removing any hope of an escape route. Embers glowed on the ground, and the heat was breaching his barrier by the time he joined Souta and Naoki, who were inside Souta's spiritual barrier.

"You shouldn't get any closer, her flames are stronger than ever before," Souta shouted over the roar of the flames.

A wind buffeted all around, catching strands of Souta's white hair. As Suzume had been gaining mastery of her flame, it had also made the untamed part of her soul more dangerous. He had hoped to never see her this way again. He thought since she was learning to master her powers, he never would. What had caused her to lose control when she had nearly mastered her ability? That was a question that would need to be answered later.

"How do we stop her?" Kaito asked.

"Only I can subdue her now, but I will need you and Naoki to distract her in the meantime."

Naoki drew both his blades, ready for Kaito's signal. Souta's barrier fell, and the flames rushed in. Kaito recoiled from the heat, but it was soon pushed back by a burst of wind from Souta. With a pathway opened through the fire, Kaito rushed toward Suzume. In retaliation, Suzume flung fire at him, which he zigzagged to avoid it.

Suzume lunged for him with a ball of flame in the palm of her hand, Kaito rolled to avoid her. She was faster than usual. When Kazue took over, her power increased, but this was unprecedented, did she always have this untapped potential within her. Kaito ran, leading Suzume on a chase around the burning courtyard. As she closed in on him, Naoki stepped into his path, drawing her after him instead.

Souta meanwhile was enclosed in his barrier, Kaito couldn't see him past the smoke clogging the air. A ball of fire zoomed dangerously close to his head, and Kaito spun to face her once more, and she was upon him reaching for him with a fiery grip. Kaito grasped her by the wrist, her flames exploded out of her and melted the ice he'd coated his skin with to protect him. His burns throbbed as they wrestled against one another. Souta's song rose on the wind, creating a tempest that blew all of them back, and extinguished Suzume's flames. Her face was screwed up in anger.

"No! You will not suppress me again!" she roared, fire flickered out of her mouth.

Kaito held onto both her arms, pinning them to her side as the last notes of Souta's song faded away, and Suzume slumped forward into his arms.

"Don't worry, I got you now," Kaito said.

Her expression softened in sleep, but for the slight furrow of her brows. He rubbed his thumb across it. Then hooking his arm under her knees, he cradled her in his arms, carrying her through the burning wreckage of the courtyard. Naoki had sheathed his swords and approached him.

"See to it that the flames are put out, and assess the damage," he ordered him.

Naoki nodded his head before turning to do as Kaito had commanded.

Most of the damage was concentrated on the outer rings of the palace. And even now, with the source gone, the flames were starting to die down. Kaito carried Suzume through the palace, yokai emerged from their hidey holes and watched them pass with soot-stained faces. Their murmurs followed him as he went.

The inner rings of the palace smelled of smoke and ash carpeted the ground like snow. Other than that, there was no damage. He brought Suzume to the room he had prepared for her, and laid her down on the futon, tucking her in up to her neck. He sat at her bedside for a few moments watching the rise and fall of her chest. He wanted to protect her, and he thought giving her more freedom to gain her own strength would be enough. But even after months of practice, she had lost control of her power and given over to her soul fragment. The damage would take weeks to repair. Not to mention the loss of life.

Footsteps approached, and Kaito stood.

Souta hovered in the doorway, his expression solemn.

"How did this happen?" Kaito growled. Was Souta preparing to betray them as well, was he working for Hisato too? Souta was loyal to that bastard Ryuu, maybe they both were working for Hisato, perhaps Tsuki and Akira's betrayal had all been part of a greater plot to destroy his palace from within, by using Suzume...

"She has been struggling to control her power without the staff," Souta said with a sigh. "Her emotions are still too tangled up in her power, and it is preventing her from performing as well as she could."

"How do I know you're not behind this?" Kaito stalked closer to him, and jabbed a finger into Souta's chest.

"Strange that she lost control for the first time in a long time while I happened to be away." Kaito bared his teeth in warning.

Souta stared back at him, his expression serene. "Would I have subdued her if I was plotting against you? I could have just left her to burn the entire palace to the ground if I wished."

Kaito deflated; he was right, of course. His nerves were rattled; first the yokai had rebelled against his plan to marry Suzume, then Akira and Tsuki and the kijo. There was a dagger aimed at his back, he just couldn't tell where it was coming from, not yet.

"Forgive me, I wasn't thinking clearly," Kaito said with a shake of his head.

Souta waved away his apology. "You've suffered much treachery, it is to be expected."

There was a knowing look in his eyes, and perhaps a hint of guilt. Souta might appear to be an old man, but a part of his soul was entwined with Kazue's, and even he shared her memories.

Kaito turned away, not wanting to chase that thought further. There were still repairs and recovery to see too, and the question that remained unanswered. If he had been drawn away not to distract from an attack, then what?

KAITO MASSAGED HIS TEMPLES AS HE SURVEYED THE MAP ON THE TABLE. Shin and Akane had returned, and much to his frustration had uncovered no new information from the kijo or who they served. Scouts had been dispatched and had searched for miles surrounding the seaside palace, but there was no hint of an oncoming attack.

Kaito drummed his fingers on the edge of the table. "What am I not seeing? Apart from Suzume's fire, everything has been quiet."

Shin leaned against the edge of the table, arms crossed over his chest. "Maybe it was simply a distraction, so Akira and Tsuki could escape."

It was too simple; there was something more, something he was missing if he could just grasp what it was.

Akane stalked around the map table and stopped at the bottom of the map, beside where the seaside palace was depicted. She ran a clawed finger along the shoreline, then into the forest and foothills where they had run into the kijo.

"What if the two incidents were unrelated?" she said, her golden eyes flickering from Kaito to Shin.

"Even if that were true, that doesn't explain what they were attempting to distract us from." Kaito glowered down at the map, as if it were the painted woods' fault for not revealing its secrets to him.

"When we found the kijo, they weren't far from their home mountain." She tapped a mountain range just northwest of the seaside palace. "What if they were sent when an opportunity presented itself," she said.

"Like a chance to kill, Suzume." Shin cupped his chin as he nodded.

"Who would dare?" Kaito snarled.

Shin and Akane shared a look between them.

"What do you know?" Kaito snapped.

Shin sighed and ran a hand through his bushy brown hair. "You can't be so blind as to not see how opposed your subjects are to you marrying the priestess, can you?"

No. He wasn't blind to it. Before she had lost control and killed dozens of yokai, he assumed given time and patience they would come around and see her charms, as he saw them, and they would accept her as their future empress. Now things were more precarious.

"Are you saying someone plotted to kill Suzume while I was away?" Kaito asked, he couldn't keep the growl from his tone. Whoever they were, he would find them and tear their guts out.

"It would appear so, and judging from the carnage, they didn't make it out alive. So there's no need to go on a murderous rampage," Shin said with a slight smirk.

Kaito's claws extended, and he clenched his hand into a fist. The hitotsume had been bitter, and he'd paid the price for it. But this went further than a singular incident. There wouldn't be enough time for him to travel to the kijo and then back before Kaito could fly there. Which meant he had allies he was working with, allies who yet might live. He would see them pay for their crimes. And be an example to all his subjects; any who dared to raise a hand to Suzume would pay the price in the end.

"I want you to find out who all was involved in this plot to assassinate Suzume," Kaito said to Shin.

"I thought you would say something like that. But even if you catch one, it doesn't change what she's done," Shin replied.

"What are you suggesting?" Kaito narrowed his eyes at Shin.

Shin put his hands up, "Don't glare at me that way. She's the one who lost control and killed your subjects."

"Because she was provoked!"

"We know that, but the yokai?" Shin shrugged.

"He's right," Akane said, "They are already slow to accept her, but now that she's killed their own, it will be next to impossible to make her your empress."

"Enough," Kaito roared as he slammed his hands down on the tabletop.

The two okami flinched at his rage. He wouldn't hear any more objections against Suzume. He was the ruler of Akatsuki, and it was his decision who he married. And as he had claimed his crown in blood, he would do whatever it took to keep Suzume.

TWELVE

Ryuu descended the mountain pass into the valley shrouded in mist. The neko's report of the spells guarding the valley had been woefully inadequate. Not surprising knowing the neko's tendency to aggravate him for his amusement. Strings of ofuda twirled in his mind, marking the first barrier. As Ryuu stepped over it, a tingle raced up his spine. This would keep out lesser yokai who might be drawn in by the faint power that this valley emanated.

The valley floor was filled with tightly packed trees. The fog created a wall of white, and it was nearly impossible to see through, as he kept moving forward. As he moved through the fog, his hand clutched Tetsuyama's hilt. A shadowy figure loomed ahead, and he removed Tetsuyama from its sheath by a few inches. As he got closer, the fog rolled back, revealing a fallen tree, which he had mistaken for a person. He sheathed Tetsuyama once more with a sigh.

For hours he trudged through the forest, the valley did not seem particularly wide from the pass, but despite following the faintest traces of spiritual energy, he had yet to discover it. The entire valley seemed to be nothing but trees, rocks, and shrubs. Had the neko gotten his revenge at last and sent him to a lost valley where he would wander forever? Even the trees were starting to all look the same to him. In fact, he jabbed his sword at a familiar shadow. It was the dead tree he had seen hours before. He had been wandering in a circle, for likely hours?

Which meant the faint trail of spiritual energy was meant to deceive him from the start. Ryuu closed his eyes and spread out his senses. A typical forest would have been teaming with the spiritual energy of flora and fauna, but it was as if this entire place were silent. As he reached out beyond the fog, he found it, a singular pathway in the mist, like a glimmering shaft of sunlight in the dark. He made his way toward it, arriving there in mere minutes.

The fog had made a sort of labyrinth, and those who did not know the pathway might become lost in it for an eternity. Intriguing. This had to be the place where the remaining piece of Kazue's soul was hidden. A bright torii arc flanked by torches marked the pathway. Ryuu approached it cautiously, this must have been where the neko had gotten and could pass no further. He raised up a hand, testing the invisible barrier that separated the fog-covered forest from the temple grounds. Sparks of spiritual energy erupted along his hand as he shoved it through, it stung but not so much so that he could not pass.

On the other side of the arch, was a basin of crystal clear water. Ryuu approached it, dipping his hand into the cold water. It was customary to wash your hands and mouth before entering the temple. He scooped up some of it and drank from the source. It was rather refreshing but lacked the presence of divine energy. Even when a lesser kami dwelled in a temple, their holy energy seeped into everything. Considering how many layers of protection this place had, he thought a powerful Kami would have dwelled here. But despite all its defenses, this place was devoid of holy energy. But as he spread out his spiritual energy searching for the presence of a kami, he felt something, like a lingering perfume after the wearer left the room. Something powerful had been, here but it was gone now.

There was a clatter, as if someone had dropped something. Ryuu turned to see a miko red and white stared at him wide-eyed. The broom she'd been presumably carrying lay on the ground at her feet.

He bowed his head in greeting. "I apologize I did not mean to frighten you."

She twirled and ran from him.

Seeing as he had passed through their defenses, he imagined they would be scared, he doubted they had many visitors. A pathway of flat stones passed through a stone wall, and onto a cluster of shrine buildings. It was a small temple composed of three buildings made of pine and stone. The roofs were freshly painted red, and the stones white. The shrine was set in front of a large boulder, tied with a string of ofuda and one flat stone where offerings and incense had been left. The style of the place was centuries old, and yet it was well maintained. Who donated to the upkeep of the shrine? A temple could not survive without the patronage of its worshipers.

The young priestess returned with an elderly woman with an austere expression and snowy white hair, who he presumed was their head priestess.

Ryuu kept his stance easy and non-threatening. These priest-esses had something to hide, and he had found them on his own. They would be on their guard, and he did not plan on giving them a reason to suspect him.

"Welcome traveler, " said the head priestess, as she drew nearer, her eyes widened, just for a moment. She must have sensed what he was. He had wondered if she were a true priestess, and had not disguised his spiritual energy to see how she reacted.

"I am glad I found this place, I seemed to have gotten lost while crossing the valley." He smiled.

"It is fortunate you found us, hidden as we are." She watched him warily now.

"Yes, indeed, if I might impose on your hospitality for one night, I am weary from my travels."

Her eyes narrowed as she studied him, and the young priestess behind her wrung her hands together. Would she turn him away or try to seal him. Half yokai, like himself, were rare, and more than once, priests and priestesses had tried to exorcise him like a yokai. Not that it was possible, one of the few benefits of his half nature was his ability to use both his human spiritual power and the yokai abilities, without being weak against either.

She inclined her head. "It would be our pleasure, please you must be hungry." She turned and led him into the temple proper, a group of priestesses ranging in age from young maidens, to late-middle-aged gathered together watching him as he passed. In particular, a pair of young women watched him with hungry gazes.

Many girls came to serve the temples around Akatsuki not because they were particularly adapted for the life, but rather because their parents had no other choice. Girls like them hungered for the lives they'd been deprived, and seeing as they likely saw so few outsiders, he was like honey to a bee. He bowed his head in their direction, flashing them a smile, that in his youth he had used to devastating effect. They blushed, turning away as they whispered and giggled together.

Beyond the main buildings was a small walled garden, and a pen that housed a few chickens and a couple fat pigs. The modest accommodations reminded him of his own youth, raised at a shrine, running barefoot in the mountains without a care in the world. It had been so long since he had thought of those days.

Ryuu was brought to a room with a view of the forest. It had snowed here recently, and dirty drifts of snow remained in the shade of the pine branches. As he drank his tea, wild birds called to one another in the branches of the trees. From his mind's eye, he surveyed the energy of the shrine. Even at their center, he still found no sign of the missing fragment, or any hint of a kami. But that elusive trace remained. What was it that this shrine was hiding.

Priestesses came to clear away his meal, and moments later, the silhouette of the head priestess appeared outside his door. Just as he had hoped.

"You master, might I enter?" she called.

"Please." He leaned back on the cushion.

She slid open the door and entered with all the grace and dignity of an empress. This was no ordinary priestess, that much was certain. Now that they were closer together, there was something familiar about her wrinkled features.

"How may I help you…"

"Hozumi Sayashi, young master," she said as she surveyed him with those dark eyes.

Ah. Now that was how he knew her. If he remembered correctly, Hozumi Sayashi was a promising miko of exceptional talent and spiritual power who, without explanation, had disappeared nearly twenty years ago.

"We met before at the Sun Shrine," Ryuu said.

"I wasn't sure it was you. Though I have aged, you have stayed exactly the same… but I suppose you were hiding your true nature, weren't you." She quirked a snowy brow.

"What a fate for us to meet here again."

"You call it fate, but I do not believe you found our shrine by accident."

Ryuu smiled. She was direct, he could admire that.

"Then perhaps we can dispatch with the formalities, as we are old friends. What is it, this shrine?"

She threaded her fingers together and cleared her throat. "This shrine? We are simply servants of the kami, like any other."

"You cannot trick me, there is no kami that dwells here, and you know it. And even if there were, what need would there be for all the protections? What are you hiding?"

She bowed her head. "There is nothing to hide. The valley is treacherous and our shrine remote, few find their way here on their own, unless they are guided here…"

He should have known he would get no honest answers from

the head priestess. Someone was paying for the upkeep of the shrine, and likely buying her silence as well.

"I suppose anything can be found if one looks hard enough for it," Ryuu replied.

She studied him for a moment before shaking her head slightly. "I hope you find your night's stay enjoyable, master Ryuu."

She rose up and left. They would not tolerate him here for long, and though he had nothing to fear from the head priestess, he would rather not fight innocents. But there would be no time to delay, the soul fragment might have been here, but if they were, they were here no longer. What he needed to find out was where they had gone.

RYUU WAITED FOR NIGHTFALL AND AFTER THE TEMPLE'S EVENING prayers before leaving his room. The temple was still; the moon cast silver moonlight upon the buildings and the boulder that served as its shrine. He approached it, expecting to find the source of the faint spiritual energy stronger here. But it was just as weak here as anywhere else. Curious, then if it weren't the missing kami, what had left this trace? Creeping along the buildings, he searched for a hint of its source. And as he got closer to the sleeping quarters of the priestesses, the remnants of strong spiritual energy got stronger.

Ryuu rested his hand on the stone of the walls and reached through the memory of that rock. It was faint, but the spiritual energy was familiar. The missing fragment had been here, but it was gone now. Where had it been taken?

"You shouldn't be here late at night," said a young woman.

Ryuu opened his eyes and spotted the two priestesses he had spotted when he first arrived.

"The head priestess will throw a fit if she catches your creeping outside our bedroom," said the second girl, fluttering her lashes.

Ryuu smiled at them. "My apologies, I suppose I couldn't sleep and lost my way in the dark."

The girl on the right linked arms with her friend and buried her face in her shoulder as she giggled.

"I'm sorry to have disturbed your sleep." He bowed and made a show of retreating.

"Don't go. Why not have a drink of sake with us?"

"I know where the head priestess keeps the ceremonial sake," said the second girl, her face lighting up.

They almost made it too easy, he almost felt guilty. These young women were perhaps a few years older than Suzume, hungry, and blinded by their youth. It was fortunate it was him they had encountered and not a more devious intruder.

"I suppose I could have a glass."

Their faces lit up.

"We'll meet you at your room shortly," the first girl instructed before they both scurried away on their errand.

Ryuu returned to his own chamber, but rather than bring them into his room, he sat on the veranda just outside. The priestesses returned, and each took seats on either side of them. One clutching the jug of sake, the other holding three glasses.

He took the jug from the priestess and then filled glasses for each of them.

"Cheers," he said.

The girls drank it down quickly, pulling a face. Had they never had sake in their life. Ryuu smirked into his cup. Despite their initial distaste, the girls made sure to keep their cups and his full. Though he drank much slower than them. And before long, both of them had a rosy glow to their cheeks, and their laughter was as free-flowing as the sake.

"Do you often drink with men who visit this shrine," Ryuu asked as he nursed his glass.

One of the girls giggled. "No one ever comes to this place, other than that hideous farmer who leers at us."

Her friend laughed uproariously. "How many times has he asked to drink with us." She laughed so hard she fell backward.

"If you don't get outsiders, who makes offerings to the kami?" Ryuu asked.

The first girl screwed her face as she considered it. "I suppose it's the man who sends the supplies twice a year."

"A patron of the shrine, do you know who he is?" Ryuu asked, leaning in closer to the priestess, and resting his hand on hers.

Her skin flushed further as she shook her head.

"Maybe its Kazue's father!" said the second girl, grabbing onto his sleeve.

Ryuu froze, hearing his mother's name had been an unexpected shock.

"That's right, I heard the head priestess say she was going to the White palace," said the first priestess grasping onto his other arm.

"Kazue?" He kept his tone neutral

The second girl leaned in to whisper.

"We all thought the head priestess was grooming her to be the next leader, but then that man came and took her away. I heard she was the emperor's bastard."

"A man took her, do you know what he looked like?" Ryuu pressed.

The second girl recoiled. "He was strange."

"There was darkness in his gaze, it was as if you were looking into bottomless pits when you stared into his eyes."

"You saw him from across the courtyard, how would you know," the second priestess reached around Ryuu to argue.

"I did too, when he went with Kazue to pack her things. Just being near him sent a chill down my spine."

Hisato. It had to be. And he'd taken her to the palace. Izume must have brought her back, to keep her close or perhaps to try and lure Suzume back there. If he went back and told her, she would only want to rush in and rescue her. If he delayed returning to Suzume, would she be in danger from the yokai of Kaito's palace? He wanted to believe she could take care of herself. The seaside palace was in the opposite direction of the white palace, if he backtracked, word might reach Izume, and she could hide the soul piece in the interim. There was only one choice, he would need to return to the White Palace and find Kazue.

Thirteen

Suzume was never leaving her futon. She burrowed deeper in her blankets as afternoon light crept across the tatami. When her eyes had first opened, flashes of memory had bombarded her, and to avoid confronting the truth, she'd stayed in bed. Though she couldn't remember much, she remembered enough that the shame wouldn't allow her to show her face. Without the staff, she couldn't control her power, and Kazue had taken control. She pulled her blankets tighter around her, as if she could block out the dawning realization as she did sunlight. Naoki had brought breakfast for her hours ago, but just the thought of eating made her stomach turn. How much damage had she caused this time, had she hurt anyone?

Arrogantly, she thought she was getting stronger. She thought she didn't have to worry about Kazue taking control of her body anymore. But when Tsuki and Akira stole the staff, they shattered all her delusions. She never had power, she was nothing and worse, a danger to others. The only option left was for her to stay buried under covers until the last soul piece was found.

Someone knocked at the door, and she froze. Had Kaito come to condemn her for the damage she caused? Were the yokai going to rise up against her and get revenge? That Hitsotsume wouldn't stop until she was dead...

The knock persisted, more urgent than before. Should she try and run? But where would she even go? Powerless as she were, she'd be picked off before she could get a mile from the palace.

"Suzume, I know you're in there," Kaito called out.

Her stomach did another flip flop. Kaito was finally starting to treat her like an equal, if he knew what she'd done, would he realize what a fraud she'd been all along. At the very least, he must be furious. She couldn't face him. She rolled away from the door and clutched the edges of her blankets tighter.

He knocked again. "Open up, or I'm coming in," he shouted, and he would make good on that threat, she bet.

"I want to be alone," she shouted back, but her voice wobbled.

The pounding stopped, and Suzume held her breath. Knowing Kaito, he'd barge here anyway. A few minutes passed, and there was no more pounding. He'd left. It should have been a relief; she wanted to be left alone. But instead, it felt unsettling. How much havoc had she caused when Kazue took over that Kaito didn't want to see her? A flash of fire and screams, was all she could remember. Perhaps she'd done something unforgivable.

Minutes stretched into hours, and he didn't return. It should have been a relief, but it only made her more anxious. Was he angry with her? Was he planning on ejecting her from his palace?

Eventually, hunger drove her out from under her covers, and she ate her cold meal, just to ease the gnawing feeling in her stomach. But it didn't go away, and Kaito still didn't return. No one did…

The loneliness was like a stone dragging her beneath the waves. If Kaito turned his back on her, then who did she have left? She pulled her knees up to her chest, as she stared out onto the endless horizon, which stretched out beyond her window. It had been a mistake to open herself to trusting others. She knew, in the end, they would only betray her, and yet she'd let herself believe the lie that she was stronger with friends. In the end, they all betrayed her, Kaito's flattery and declarations of love were nothing but words. She was the only one she could rely on.

The thought had her on her feet in seconds, and she paced the length of her chamber. Why was she sitting around here, waiting for Kaito to come and comfort her? She didn't need him, she didn't need Tsuki and Akira or any of them. If she didn't have the staff, then she couldn't fight. What was the point of waiting around for Hisato to come and find her? She would get on a boat and run as far away as she could, where no one could find her.

She headed for the door and pressed her ear against it. If Kaito wanted to see her punished for what she did, she might be guarded. At the least, Naoki might be lurking around. She strained but didn't hear a sound except for the distant crash of waves on the shore and the wind's howls. She slowly opened her door, the courtyard was still, as the sun sunk on the horizon, it cast long shadows. The sakura tree was dormant again, all the petals had fallen but for a single stubborn blossom clinging to the highest branches.

"About time you came out," Kaito said.

Suzume jumped in the air and clutched at her chest. Kaito was crouched on the ground beside her door. Had he been there ever since the afternoon? That wasn't possible, why would he wait around for her?

"What are you doing there?"

"Waiting for you." He stood, and there was a lazy smile on his lips.

"All day?"

"I wanted to be there for you when you were ready to talk," he said with a shrug.

Her mouth opened and closed. Had Kaito been possessed like Akira and Tsuki? Because this couldn't be the Kaito she knew.

"Why didn't you just barge your way in like you normally do?" she asked.

He quirked an eyebrow. "You told me you wanted to be left alone."

Now she was certain this was a trick.

"That's never stopped you before," she replied.

Kaito rubbed the back of his neck. "Believe me, I wanted to go in there and drag you out of bed. But more than that, I was afraid if I did, it would push you away."

Suzume inhaled sharply. He'd been listening to what she said, did that mean he was sincere? The part of her who had only known lies and deception wanted to reject even the idea. But the lonely part of her was desperate for it to be true.

"Come on, I want to show you something." He held out his hand for her. It was up to her to take it.

Her stomach flipped, and she took it. His touch was warm, and the jolt raced up her arm. Before, when they touched, it was a clash of fire and ice. Now she just felt a pleasant warmth that was consuming her body, she never wanted to let go of him. He led her through the palace, past scorched buildings. Seeing them, she flinched. It was her fault, all the months of reconstruction were destroyed in a single afternoon. She wanted to return to her blanket cocoon. Kaito must have sensed her resistance, because he squeezed her hand tighter

"If this upsets you, we can go back until you're ready." His expression was sincere, more so than it had ever been before.

As much as she didn't want to face what she'd done when Kazue had taken control of her, she felt more confident when Kaito held her hand.

"No, let's keep going."

He nodded, pulling her closer, so that their shoulders brushed against one another as they walked. The further they got away from the inner ring of the palace, the worse the damage was. The outer buildings that housed the majority of the yokai were charred, and one roof had collapsed. The main courtyard was blackened but for a single place in the middle. It had to be where she was standing when it happened. The halls and courtyard were eerily empty as if she and Kaito were the only ones left.

"Where is everyone?" she asked. She hadn't killed them all, had she?

"I told them all to remain indoors for now." There was an edge to his tone. Was he upset with her or the yokai? She wasn't sure.

They entered the training grounds. The sparring pit was sprinkled with ash, and the side of the armory was scorched, but otherwise still standing. Kaito led her to the center of the sparring ring and turned to face her, taking both of her hands into his.

"Why did you bring me here?" she asked, her eyes scanning over the destruction she had wrought.

"We haven't sparred in a while." Kaito flashed her a smile.

She pulled her hand from his. Was all of this a joke to him? Her pulse raced. What if she lost control again and finished burning the palace to the ground?

"That's not funny," she said.

"It wasn't meant to be a joke." Kaito strolled away from her and picked up one of the training staffs that Ryuu used when they sparred together. He grabbed one and threw it to her, and she caught it.

"Because you haven't forgotten anything that bastard taught you."

She frowned at him. She'd caught the staff on reflex, it was as easy as breathing now. But this wasn't the same, this wasn't her staff. And though Kazue was dormant now. She knew she was there just beneath the surface, waiting for her opportunity to take over again.

She dropped the staff on the ground. "I'm not doing this"

He strolled closer to her with his own practice staff.

"I know you're afraid, two people you trusted turned on you. And maybe you're even scared about what you're capable of.

But I've seen you get stronger, and I know you don't need a piece of wood to do it."

She scowled at him. "It wasn't just a piece of wood; it channeled my power, it—" Her voice caught, and she growled in frustration. Why couldn't he understand? She wasn't Kazue; she wasn't naturally gifted. It had taken months of hard work to get this far, and then in an instant, it was all gone.

"One round." He held up a single finger.

"And what if I burn the rest of the palace?"

"I'll put it out." He twirled his fingers, and an icicle formed in his hands, then with a flick of his wrist, it burst into mist.

Suzume inhaled through her nose. This was stupid. At the least, Kaito was going to knock her on her backside; at the worst case, she'd lose control again. And yet a voice nagged at the back of her mind. What if it wasn't over, what if she could find a way to control it.

"Just one round," she said.

Kaito smiled as they both got into position, they bowed to one another before the fight was on. Typically when she sparred with Ryuu, she started out on the offensive, but without her staff, she felt less sure and decided to take a defensive stance instead, circling Kaito, her hands clenched around her practice staff. Kaito rushed her, and she thrust her arms up to block.

"Good," Kaito said, their faces were inches apart, his lips tantalizingly close.

She shoved him away, before she let those thoughts continue further down that path. This was a fight, nothing else. They circled one another again. Kaito tapped his staff against hers.

She blocked and backed away. Over and over again, he repeated the same attack. He was toying with her, trying to lure her into an offensive maneuver. Even though there were no sparks, no indications Kazue would take over, the fear held her back, she was tangled up, too scared to dare strike first.

Kaito's repeated attacks kept her on the move, the attacks though repetitive, were distracting, and before long, some of that fear melted away as she lost herself in the fight. He turned, exposing his side, it was the perfect opening for an attack. It had to be a feint. She resisted the temptation, and kept on the defensive. But he too had changed strategies and went on the defensive, and they watched one another warily, feinting to draw the other into striking.

"Are you going to make a move?" he asked.

"I will, when you do," she taunted back.

"Well that's the problem, I said I would wait for you to come to me first."

Her skin flushed, he was teasing her, trying to put her off her guard.

"What will you do if I never come to you?"

He smirked. "Die of longing for you."

Her heart stuttered in her chest. Kaito lunged, and she dodged, but as he came close, he grazed past her, brushing his hand along her arm, and the gooseflesh rose up along her arm.

"Did you ask me to spar just so you could tease me?"

"I asked you to spar cause I wanted to see how you fought first hand." He tapped her staff again, once more exposing his left side. She was too flustered to overthink, and thrust forward, knocking him onto his back foot.

It was time to stop playing nice. She swung toward Kaito, and he stumbled back a few steps to avoid getting struck upside the head. Though she had enough sense and control to not actually strike him. While she had him on the back foot, she used a combo of strikes, Ryuu had taught her that knocked Kaito's staff from his hands. It went sailing through the air, and Kaito watched it fly, his mouth hanging open.

She'd won. Suzume panted for breath as she smiled. He'd likely let her win, but it still felt good.

Kaito stared at the staff where it was on the ground. "You disarmed me."

She shook her head. "You let me win."

"No, I didn't." Was that awe in his voice? It couldn't be. She'd never won a skirmish against Ryuu, how could she possibly win against Kaito?

She studied him for a moment. He must have given her a win because he wanted to make her feel better, like the way Tsuki had let her win the race because she was angry... Actually best not to think about him right now.

Kaito took a step closer to her. "I'm serious, I wasn't expecting that combo. You genuinely caught me off guard."

She stared at him for a few moments, her brain seemed unable to catch up with her mouth.

"You're lying."

Kaito cupped her cheek and smiled at her. "You've improved a lot, I hate to admit it, but that bastard is doing a good job teaching you."

She pulled away. "I know you're trying to cheer me up. I know that Kazue's staff was where all the strength really came from. Without it, I'm nothing."

"That's not true."

"How can you say that? You saw what I did because I lost control..." She gestured toward the palace before letting her hand fall to her side. What was she thinking, she'd never be his equal. It had been greed, which made her think she could ever master Kazue's power.

"Do you know why I chose you as my empress?" Kaito asked.

Hearing those words again, her heart stuttered once more. Was he trying to kill her? Or maybe just distract her again.

"Because you want to make an alliance with the emperor," she replied.

"That was just an excuse that I gave the yokai. The real reason is that I know you are what my kingdom needs. No matter the danger, you are not afraid, no matter how many times you're knocked down, you get back up again."

Her skin flushed. "What if I told you I'm always afraid, that I don't want to keep fighting?"

"If you're weary, then lean on me."

He approached her once more, though this time he didn't try and touch her. The space between them was charged. It was drawing them closer together, stealing the breath from her lungs, and filling her with a yearning for contact. She didn't want to be alone anymore. More than anything, she wanted him. The realization struck her like a lightning strike. She'd been running from it for so long, but there was nowhere else to go.

Some sort of madness must have come over her. She closed the distance between them, and grabbed onto the front of Kaito's haori and pressed her lips against his. His hand slid around her waist and drew her closer. Sparks erupted along her entire body, as they merged with the ice of his touch. She was fire, and he was ice, but when they were together, those same sparks turned to molten in her veins. Her hands grasped at his back hungry, desperate for more of him, all of him. There was a blaze in her that he had awoken, that passed between their lips. And as she had in that moment when his power had passed into her on the battlefield, she felt whole and complete. Even if she lost everything else, she had wanted for nothing else. At least she had him.

FOURTEEN

Rin crouched in the shadows of a barren tree. A bitterly cold wind blew off the mountain, and a chill ran down her spine. Hikaru's teeth chattered, and he pulled up the collar of his jacket to block it out. Though Mori had equipped them for their quest. She couldn't help but worry that the challenge was too much for Hikaru. She scooted in closer to him and created a fox flame in her hand to warm him. Hikaru looked at her, with a shy smile.

"I'm fine, don't worry."

She forced a smile for his sake. This wasn't going to be as easy a rescue mission as she would have hoped. The yuki onna were typically solitary yokai, living in mountain ranges and other snowy areas, where they would capture lost travelers and drain them of their spiritual energy. But the yuki onna of the tengu mountain were different. They had gathered together, and built a glittering ice palace. It caught the rays of the noonday sun and rainbows reflected on the freshly fallen snow on the ground.

Yuki onna in icy blue kimono patrolled the perimeter, and surrounding the castle was a barren field of snow. There was no way to approach it without being seen immediately. But according to Mori, his younger brother was trapped inside there somewhere. If she wanted to get him out and win the Tengu Elder's favor, they'd have to get him out. To get in, they'd need disguises.

"I have a plan. We'll go in disguised as yuki onna, find the prince and then slip him out in disguise as well."

"You're right, I noticed there seems to be a lot of yuki onna arriving. We can use that as part of our cover, they shouldn't scrutinize us too closely."

"My thoughts exactly."

Rin reached into her sleeve and withdrew a leaf, which she would use as an anchor for Hikaru's disguise. She concentrated her fox fire into the leaf and envisioned the form that Hikaru would take. And then she placed the leaf against his forehead. As soon as she did, her illusion magic transformed Hikaru from a handsome man, to a beautiful woman with skin as pale as snow and ebony hair.

"How do I look, am I beautiful?" he asked, fluttered his long fake lashes at her.

She chuckled, and it dispelled some of her nerves. Rin exhaled and unclenched her jaw. The yuki onna were predatory yokai, if they sensed fear on her, it might destroy their cover. A single yuki onna would be no match for her fox fire, but with how many she'd seen guarding and entering, they'd be overwhelmed in an instant if their cover was blown. Her spiritual energy was strong enough to disguise them both, as long as they remained close together. If they were separated… Well, she didn't want to think about that.

"Ready?" she asked Hikaru.

He reached for his bow and arrow and hid them in the hollow of a fallen tree nearby. Yuki onna fought with their ice, and didn't use a bow and arrow. Though it would leave them vulnerable, they couldn't risk breaking the illusion.

"As ready as I'll ever be," he said grimly.

She reached for his hand and gave it a squeeze. She hated bringing him into a dangerous situation. They'd fought many yokai together, but after they'd been separated for decades, she was more afraid than ever of losing him. But she knew him well enough to know, he wouldn't let her do this alone. They just had to be quick, get in, get the prince, and get out.

Rin took a deep breath again. And before she could second guess herself, they exited the forest onto the road, where a stream of yuki made their way toward the palace. No one gave them a second glance as they approached the gates. But as they passed through into the courtyard, Hikaru gasped.

Rin's eyes grew wide. From the outside, the palace was an icy blue, inside was a dream space of shifting light and color. All very cold. Yuki onna with their pale skin, glowed in the shafts of light coming through cleverly made hanging ice, which caught the light and illuminated the spaces.

Clusters of yuki onna gathered around chatting amongst themselves. Their voices were sweet but seductive and their beauty as sharp as a knife. Hikaru's head kept drifting in their direction, unable to resist their charms. This was how they lured men in, with their songs, their magnetic auras, and this was without them trying. How much more intense would the pull be if they knew outsiders were in their midst.

Rin tugged Hikaru away from the group, and they headed into the building beyond the courtyard. She strode confidently through the crowd, as if she knew exactly where she was going, so no one tried to stop them and ask them where they were headed.

Inside the walls of the palace, was an icy labyrinth. If the tengu prince was here, where would he be kept?

"Do you suppose they have a prison somewhere?" Hikaru reasoned.

In this glimmering palace of ice, it was hard to imagine a prison. Thinking like a yuki onna, they lured men in with their beauty and their voices, and only once they had them did they expose their true faces. Perhaps they were keeping the tengu prince somewhere hidden, somewhere he wouldn't destroy the illusion of this place.

"There must be a secret entrance, or somewhere they're hiding him," Rin said.

They had already turned down a few hallways, and ignored the numerous doors that lined the halls. The cold was already starting to seep into her bones. Her fingers were numb with it; she could only imagine how much worse it was for Hikaru. And what of the tengu prince? The tengu lived on mountain tops, but even he must have been nearly frozen solid after being trapped here for centuries, how had he not been frozen solid? Unless that was exactly what had happened to him...

"You don't think, they've got him frozen into an ice block, do you?" Rin whispered to Hikaru as another pair of yuki onna passed them by.

Hikaru raked a hand through his hair; it was uncanny seeing a yuki onna do that. He rubbed the spot on the top of his head, where one of his twin scars marked where his kitsune ears had been. He always touched them when he was thinking.

"They wouldn't want to kill him, but tengu are strong, it might be how they've kept him so long here." He gestured around the room.

"How do you find a frozen tengu prince in a palace of ice?" Rin mused aloud.

"What are you two doing there?" said an unfamiliar voice. Rin nearly leaped out of her skin and swiveled toward the yuki onna, who was striding toward them. Had they been caught already? She assumed they were alone, and no one would overhear them. She stepped in front of Hikaru, prepared to transform into her kitsune form if necessary.

"We seem to have lost our way, we were looking for the main hall." She plastered on a fake smile, and prayed some Kami would be listening and save them.

The yuki onna narrowed ice-blue eyes at Rin. Did she see through their disguises?

"You two..."

Rin clenched her hand into a fist, prepared to unleash her fox flames.

"Where are you from, I don't think I've met you before..."

"We're from the southern mountain range," Hikaru said.

"Ah. That's why I've never seen you before." The yuki onna shook her head.

Rin relaxed, but only slightly.

"Well it's a good thing I found you, the meeting is just about to start. Come." She waved for them to follow as she strode down the opposite way down the corridor.

Rin and Hikaru shared a look. They couldn't refuse her without arising suspicion. For now, they would have to play along until they could slip away and go find the tengu prince.

They followed the yuki onna through the twisted corridors, where she led them to a large audience room. The walls were made of ice as the rest of the palace was, and long icicles hung from the ceiling and caught sunlight coming through the windows at the top, casting rainbows of colors all around the room. And at the end of the hall was a massive pillar of ice that reached from floor to ceiling and was four men wide. Suspended in the center was the tengu prince his wings extended as if he'd been frozen mid-flight.

Rin covered her mouth when she saw it. They had really frozen him solid.

"Is it your first time seeing him?" the yuki onna asked.

Rin hadn't meant to react this way. She thought they would have kept him hidden. Instead, they were flaunting him, using his frozen body as a decoration.

"Is he alive?" Rin asked, there was no need to disguise the tremor in her voice.

"I didn't believe it the first time I saw it, but he lives in empress

Toku's ice," the yuki onna remarked, shaking her head in amazement.

Empress Toku? Rin had never heard of a leader of the yuki onna before, but she didn't know they'd built this palace either. Many things had changed since the fall of The Dragon, the different clans had fractured and warred with one another, and it seemed when this Toku had captured the tengu prince, she had risen to the role of empress. Getting the tengu prince out was going to be more difficult than she expected.

A group of yuki onna waved them and their escort over. "Who's your friend." They narrowed their gazes at Rin and Hikaru, could they see through the illusion. She grabbed Hikaru's hand, discreetly hoping to strengthen it. She'd let her guard down for a moment when she saw the tengu, that couldn't happen again.

"They're from the southern mountains," said their escort.

These new yuki onna looked more suspicious, but before they could question them further, a cheer rose up among the gathered yuki onna. And all eyes turned to the front of the room. A yuki onna took the stage standing in front of the frozen tengu prince. All yuki onna were beautiful, but there was something more beautiful about this one. Perhaps it was the sense of power that she carried, or the fierce angles of her face or the ruby red lips. But there was no doubt, this had to be queen Toku.

"Sisters!" Toku's melodic voice seemed to boom through the room. "At last, our clan is united for the first time in centuries."

More cheers rippled through the crowd.

She held up her hands again, and the crowd fell silent.

"Though it should be a joyous celebration. I have gathered you here for a purpose. A pretender sits on the throne of Akatsuki."

A hiss went through the crowd.

A pretender? Rin looked at Hikaru, he was frowning as well. She couldn't mean Kaito, could they?

"This so-called dragon would have us all believe he is The Great Dragon returned. My sisters, I ask you, can we suffer this liar to remain?"

"No!" they shouted. The air was getting colder, and Rin shivered. Hikaru trembled beside her as the temperature dropped. Rin pressed closer to him, trying to share the warmth of her body as best as she could.

If the yuki onna were to attack, she felt confident Kaito's army could defeat them. Though she was outnumbered now, they were no match for Kaito's army.

"Sisters, we have grown stronger, we captured the tengu prince." She gestured to the frozen tengu behind her. "It is time all of Akatuski recognizes our true strength!"

They roared with approval.

There was a smug smile on Toku's face. If Rin could stay long enough to learn their plans, she could return to Kaito and warn him. That was after they got the tengu prince out of ice.

"I asked you all here because the time to act is now. Our allies in the north have reached out to us to march upon this pretender and remove him from his throne."

The yuki onna were devolving into a frenzy. Their hunger for the battle ahead was palpable. It was time to escape, and reassess. Rin grasped Hikaru's hand, and they started backing away. But she didn't get a few steps before she ran into something solid.

They were surrounded by yuki onna. While she'd been listening to their speech, they'd closed in around them.

"Where do you think you're going?" They smiled.

"I just realized I forgot something." Rin gestured for the door.

"You're not one of us."

Her heart clenched. No.

"Are you a spy?" asked the yuki onna to her left.

Rin forced a smile. "I don't know what you're talking about."

She tried to shove her way past the yuki onna, but they pushed her back.

"You're not going anywhere."

FIFTEEN

The priest howled as his forehead burst. A pair of black curved horns dripping with blood grew out of the tear in his skin. Tsuki let go of the priest, and he crumbled to the ground, grasping his abdomen. He wriggled as if live snakes were crawling under his skin. Though he wanted to look away, he couldn't. Kazue was the one who ordered he attack the shrine, that he hold the poor bastard while she forced the black stone in his mouth. If he weren't a coward, he would have refused, or tried to stop her. But running away meant losing himself entirely. Even now, he felt the darkness crawling around him, like an insect burrowing under his skin. Just like this unfortunate soul. Only he wouldn't lose himself to the oblivion of becoming a hybrid, every moment he had left the darkness clawing him inside was waiting to consume him and Akira whole.

"There's no use in regretting," Akira said.

"And there's no honor in slaughtering the defenseless," Tsuki replied. He and Akira had disagreed before, but this time it felt different. She'd never been this callous before; she was too willing to forgive Kazue's transgressions.

The bodies of the slain priests lay scattered on the ground. Kazue said they were to teach the others not to resist. To him, they were the lucky ones; at least they wouldn't be transformed into monsters by Kazue's song.

They moved down the line, transforming the remaining priests left in the palace. Tsuki held them while Kazue sang. Some begged for mercy, others mumbled prayers, hands pressed together and eyes closed. The kami were gone. They had been for a long time. The first Kazue had rounded them all up to create this monster who stood before him.

Nothing human remained in this temple, and a small group of new hybrids, relearned to walk with the new strength of their disfigured bodies. The wounds where scales, claws, and horns had burst through their flesh wept blood.

"The transformation is so much more successful when we use priests and priestesses," Kazue remarked as if they were discussing the weather.

Even the original Kazue had not been this cold or calculating nor had the same mad glint in her eye. Though she claimed they were the same, he saw only echoes of the woman he remembered. This Kazue was different, more bloodthirsty, and more terrifying than her namesake.

"And what will you do with them?" Tsuki asked her. "What's the point of all this?"

She stroked the scaly green cheek of one of her creations.

"We are creating the perfect world, one in which there are no yokai, no humans. A world where we can coexist." She turned to

Tsuki with a too-wide smile. It was the smile of a madwoman, blinded by her own twisted visions. Had Hisato done this to her, or was she as delusional as him, tortured by memories that didn't belong to her and a power that shouldn't be contained by a human body. Which reminded him, he assumed Hisato would show himself by now, but he'd been mysteriously scarce. When he tried to ask Kazue about him, she avoided the subject. They must be plotting something together, if only he could find out what.

"And what good would it do if we know. It's not as if we can return to Suzume."

Kazue left the hybrids to their transformation, and Tsuki followed her without responding to Akira. She might have given up on escape, but he wasn't ready to give in yet.

"Don't do anything reckless, do you want us to end up like those abominations?" Akira scolded him.

He took a deep breath to quiet the rage that threatened to take hold of him. He never had reason to hide his thoughts from Akira before, and he had to consciously shield his desires from her. If he didn't, then she might try and stop him. While Kazue held the staff, they were bound to serve her, and because she could read their thoughts when it pleased her, they couldn't plot together. But he'd tested it, only when he shared his thoughts with Akira was Kazue able to hear them. Akira had given up, but he would save them both.

Kazue entered the shrine, and knelt before the icon of the kami to pray. Tsuki and Akira stood on guard outside. Not that anything could get through these hybrids to reach her. And even if they did, he would have no choice but to destroy them if they tried.

The temple was a small one, the scent of the ocean wafted on the air. They weren't far from The Dragon's seaside palace. Would Kazue take these hybrids and march them onto the palace to capture Suzume?

"Brother, you must give up on your delusions of returning to Suzume. Even if we could. They would never welcome us back. Kazue made sure of that."

Tsuki balled his hand into a fist. For the entirety of his long life, he never much cared for anyone other than himself or Akira. He lived for the sword in his hand, the rush of battle. But being wielded by Kazue as a tool to harm the defenseless didn't sit right with him. There must be something they could do, he couldn't just roll over and accept his fate. Wind blew in off the ocean, and ruffled his hair and the garden nearby. His eye was drawn to a plant the priest had been growing. It was one he recognized which had grown wild like a weed from the mountain where Akira and he had grown up.

When consumed, it was a strong sedative. While Kazue was absorbed in her prayers and shielding his thoughts from Akira, he leaned over the garden wall and plucked a few leaves of the plant, stuffing them into his pocket. If he could slip this into Kazue's evening tea, then he could steal the staff and give them the opportunity to escape back to Suzume and the others.

"Please do not tell me you're thinking of doing what I think you are."

"Don't, she'll hear," Tsuki warned her.

"I can't let you destroy us both." He could feel Akira's sneer inside his mind.

She tried to wrestle control of the body they shared from him, but Tsuki clung on tight. Akira gave up the fight when Kazue emerged from inside the shrine. She narrowed her eyes at him. Tsuki had to keep his mind blank, not let anything reveal itself on his face. Did she suspect? Had she heard him and Akira arguing.

She turned to look up at the gray clouds gathering on the horizon. "It seems like it might rain, I think I'll take my tea early today."

Tsuki bobbed his head and went to fetch her tea. As he pulled the kettle off the fire, he tore a few leaves into her cup and stirred it around.

"This cannot possibly work," Akira said. But she didn't try to stop him, she must recognize this was the only way they were going to escape her.

He brought the cup to Kazue, who sat upon the veranda, watching the ambling hybrids as they wandered the yard. Trails of blood had stained the ground where the hybrids had transformed, and one had died from his transformation. His mangled body was trampled under the feet of the others. Flies gathered on the corpses of the fallen, buzzing around their eyes and open mouths.

She took the cup from him and inhaled the aroma of her tea. The plant should be odorless, but he still held his breath just in case. Then she brought the cup to her lips. His hungry gaze strayed to the staff, which she wore on her back at all times.

She took a long drink, then said, "Thank you, Tsuki for this tonic, I have had trouble sleeping."

His blood ran cold, as he reached for his sword.

She took another sip of her tea. "Don't bother."

"What you're doing is barbaric. I won't help you make more of these things." He threw his arm toward the bloody temple.

"If you are so weary of killing priests, then I have a new job for you, go and bring me Suzume."

THE MOON HUNG HEAVY IN THE SKY LIKE A RIPE PEACH, A DUSTING OF stars were sprinkled across the inky horizon. It was the perfect kind of night for a moonlit stroll. Though his days might be taken up with rebuilding his kingdom, he wanted his nights to be filled by Suzume. The halls between their rooms were vacant, just as he'd ordered. He didn't want to run into Shin. He had noticed Kaito's good mood and had come to the logical conclusion about Suzume and him. The rest of the afternoon's strategy meeting had been filled up with Shin trying to wheedle details out of him. But he wasn't one to kiss and tell.

It still felt surreal. After all the uncertainty, and waiting, she had chosen him; she had come to him first. Once his kingdom was whole again, he would have nothing to want for.

Wind swayed through the branches of the stark sakura tree. When Hikaru returned from his mission, he would need to ask him to have it bloom once more to celebrate. Was it too soon to start planning their wedding ceremony? Ideally, the entirety of Akatsuki would attend, including her family. But first, he would have to get the emperor to agree. All the political machinations would take too long. He wasn't sure how much longer he could wait until she was his completely.

The inner palace was very still tonight. Not a thing moved or breathed, and it set him on edge. It was too quiet. Kaito spread out his spiritual energy seeking out Naoki, who should be guarding Suzume from the shadows, but as he drew in closer, he found nothing. Not even a hint. Suzume's door was slightly ajar, and something was moving inside.

Kaito flexed his claws and crept closer. Whoever was inside, they were cloaking their energy so he couldn't attain a clear reading. This wasn't some lesser yokai. Not wanting to give away, he'd sensed them, Kaito knocked on the door.

"Suzume, can I come in?"

There was no answer, not that he expected one.

"Don't be shy, it's just me," he said as he slid the door open.

Inside was pitch black. Suzume's bedding was tousled, and her clothes strewn across the ground. But no sign of a struggle. Whoever they were, they hadn't run into Suzume yet. It was fortunate he got here first.

Kaito crossed the room, as casually as possible.

"Are you hiding?" he called out as he pretended to scan the room for Suzume.

At the empty futon, he crouched down and spread out his senses to feel for the intruder. Their energy was concentrated in the corner. Kaito sprung up and lunged for the shadowy corner, catching the intruder by the throat and pinned them to the wall.

"It's not very honorable to attack while your opponent's back is —" Kaito froze.

"Miss me?" Tsuki smirked, and then kicked, landing a blow on Kaito's shin.

The kick caught him by surprise, and he let go of Tsuki.

"You dare come back here," Kaito growled as he chased the fleeing Tsuki.

"It wasn't my choice, she ordered me to do it," Tsuki said.

"Like I would believe anything a traitor like you has to say." Kaito swung for Tsuki's head with his claws, but Tsuki dodged and ran to the other end of the room again.

"I never wanted to hurt Suzume, but she—" His words were cut off as he wrapped his hands around his throat.

Kaito rushed toward him, as Tsuki wrestled with himself and landed a punch on Tsuki that sent him stumbling backward. He grimaced as his features fluctuated between Tsuki to Akira and back again.

Kaito slammed him up against the wall. "Why did you come back, are you here to try and kill Suzume this time?"

Tsuki's face was twisted in pain. "It's—"

The words were cut off as Akira came to the surface. Kaito was thrown backward.

A shimmering red barrier separated him from Akira, he surged toward the barrier, slamming his fists against it. But he couldn't get through it. Akira ran for the exit. He had to stop them before they hurt Suzume.

He paced behind the barrier like a caged animal, every few minutes testing the limits by slamming his hands against it. But try as he might, he couldn't get past it. Even now, while he was trapped here, Suzume might be being carried away by Akira and Tsuki.

From the hall beyond the door, he heard footsteps approaching. Kaito pressed against the barrier.

"Who's there?"

"Kaito? What are you doing in my room?" Suzume appeared in the doorway, looking confused but unharmed.

Kaito exhaled a breath he'd been holding, Naoki and Souta were right behind her.

"Are you hurt?" Kaito asked, pressing his hands against the barrier.

She frowned. "I'm fine, what happened here."

"Akira happened," Kaito bit out the words.

Souta approached the barrier and pressed his hand against it, with a few mumbled words it dissolved. Kaito bolted for Suzume and gathered her up in his arms, he needed to be certain she was unharmed.

"What's gotten into you?" She pulled from his embrace, looking over at Souta and Naoki.

Kaito pressed his lips against her hair. "I was worried they'd hurt you."

She relaxed against him, her hand resting on his back. "I'm fine, there's no reason to worry," Suzume said as he held her.

He didn't want to let her go, but Akira and Tsuki were still out there.

"Gather a search party, find Akira and Tsuki," Kaito ordered Naoki.

He bowed and turned to obey his command. They couldn't have gotten far. He would make sure they were captured, and then he would punish them for daring to betray him.

Sixteen

Suzume paced back and forth in the map room. Kaito leaned casually against the map table, arms crossed over his chest. He was watching her as she paced, she could feel his eyes on her burning her up. She kept avoiding looking at him because whenever their eyes met, she thought of their kiss. Then her face flushed, and her stomach did flip flops.

"You're going to wear a hole in the floor at this rate," Kaito said.

She glanced at him intending to refute his statement, but the words were dried up in her throat.

A blush crept up over her neck and cheeks; he was smirking at her as if he could guess exactly what she was thinking. Did he know how she kept reliving the feeling of his hands on her waist, or how she thought about the reasons why her entire body felt aflame when his lips parted hers? Now was definitely not the time for that. She turned back to the map, as if the depictions of mountain ranges, rivers, and coastlines were of intense interest.

She cleared her throat. "The scouts should be back by now."

Kaito joined her at the map's edge, close enough that his arm brushed against hers. Her heart sped up. How was she supposed to focus on finding Akira and Tsuki, when Kaito was slowly driving her to madness? If he kept this up, she was going to be a pile of goo on the floor in a few minutes.

"Don't worry, we won't let them get away again," he said as his finger traced up her arm.

Gooseflesh pebbled her skin, and her heart raced faster. At this rate, her heart was likely to beat out of her chest. The doors at the back of the room flew open, and Suzume jerked away from him. Seeing as their romantic relationship was so new, she wasn't ready to flaunt it in front of the others. Shin must have noticed, though, because there was a small quirk at the corner of his mouth.

"What do you have to report?" Kaito asked him, as he and his mate Akane, who'd been part of the scouting party looking for Akira and Tsuki, entered.

Akane met Suzume's eyes and gave her a knowing look. Suzume dropped her gaze to the floor, but she couldn't keep a smile from her face. She never thought she could be this happy. The happy fluttering in her stomach never quite went away since she'd admitted to herself how she felt for Kaito.

"The shrine is swarming with hybrids, at least fifty, but there could be more hidden," Akane reported.

"We've got them outnumbered, that's good," Kaito replied, rubbing his chin.

"I would advise caution, I feel uneasy about it. Apart from a few guards, there were no other protections around the shrine, it's almost as if they want us to attack."

"What do you think?" Kaito asked her.

It was a valid concern, when she'd first encountered the last piece of Kazue's soul, it had been during a hybrid attack. Maybe it hadn't been a coincidence, and they were working with Hisato; perhaps they were even the reason Tsuki and Akira had betrayed her. That day they'd gone missing while she fought the hybrids. Chasing after them was a risk, but it might also lead them to the last piece of Kazue's soul.

"I think we'll have to take the chance," she said.

"I agree," Kaito said. "Let's prepare the warriors for an attack."

Shin bowed, and he and Akane left to prepare. Things moved in a whirlwind after that, an attack was organized, plans made, and they were all so busy there was no time for second thoughts or doubts. Not until she was looking at the army before her did the reality settle upon her. They were going to attack Hisato's hybrids, they might finally be able to find the last piece of Kazue's soul.

Once they were all together, they would be strong enough to defeat Hisato. From the moment she had first discovered her power, she never thought she could live a normal life again. She had given up on thinking about the future, what happened after. But for the first time, she started to think about what came next. A life, not the one she had planned for herself, but a good one none the less, one with Kaito?

She snuck a glance at Kaito from the corner of her eye. He had asked her to marry him, to become his empress. What would it be like to rule at his side, a world where yokai and humans could co-exist...

Doubt started to creep in, and Suzume clutched her temporary staff in her hand. She'd been practicing with Souta after Kaito, and her sparred. She was feeling more confident, and her powers were coming easier again. But that was in the practice yard, what if in an actual battle she froze up, or worse lost control.

Kaito grabbed Suzume's hand and squeezed. She met his gaze, and he gave her an encouraging smile.

"Don't worry, I'll be here for you."

That was right, she wasn't going to do any of this alone. She had Kaito, Souta, and Naoki on her side, besides Kaito's army, to fight alongside them. They would win. They had to.

They were approaching their destination, a small cove on the beach where they could prepare for their attack. This was also where their group would split apart. As they drew closer, Suzume felt the pull of the last soul piece. They were there. This was it.

"Be safe," Kaito said as he cupped her cheek, drawing her attention to him.

The rest of the world felt as if it fell away when she looked into his eyes. She leaned into his hand. Kaito's words gave her courage. She never thought she could find comfort in another person, but Kaito's belief in her made her feel stronger, more certain that she could face any challenge.

"Worried I'll get hurt?" she asked, but there was a tremor to her voice that she couldn't hide.

He shook his head. "You're more than capable, but I couldn't stand it if you were to get hurt."

She exhaled sharply, something swelled in her chest that was hard to define. Was this what it meant to have someone to care for you? Someone who loved you?

"Time to go," Souta said.

She let Kaito's hand slip from hers, giving him one lingering look before following Souta. Kaito and the army would be attacking from the front, while Suzume and a smaller group would be sneaking in around the back, trying to find the last soul piece and getting them out before Hisato realized they'd taken them. She kept watching Kaito until they were over a rise and out of sight.

Once she could no longer see him, she focused on the task at hand. She would need to clear her mind of all other things, there was no time for distraction. But when all the battles were over, she hoped they could share more moments together and start planning for their future, together.

Kaito led his army toward the temple. It was smaller and more run-down than he had pictured. A few scattered shrine buildings with peeling paint, and scattered rocks were all the cover it could afford. But the hybrids shambling about the grounds, were not trying to disguise their numbers. A few well-placed archers could thin their numbers considerably. It all felt too easy, which only made him wary.

Shin approached. "What are your orders?" he asked.

"We lure them out to us. Have archers shoot from above and provide cover."

"As you wish." Shin pivoted on his heel and went to do as Kaito commanded.

When Tsuki had attacked, he had said she ordered them to attack Suzume. In the moment, he had thought nothing of it. But now he wondered, could it have been some sort of warning or a trap. They had led their army straight to them, and there was nothing to stop them from sweeping in and destroying them. He knew Hisato, he was cunning. They would take every precaution possible until he could be certain.

The archers were in position, just awaiting his signal. A hybrid stumbled across a courtyard in the temple. Kaito held his hand up and gave the signal to fire. A single arrow sailed through the air and struck the eye of the hybrid. It swung around and roared, alerting the other Hybrids, who, like a pack of wild animals, started to charge in the direction the arrow had been fired from.

They were drawing closer. Some dripping blood, their forms disfigured and terrifying. Some of his yokai warriors had never seen them before, and they recoiled from them. The scent of rotting flesh preceded them, and it turned his stomach.

"Hold," Kaito ordered the army

The yokai shifted restlessly, he could feel their fear and hunger. The hybrids were nearly upon them now, he could see the whites of their bloodshot eyes.

"Now."

A volley of arrows sailed through the sky and rained down upon the hybrids. Their bodies bristling with arrows, they continued without stopping. Fear rippled through the yokai, and they were slow to attack. It was up to him to lead the way; with a shout, he led the charge. Kaito plunged himself into the fray and swung his sword, hacking into the hybrids who bled thick black blood. The yokai followed him, Shin and Akane in wolf form tore at the hybrids with powerful jaws. While the rest attacked with sword, claw, and fang.

Kaito waded through the chaos, searching out his true opponent. Today would be the day he got his vengeance against Akira and Tsuki for their betrayal.

A hybrid rushed toward him, and Kaito sliced through it, and it sprayed black ichor on his face, which he wiped away. The grunts, growls, and clang of metal was a cacophony around him, and his vision was obstructed by the clash of bodies. Dust had been kicked up by the numerous stomping feet.

Tsuki fought at the edge of the fray. Kaito charged toward them, dodging hybrids on his way. They swung their sword cutting through yokai, severing them in half with ease. It shouldn't have been possible. When they turned toward him, their eyes were without pupils and entirely black. They collided on the battlefield, and the force of it threw them both backward. Kaito's skin prickled with energy, he could sense something in them that he'd never felt before, it was dark and spreading.

They traded blows, their power too easily matched, and neither one losing ground. Each time Kaito thought he was getting the upper hand, they would slip out from beneath his grip. The fight continued to rage around them, but it had faded to nothing but a dull roar for him.

Tsuki rushed toward him and swung his blade high, Kaito dodged slicing a deep gash along his side. It didn't slow Tsuki, and instead, he thrust at Kaito catching his dominant shoulder.

His grip on his blade slackened as the black-eyed creature with Akira and Tsuki's face bolted toward him again.

Kaito growled and rammed an elbow into their gut, forcing him to drop his sword. Kaito swung a punch, and missed, only to get caught by an uppercut that sent him stumbling backward. Before he had time to recover, he was on top of him again. They shoved him to the ground and pinned him there with a foot on his chest.

Tsuki smirked down at him. Kaito grabbed his leg and yanked it out from under him, bringing Tsuki or whoever he was onto the ground with him. They wrestled, neither one was able to pin the other.

A song rose over the chaos of the battle. It rattled in his skull and made his head throb. Suzume must have unleashed her song of destruction. He slapped his hands over his ears to block out the sound. Tsuki fell on all fours and screamed, his skin bubbling and twisting. For some reason, it was hitting him harder. Had Suzume learned to control her song that well?

He scanned the crowd for her, but instead spotted a priestess with glowing blue eyes. Tsuki and Akira lay unconscious or dead on the ground. And the woman strode toward them, in her hand was a staff. Kazue's staff.

Kaito reached for his sword, which had fallen on the ground before leaping to his feet and drawing it on the woman.

She stood back, watching him, eyes wide. And behind her, Souta and Suzume ran toward him.

"It's really you," the woman said.

"And who are you?" Kaito nodded at Suzume, who closed in

from behind, her hand raised, prepared to subdue the woman if necessary.

"Kaito, do you really not recognize me?" Her expression was hurt.

He had never seen this woman in his life, though he suspected this was the missing piece of Kazue's soul. Hisato must have had her this entire time, perhaps even planned to use her against them.

Suzume was closing in behind her. Just another few feet. This woman couldn't be trusted if she had Suzume's staff.

"I gave you that name, don't you remember?" she asked as she took a step toward him.

Kaito pointed his blade at her throat. He wasn't fool enough to fall for Hisato's tricks.

"I've never met you before in my life," Kaito stuttered.

"Not in this life, but you knew me before. I hoped you would recognize me."

"You're the water of Kazue's soul," Kaito said.

"No. I am Kazue. The day by the waterfall, when you first told me you loved me, do you remember the promise we made?"

Kaito was struck cold as he took a second look at the woman standing before him. It couldn't be. It had to be a trick. He'd never told anyone about that day...

A song rose up on the air, and Kaito turned as Souta and Suzume closed in. The water of Kazue's soul turned as well, her eyes wide with panic.

"Save me—" she reached for him, but the song had already taken hold. She pitched forward, and on impulse, he ran forward, catching her before she could fall.

Her eyes were fluttering closed. "You promised we would find one another again in my next life…"

Kaito's heart thumped in his chest, the old promise that he had long ago buried brought back to light. It couldn't be real. This woman couldn't be Kazue's rebirth, it was impossible because Kazue had torn her soul apart. And yet she held a memory no other soul fragment had.

"We did it," Souta said as he picked up Suzume's staff off the ground and handed it to her.

She took it without a word, her eyes were trained on him. She had heard everything this woman said. He wanted to explain, to assure her it meant nothing. But she pivoted on her foot and marched away before he could get a word out.

"Take her back to the palace. We'll keep her locked up until we know if we can trust her or not," Kaito handed her over to Shin, who had joined them looking for orders.

Even if Kazue had been reborn, this changed nothing. His heart belonged to Suzume. But why did he feel so guilty?

SEVENTEEN

The yuki onna fanned out around Rin and Hikaru. The temperature dropped, and her breath came out in clouds of vapor, and a shiver ran up her spine. Hikaru was trembling with the cold. If it got any colder, he might end up a solid block of ice like the tengu prince. Behind her, the Queen of the yuki onna continued her speech, for now, the bulk of the crowd's attention was on her. If she could just get through this group, they could get away unscathed, but that meant abandoning their mission to rescue the tengu prince.

"Follow my lead," Rin whispered to Hikaru.

He gave her the barest nod of his head.

"Sisters, I think there's been a misunderstanding." Rin held up her hands in surrender, she'd talked her way out of worse predicaments. Maybe she could get out of this one as well.

The yuki onna in front of her smiled and revealed rows of jagged pointed teeth.

"There is no misunderstanding. One of our sisters wouldn't be affected by the cold as you are," said the yuki onna directly in front of her.

With each breath Rin took, she exposed herself, none of the yuki onna's breath clouded in the air.

Rin forced a laugh and shook her head. "What do you mean?"

They closed in closer around them, their faces transforming from pale and deadly beauties to pupiless eyes and mouths too full of sharp teeth. Their hands were tipped in long claw-like fingernails that they reached for them with.

Rin and Hikaru backed away, but the yuki onna who had been previously watching the yuki onna queen had turned toward them, hunger in their gazes.

"It seems we have a guest, sisters," the yuki onna queen said.

Rin took hold of Hikaru's hand and squeezed and, with her other hand, reached into the sleeve of her kimono, where she had hidden away a leaf.

"Looks like we came at a bad time. We'll see ourselves out then." She tossed the leaf into the air before striking it with her fox fire. It exploded in a blue smoke that filled the air. For anyone but her, it would blind them for several minutes. Just enough time to escape.

Rin pulled Hikaru through the smoke, weaving their way through the yuki onna, who were scrambling to find her in the dark, while colliding with one another.

"Find them. Don't let them escape," the queen screeched.

Past the fumbling and howling yuki onna was the door out of the audience hall. The smoke was starting to thin, but it should give them enough time to escape. Once they were out of the palace, she could transform and run far away, from the yuki onna and from even the tengu and the alliance.

Hikaru must have sensed her indecision because he squeezed her hand. Saying without words that he trusted her decision, whatever it might be. If the yuki onna had allied with Ai, The Dragon's rule would be threatened. And until there was peace, neither she nor Hikaru could rest. As much as she wanted to make their own safety a priority, she had no choice but to stay and rescue the tengu prince.

Rin drew another leaf from her sleeve and infused it with fox fire. They would need new disguises. Turning away from the door, she led Hikaru over to the side of the hall, dodging blinded yuki onna as they went. They pressed their backs against the pillars.

The yuki onna were flowing toward the exit, assuming that they had used the distraction to make their escape. She hoped she was making the right decision.

"Keep your eyes closed, and whatever you do, don't move," Rin whispered in Hikaru's ear. She placed the leaf against his forehead.

The smoke had dissipated, and the yuki onna squinted in the gloom. Rin disguised herself, closing her eyes tight. Her fox magic could make them invisible for a short period of time, as long as no one touched them, and they didn't move, they would appear as if they were part of the pillars.

Footsteps approached, ice crept over her skin. And Rin held her breath so it wouldn't give her away once more. She could feel a yuki onna beside her, the icy touch of her spiritual energy raised the gooseflesh on her arm. Just an inch more and she would brush against Rin, and her disguise would be ruined.

"They must have fled for the forest. Capture them and bring them to me," the yuki onna queen commanded.

The cold receded, and footsteps raced out of the audience hall. She held her breath until she was certain they were alone again. The dim sound of shouts faded until there was nothing but the sound of wind whistling over the roof of the audience hall. Rin risked opening her eyes and peered around the pillar.

The yuki onna had almost all left, but for a pair of guards standing on either side of the tengu prince. Two yuki onna she could handle. There wasn't much time to waste, before long they would realize they were hiding here right under their noses. For now, their heads were turned away, looking to the exit prepared for someone to storm through. Rin tapped Hikaru on the shoulder and made a silent signal for him to follow her. They stayed behind the pillars, darting from one to the other until they were right beside the guards.

Rin and Hikaru moved slowly behind them, and with a silent exchange, they each struck the yuki onna knocking them unconscious. The yuki onna crumbled to the ground. Once that was out of the way, they dragged them from the audience hall. At the door to the hall, Rin looked both ways. Across from the audience hall was another room. Voices echoed down the long hall, and she hesitated, her heart in her throat. But instead of coming closer, it was moving away. Once she was certain they wouldn't come any closer, she placed both the yuki onna in the other room and closed the door.

She and Hikaru returned to the audience hall, where they

barred the door with a barrier Hikaru created. The green light of his spiritual energy sparkled.

"We don't have much time," Hikaru said.

"We'll have to get the prince out quickly then." Rin gave him a smile to reassure him. But the screams of the hunting yuki onna had her rattled. If she couldn't figure out a way to melt this ice and get the prince out, they would be torn apart.

The motionless tengu prince suspended in ice loomed over her at the far end of the hall. She paced around the pillar of ice, searching for a weak spot. It was solid ice straight through. It was possible he was dead, could he be brought back after being trapped in ice so long? She might have condemned them both for a doomed mission.

Rin shook herself. She couldn't think that way. They'd come this far; she just had to break through the ice. And the best thing for that was fire. She transformed into her kitsune form and backed up a few feet away from the column of ice.

"Stay back, it's going to get hot," Rin said to Hikaru.

He took guard behind her and watched the door. Rin gathered up her spiritual energy, funneling everything into her fox flame, feeding it higher and hotter than she had ever done before. Then once it had built up, she unleashed it upon the pillar of ice. A blaze of fire poured from her mouth, striking the pillar. Water dripped along it slowly, creating a small divot. It was too slow, she needed more power.

Rin concentrated more power into her flame, making it hot enough that even the icy walls started to sweat. It forced Hikaru closer to the door, and even warmed her face. Water gushed from the growing hole in the pillar, and ran in a river soaking her feet.

Shrieks grew closer. The yuki onna must have sensed her fox fire.

"I'll go guard the door, you get him out," Hikaru said, and he jogged over to the door.

A loud bang slammed against the door.

Little by little, she was breaking through the pillar. But it still wasn't enough. The wail of the yuki onna echoed through the audience hall. It felt as if they were all around her. Cold crept over her; the river of melted ice started to freeze her feet in place. The temperature was dropping, they were trying to freeze them inside. She was going too slow, they wouldn't get him out in time. And even when they did, how would they escape. The animal side of her wanted to flee, to put her own life above a stranger's.

"Don't give up, we're nearly there," Hikaru cheered.

She had exposed the tengu prince's hand from the ice. And the digits twitched slightly. Rin raised the fire up higher as to not burn the prince in the process of freeing him. She could do this, just a little bit more.

The audience hall shook, and ice fell from the ceiling. She could hear the yuki onna, they had surrounded the audience hall on all sides. If they didn't freeze them to death, they would tear apart their own palace to reach them.

Hikaru fell back closer to her, and encased them and the tengu prince's prison in a shimmering green barrier. He didn't need to say it, but his first barrier would be breached soon. This was their last line of defense.

Rin returned her attention to melting the pillar. But her energy was not limitless. She'd managed to melt most of his abdomen, and the tengu prince's arms were free. Instead, she moved closer to the pillar, circling around it, trying to melt more and more of the ice. The tengu prince bent and flexed, he was waking up.

A crack sounded, and Rin resisted the urge to turn and look. She focused all her flagging energy on melting what remained of the pillar. Ice crept over Hikaru's barrier, covering it in frost and obscuring her view beyond it. But even that could not block out the cries of the yuki onna, both beautiful and terrifying. It was a song that had led countless men to their deaths. Their ice slammed against Hikaru's barrier, and sweat beaded on his forehead as he concentrated on keeping it up.

The tip of the tengu prince's wing was free, and water was rushing from the ice, flooding the barrier, with nowhere else to go it was reaching up to her ankles now.

Hikaru cried out as his barrier fell. He collapsed onto his knees, and Rin abandoned melting the prince and shot a blast of fire at the swarm of yuki onna that were coming toward them. They recoiled from the fire, long enough for Hikaru to create a wall of earth which cut the audience hall in half. But it had taken too much out of him, and he was pale and shaking as he grabbed onto the edge of her collar to stand. He leaned too heavily on her. Rin too was running low on energy.

The tengu prince's prison continued to melt, but by the time she broke him free, she wouldn't be strong enough to escape. On the other side of the earthen wall, the yuki raged, and dust fell down from the walls. It wouldn't be long before they were able to break through here as well.

A loud crack echoed through the chamber, and ice sprayed over Rin and Hikaru. She blocked Hikaru's body on instinct, and prepared herself for the swarm of yuki onna breaking through Hikaru's last defense. But the screams continued, still muffled by earth.

Rin looked over her shoulder and found the tengu prince standing in the remains of the ice pillar his black wings extended outward and dripping. Ice clung to his ebony hair, and his haori and hakama were soaked, but he was alive. They'd done it; they freed him.

The earthen wall shuddered once more.

The tengu prince tested his wings, flinging droplets of water onto the walls.

"I'm alive—" He looked around the room.

"But you're not safe yet, we have to get out of here," Rin said as she searched for an escape.

"I can fly us out of here if you can create an escape for us." He pointed upward.

The entire palace was made of ice. If she could concentrate one last blast of fox fire, she might be able to burn a hole in the ceiling large enough for them to fly through. But she suddenly felt very tired, she'd used more energy than she normally would. Hikaru wrapped his arm around her neck. And the feel of his body close to her gave her the strength she needed.

She tilted her head up toward the roof and let the fire flow from her. Water fell down from the ceiling drenching her fur. Sunlight spilled through as the hole grew wider and wider until it was large enough for the wingspan of the tengu prince. Rin collapsed, panting for breath. Her internal fox fire was nothing more than a tiny ember burning inside her. She had only enough energy to take on her human-like form.

The tengu prince held out his hands to Rin and Hikaru. "Let's fly."

He wrapped an arm around her waist and Hikaru's, bringing them close. And with a few beats of his wings, they were lifted into the air and toward the hole in the roof. As they got close, yuki onna swarmed toward it. But the beat of his wings, sent them flying backward and they were able to take to the sky and over the treetops.

The screams of the yuki onna followed them before eventually fading to nothing. It wasn't until the landscape changed, the forest thinning did Rin let go of the breath she'd been holding. Wind rushed over her, and the horizon was endless before her as she threw her head back and laughed. They'd done it, they'd really done it.

EIGHTEEN

The staff came down with a sharp rap on Suzume's knuckles. She should have seen that coming, she'd left herself wide open for that attack. She hissed and blew on her stinging digits.

"You need to focus," Souta scolded.

It was the third time he had caught her unawares like that. But she couldn't help it. Her thoughts kept circling. No matter how she tried to distract herself, she kept thinking about the tender way Kaito had looked at the Water of Kazue's soul. She wanted to convince herself that it was all in her head. But when he had caught her, it had made her chest tight. And what did she mean by "remember the promise they'd made." Did that woman remember something of Kazue's life that Suzume didn't? She'd never wanted Kazue's memories, but right now, she wished she did.

"Instead of battering your body, why don't you tell me what's been on your mind?"

Souta gave her a kind, grandfatherly smile. He was nothing like her own grandfather, because she had been born a girl, he'd never wanted anything to do with her. If she hadn't been born as a princess, perhaps she could have been born to a family with someone like Souta as her grandfather. Though she'd been resistant to opening up to him, his advice that night she thought of running away had helped a lot. And now that she thought about it, unlike her, he had memories of Kazue's life. Maybe he knew about this promise.

"You have Kazue's memories, do you know anything about a promise between Kaito and Kazue?"

Souta hesitated and frowned, as if he were measuring his words. "Most of what I retained that was Kazue's feels like half-remembered dreams. They're often vague and hit me at random, a scent that evokes an image. A phrase that awakens an emotion."

"So, you're saying you don't remember a promise?" Why did he love talking in riddles so much?

He smiled and placed his hands on her shoulders. "Whatever happened to Kazue in the past is nothing but dust on the wind. It matters not, you need only look to the future."

She looked down at her hands clenched around the staff. She had it back; the last piece of Kazue's soul was with them, and yet she still felt empty. There was something else she was missing, a gnawing feeling at the back of her mind that she couldn't quite pinpoint.

"Why don't I have any of her memories when the rest of you do?" It wasn't that she wanted to relive Kaito and Kazue's past, but it ate at her that this woman had something with Kaito she could never have. Kaito wouldn't have looked at her that way if it weren't for the memory of that promise.

"I cannot be certain, but I believe when Ryuu bound your power as an infant, the divide that kept you from melding with Kazue, also kept her memories from you."

Suzume sighed heavily. She supposed that made sense. But it also meant, she might never be able to reach Kazue's memories. Maybe Souta was right, and she should just let the past stay in the past. The water of Kazue's soul was locked away, and Kaito had told her that he loved her for who she was, not because she had a piece of Kazue's soul within her. She had to trust him.

"Why don't you get some rest, and we'll continue your practice tomorrow," Souta said.

She wasn't going to get anywhere practicing in this headspace anyway. She headed for the exit of the training grounds, where Naoki had been on guard.

"I have a favor to ask," Naoki said.

He so rarely asked for anything, or said anything for that matter that she was immediately intrigued.

"What is it?" Suzume asked.

"Akira and Tsuki have asked for you to speak with them."

She recoiled at the statement. The last thing she wanted to do was to speak with them. As far as she cared, they could rot in a cell forever. They'd not only stolen from her, but betrayed her trust. She thought they were her friends, and once it was convenient, they had turned to Hisato. And now that they were at her mercy. Well, she had none left to give to them.

"I'd rather not." She strode through toward the courtyard, but Naoki didn't follow. There were yokai lingering around the courtyard, and after she had set the palace on fire and killed several yokai, she was afraid to go near them without a guard.

She turned back to Naoki. "Let's go," she gestured to the courtyard.

Naoki was unmovable as a mountain. "I think you should at least hear what they have to say."

He never pushed his own agenda upon her before. If she wanted, she could order him to obey, to never speak their names in her presence ever again. Tsuki and Akira were his children, but all this time they'd been together, he'd never really shown any interest in their well-being. Even when they'd betrayed her, he hadn't spoken out in their defense. Why now? She had to admit, seeing as Naoki was being uncharacteristically stubborn, she was curious.

She crossed her arms over her chest. "I'll listen to what they have to say, but I make no promises."

Naoki inclined his head to her, his expression still a blank mask.

The prison of the seaside palace was underground. The stairway led downward into a dark pit, the walls dripping with water from the ocean, and there was a strong scent of salt and fish. As of now, the only prisoners who were being held in these walls were Akira and Tsuki, and the water of Kazue's cell. Extra layers of protection had been placed around the water of Kazue's soul's cell. But as Suzume got closer, she felt the call. A deep yearning in her core, to be reunited, to be made whole once more. Flames flickered along her skin, as if the Kazue inside her was waking and stirring.

The water of Kazue's soul must have felt it as well, because as Suzume passed her cell, she came to the bars, watching Suzume with wide dark eyes, framed by long lashes.

She spoke not a word as Suzume passed, which made her all the more eerie. It wasn't certain if she were working for Hisato, or if she had been his prisoner. Suzume was glad she remained in that cell, because she wasn't ready to confront her, not yet. Suzume passed her cell by and went to the end of the hall where Akira and Tsuki were being kept. Akira had control of the body they shared, and was kneeling against the far wall on a dirty pile of straw. But despite their dreary surroundings, Akira still held her head like a queen.

"Thank you for coming," Akira said in greeting. She didn't bother to get up. Did she have no remorse at all for what she had done?

"Naoki says you have something to say. Well, do it quickly."

Akira did not even flinch. If anything, it only made her angrier.

"We wanted to explain why we did what we did."

This was it. Would it change anything, maybe not? But maybe it would ease some of the anger that continued to bubble inside her.

"The day of the hybrid attacked, we met the last piece of Kazue's soul."

Suzume's gaze flicked over to the cell which held the last piece of Kazue's soul. She was watching them, her expression impossible to read. Then she hadn't been mistaken, it was the water of Kazue's soul that had saved her that day on the beach.

"Why didn't you tell me back then, you knew we were looking for her?" Suzume asked Akira and Tsuki.

"That day, she infected us with something. A darkness that threatened to destroy us from the inside out. We had no choice."

"You did have a choice," Suzume's voice rose, the anger was boiling inside her. "We could have tried to find a cure together."

"Just how you're quick to rely on others?" Akira arched a brow.

It was like a slap to the face. Was their entire friendship a lie. Had they only helped her until she was no longer useful to them, until someone more powerful came along.

"Don't be cruel, Akira," Tsuki scolded, taking control of their body. He moved closer to the bars and grasped them, looking at Suzume with what was meant to be a sincere expression. "Suzume, believe me, I wanted to tell you, but Akira wouldn't let me."

She shook her head. They were both liars. "I don't care what your intentions were. You stole from me and didn't tell me the truth when it mattered most. Were you ever really my friends?"

Tsuki lowered his gaze. It was all the confirmation she needed. She turned to walk away, and Suzume passed by Kazue's cell. She lingered there for a moment.

"Do you have anything to say for yourself?"

The water of Kazue's soul canted her head to the side. "I only tried to get back what I thought was mine."

Suzume unconsciously reached for her staff on her back. "How can you say it's yours, this belonged to Kazue."

"But I am Kazue."

A creeping sensation was crawling over her skin. There was so much conviction in this woman's gaze it terrified her.

"Kazue died hundreds of years ago."

"Yes, on the mountain top where she split her soul apart to gain immortality. But one part of her soul was reborn in me. I am her reincarnation."

Suzume took a step back. That wasn't possible. Kazue had never really died, she couldn't be reborn. Souta's words came rushing back to her. She'd had her fire ability suppressed when she was young, but what if this woman had been born with the water of her soul within her, then the memories of her past life would have seeped into her soul, to where you couldn't tell where one part started and the other ended.

She didn't want to face her and instead turned and strode out of the dungeon. She didn't even turn to make sure Naoki was with her. She walked blindly. She had to get far away and now. If Kazue was reincarnated, what did that mean for her and Kaito? Would he choose to go back to the woman he had first loved?

Who was she to get between them?

"Whoa, where are you going in a hurry?"

Suzume glanced up to see Kaito, his hands on her shoulders. He couldn't know about Kazue; she would only lose him if he learned the truth. The idea of losing someone else she loved, she couldn't bear it.

"I was looking for you, actually." She forced a smile on her face.

"Oh were you," he cupped the back of her neck, and she tilted her head up to kiss him.

She wrapped her arms around his neck, pulling him closer. She couldn't keep him close enough. She was terrified if she let him go, she would never get him back again.

"Did you miss me, it's only been one afternoon?" he said against her lips.

"Let's go back to your room," she said, panting for breath.

He growled at the back of his throat. "What's gotten into you?"

She kissed him again, putting all her need and desperation into it. There were no more protests from Kaito as they hurried back to his room. And for a while, she got lost in the oblivion of his embrace.

When they were finished, Kaito's eyes slid closed, and she studied his sleep face, tracing his jawline with her finger. Kazue might have his past, but she had his present, and she wouldn't give that up without a fight.

At some point, she dozed off, because the next thing she knew she was waking in a tangle of sheets, she reached for Kaito but found only a warm spot where he had been. She sat up, clutching a blanket to cover her naked body. Kaito was up and getting dressed.

"Are you going somewhere?" she asked.

Kaito turned as if he hadn't realized she was there. "Duty calls. A few of my emissaries have returned from their missions, and I need to hear their reports."

"That sounds boring, why don't you spend all day in bed with me?" Suzume said in her most seductive tone she could manage. The thought of him leaving her filled her with fear. She wanted to keep him close, by any means necessary.

"Oh?" He quirked a brow and sauntered over to her. He strad-dled her over the sheets. "That does sound much better."

Suzume wrapped her arms around him, pulling him close as he kissed her.

Someone knocked on the door, and Kaito sighed.

"Ignore them," she whispered against him.

He sat back. "I can't, believe me, I want to very much. But this is important."

He was leaving her. Panic tightened her throat. She'd never clung to anyone before, but right now, she was feeling very vulnerable. Letting him in it had cracked her open and exposed her soft interior. "What is so important that it can't wait?" She didn't mean to, but her tone rose.

The knock persisted.

"I'll be there in a minute," he snapped at the door and then frowned at her. "I thought you understood, I'm the ruler of Akatsuki, I have responsibilities."

"Then, I'll come with you." She grabbed onto his hand.

Kaito pulled away gently. "You know that's not a good idea, it would only be a distraction to the council." He kissed her fore-head once more. "Wait for me, eat breakfast, you'll need your energy for later."

He strode to the door without another word. Suzume stared at it for several long minutes. Never in her life had she begged someone. What was he doing to her? Did she have no shame? Without meaning to, she'd let Kaito worm his way inside her heart. Her feelings for him had blinded her, it was making her weak and desperate. And though she swore she would never become her, she realized she was becoming her mother.

NINETEEN

There was nowhere Ryuu could call home. Rin and Hikaru, who had raised him, had done their best to make him feel welcome and loved. But from a young age, he had been restless and eager to see the wider world. Along his travels, he thought uniting the humans of Akatsuki under his rule would fill the emptiness inside him. But after decades of rulership, unchanged and unaging while those around him grew old and then died, the emptiness only grew. He gave up his position of emperor and retired to the White Palace, where for a time he had been happy, but that soon lost its glimmer. As a half-yokai, he aged much slower, and there was no escaping death for mortals.

He'd left the temple, wandered the countryside, assuming new names and faces until curiosity brought him back to the White Palace, this time, he did not reveal his true identity. And instead lived under an assumed name, and for once, he was happy. And so for centuries, disappearing for decades when he became restless. No matter how far he roamed, he always came back here, this was his home. He knew it like an extension of himself because, in a way, it was a part of him. When a kami dwelled in a temple, their spiritual energy became entwined with their shrine. For Ryuu, it was much the same. And when he entered the temple grounds, the air felt charged. There was an uneasiness that had seeped into the very soul of these sacred grounds, and it flowed back to him on his return.

Priests sweeping the steps greeted him with a smile. Nothing had physically changed, but the deeper into the shrine grounds he went, the more the uneasy feeling choked his throat. He'd only intended to make a quick stop, gather his things from his quarters before heading to the White Palace, but something told him he should speak with the head priest first.

The current head priest, Nariuji's quarters were at the heart of the temple. Ryuu rapped on the door with his knuckles. The unsettled feeling was worse here. As if the concerns of the head priest were polluting the entire temple. Things must be serious if even Nariuji was rattled. He was typically a very serene individual.

"Come in," came a rasping voice.

Ryuu slid open the door. The head priest sat behind his desk and twirled the end of his long white beard. His bushy brows were furrowed as he studied the letter on the table in front of him. Ryuu recognized the seal at the bottom, it was from the minister of religion. One of the highest-ranking officials and advisor to the emperor.

"Am I interrupting?" Ryuu asked.

The old man's eyes snapped up toward him, and a smile broke out across his face. "Ryuu, I thought we had seen the last of you when you left months ago."

He gestured for Ryuu to take a seat across from him, and Ryuu settled himself onto the cushion opposite from the elderly head priest. Few could sense his true nature, and to most, Ryuu kept that side of himself hidden. But Ryuu still remembered the wiry young man who'd first come to the temple from his fishing village. Straight away, he'd seen through Ryuu's disguise and kept it a secret from the others without Ryuu needing to make threats. The decades passed to fast; in the blink of an eye, humans aged and died. Just thinking of it filled him with wistful regrets. He should have stayed around longer, gotten to know Nariuji better.

"I won't be back long, I'm afraid," Ryuu said.

There was a knock at the door.

"That'll be my tea, will you share a cup with me?" Nariuji asked.

Ryuu nodded.

"Come," Nariuji said to the acolyte outside.

They entered with a pot and two cups. Word spread fast in the temple, and it had likely already leaked outside the palace. His absence would not have gone unnoticed by the emperor. It would not surprise him if he were summoned to the White Palace soon.

The acolyte set the tea kettle and the two glasses down and then lifted the pot to pour for them both, but Ryuu dismissed them with a wave. He set the pot back down, before bowing and exiting the room. Ryuu filled the glasses for him, and the head priest, and the fragment aroma of herbal tea filled the room. Nariuji took his glass and inhaled the steam.

"I should be the one serving you, not the other way around," Nariuji remarked before taking a sip.

"Nonsense, you are head priest here," Ryuu replied, he held onto his glass but didn't drink. His attention was on the acolyte that continued to linger just outside the door. He would need to be careful with his words.

The head priest set down his glass with a gentle thud, his expression was grave. "Since you're back, I assume there is something you are seeking."

"Is it so hard to believe, I would merely wish to visit with an old friend?" Ryuu asked.

The head priest gave him a wry smile. "I'm too old to fall for your flattery. You disappeared without a word around the same time as princess Suzume, and with the emperor's... condition getting worse, you'd have me believe you come just for a friendly visit?" He tsked.

"You've caught me," Ryuu twisted his cup in his hands to kill time. "The emperor is unwell then?" Ryuu said carefully. Though he had nothing to fear from the emperor, he didn't want treason accusations to impede his search for the missing soul piece.

The head priest sighed heavily. "I thought you'd left to escape the uproar at the palace. The empress has been sent away, along with the crown prince and younger princes."

Ryuu's eyes widened. The emperor had never been an impulsive man, and everything he did was done with strategy and purpose. The empress' family was one of the most powerful clans, sending her and her sons away was as good as declaring them illegitimate. The empress' family would be out for blood. What was he thinking?

"Why was she sent away?" Ryuu asked.

"Officially, for her health. The court physician thought she needed rest. The crown prince joined her and his younger brothers, to assure she was getting everything she needed. She and the princes are staying at a mountain shrine in the north." The head priest looked at Ryuu, saying more with his gaze than words could.

"And unofficially?" Ryuu prompted.

"The empress expressed concerns about the emperor's war against the yokai. There are those at court that see this war as insanity. They think he is chasing his own delusions."

For the common courtier, the yokai were nothing but fairy tales, and to declare war on them, the emperor must have seemed like madness. The emperor knew as much and had been trying to keep the efforts private. It seemed the secret was out. Even if it was and the empress, or her family opposed, the emperor was not so afraid of distension to banish the empress over. There was more to it that Nariuji wasn't saying or potentially couldn't say. He must know that they were being listened to. This feeling of dread that was soaked into the temple, must have been coming from the head priest whose prayers and leadership guided the temple.

"I feel a visit to the emperor is overdue. He must be grieved to be without his beloved wife," Ryuu said.

"He is not often alone, Consort Izume has returned to the main palace. And rumor has it she is staying in the empress' old quarters."

And there it was, just as he feared, Izume had sunk her claws into the emperor and ousted the empress just as she had always wished. Once more, he regretted not seeing her ambitions sooner.

"It is fortunate he's not alone then." Ryuu pulled a piece of paper off the head priest's desk and wrote a quick note: the energy at the temple is there anything else I should know? Have you encountered an exceptionally powerful priest or priestess?

He slid it across to the head priest who glanced it over.

"That he is. I hope you will stay awhile now that you're here. The temple is not the same without you," Nariuji said as she scribbled a reply.

He slid it back across the table, and it read: No one has come to the white palace, but priests are going missing. I do not know where to, anyone I send to investigate never comes back. Tread carefully, the emperor is not himself.

"I will be here a while, I think," Ryuu said as he brought the note to the nearby brazier and lit it on fire.

Nariuji watched him with a sad gaze. How many priests had gone missing, he wondered, and where? The more he tugged at the thread, the more it unraveled a deeper mystery. Ryuu made his goodbyes and then headed for his room. After washing and changing into court attire, he would need to request to see the emperor. His strange behavior was a concern.

A royal messenger was awaiting him outside his chamber. It seemed the emperor had beat him to the invitation.

The messenger bowed to him. "The emperor has requested your company at dinner," said the messenger.

"Tell him I gladly accept," Ryuu said.

The messenger nodded and hurried away. Had the emperor set spies in the white temple to wait for his return? He might very well be walking straight into a trap. The neko was waiting for him in his room. When he had left the hidden shrine, he had summoned him through their bond, and it was a good thing too, there was work to be done.

The neko stuck a claw in his cat ear and dug at earwax. "I hope you're not planning on staying here long. The energy here is making my skin crawl."

Even the neko could sense it. The situation was more serious than he'd originally thought.

"Then you'll be glad to know I have a mission for you. Priests are going missing, I want you to find out where they're going."

"Delightful, more priests." With a snap of his fingers, he took on the form of a cat. "Open the door, would you?" the neko meowed.

Ryuu slid the door open, and the neko sauntered out. With that taken care of, he could prepare for dinner. Ryuu washed and donned his court silks and headed out to the White Palace.

When he arrived at the gates of the palace, he noted the guard had been doubled. Inside the walls of the palace was no better. Winter was always a subdued time at the White Palace, many ministers and government officials retired to their homes for the cold months. But even for winter, the palace was empty. The courtiers he passed seemed on edge, glancing over their shoulder as if waiting for a dagger to strike them in the back.

When he reached the emperor's quarters, a servant announced him before opening the double doors and showing him inside. The emperor was already seated and wore his less formal haori and hakama. If Ryuu didn't know better, he might almost believe that this was a meal to be shared between equals. But though the emperor heeded his advice when he gave it, he, like many of his successors, were wary of him. When the crown prince became emperor, they learned the family's secret. The first emperor had been a half yokai and yet still lived. As a rule, Ryuu did not meddle in politics, and left the emperors to rule on their own. But no matter how he distanced himself, there was always an undercurrent of unease between him and those that sat on the throne.

"Our Ryuu, you've returned at last." The emperor stood to greet him, throwing out his arms to embrace him.

He could not think of a time the emperor had ever greeted him so warmly. But not wanting to give offense, he accepted the warm gesture, with a measure of wariness. He'd left Tetsuyama back at the temple, no one, even a former emperor, could wear a blade in the presence of the emperor. Now he was second-guessing his decision to do so.

"I am sorry for returning so late, my emperor," Ryuu said, bowing low.

The emperor waved away his apologies. "We are old friends, are we not? There's no need for such formalities."

Given everything that the head priest had said, he thought the emperor would be suspicious of him, or at the least less in control of his sanity. But the emperor seemed unchanged from when he'd last seen him.

The emperor gestured for Ryuu to sit at one end of the table as he took his place on the other end. Servants entered with steaming plates of baked fish, fragrant soups, and pickled vegetables. Three bowls of rice were set out along with accompanying chopsticks.

"Are we expecting a third?" Ryuu asked.

The emperor glanced at the empty seat, and a smile spread his face. "Yes we are, she should be here any minute."

He wouldn't.

"Empress Consort Izume has arrived," bellowed the servant.

"There she is now." The emperor stood as the doors were flung open.

Ryuu schooled his face, not willing to give anything away, despite the rumors he had not expected the emperor to flaunt his consort this way. Did he know they had been lovers once? Izume entered dripping in layers of silk, her ebony hair pulled back with a jade comb, carved into the shape of sakura blossoms. There was an ethereal smile on her lips that brought him back to the days when she'd been a girl living at her father's manor outside the scheming and politics of the White Palace, back when he had fallen in love with her.

But it wasn't directed at him, her dark eyes skimmed right past him and came to rest instead on the emperor. The way her eyes lit up, it was as if he were the only man in the room. The emperor rose up to greet her, and took her hand to lead her to the place just beside him.

Now he knew why she was here. Izume had done this, to remind him that she had moved on. That she had chosen the emperor. It stung, she'd hurt him so many times, and he thought he would learn better, yet he never did.

"Ryuu isn't empress consort Izume, a vision?" the emperor asked.

She smirked at him, one painted brow arched. That smile which had once driven him mad, now just twisted like a knife in his gut. Knowing her, she was already aware of what he was after, and had orchestrated this dinner to taunt him.

"She is radiant, as always." He bowed to her.

The emperor and Izume took their seats.

"Izume has done great things for the kingdom, she found a priestess of immense power. We are close to destroying the yokai, tomorrow I will show you our army she helped us create."

That powerful priestess could only be the missing soul piece. And these soldiers, was the emperor using hybrids to fight the yokai? Why tell him that, Izume wasn't this careless.

"I would very much like to meet this priestess," Ryuu said, doing his best to avoid looking at Izume.

"That won't be possible, I'm afraid. She has never been seen by a man. She was raised in a remote temple, and both her body and soul are pure. We cannot risk a man's lude gaze falling upon her and risking her purity." She laughed.

"I see." Was that how she had kept the emperor away from her? At least one thing was confirmed, the last piece of Kazue's soul was here. And no matter what, he would find her. Izume could play her games, but he was a master at this, and he never lost.

TWENTY

The meetings seemed to drag on for an eternity. As Kaito's emissary droned on about the details of the alliance he had made, his mind drifted to the woman in the cells below the palace. The promise he made to Kazue had been buried in the farthest reaches of his mind. When he first met Kazue, he was certain she was his destiny. But the reality of a love between a yokai and a human was it must come to an end. He had sworn to her that when the time came that they must part, he would find her again, in the next life. There was no next life for Kazue, and even if there were, he had Suzume, he wouldn't turn on her for a painful memory.

"My Dragon?" said the emissary.

Kaito blinked at the council members who surrounded him, he hadn't the slightest idea what they'd been saying.

"Very good," Shin coughed into his hand.

"Yes, that all sounds good," Kaito said with an authoritative tone.

The emissary bowed his head. "I am glad you are pleased with my work, My dragon…"

The emissary continued with his prattling. He'd forgotten just how tedious these sorts of proceedings were. It would have been much better to stay in bed with Suzume all day. That was right, this woman, the water of Kazue's soul, who was she but another powerful priestess. She was no different than Hikaru and Souta. She might remember the promise Kazue, and he had made, but that didn't matter. What was past was past.

When the emissary finished his long ramblings, and other matters were dealt with, Kaito rose, at last, eager to be free and return to Suzume.

"There is the matter of the captured priestess," said one of the councilors.

"What about her?" Kaito snapped.

"We must decide what will be done with her," said a councilor.

"We cannot allow another dangerous priestess to live in the seaside palace," said the oni councilor.

Their prejudices were a problem. If they harbored this much hate for the water of Kazue's soul, it might continue to spill over onto Suzume.

"As of now, we are not certain where her allegiances lie, she could very well be an ally in our fight against Hisato."

"I don't like it. The one untamed priestess nearly burned the palace to the ground," groused the Oni as he brought a fist down on the table.

Kaito stood. "You remember who you are speaking of, she is my future empress."

The oni glared at him but said no more. Though he wasn't sure he could trust the water of Kazue's soul. He also couldn't avoid her forever, running from the memories she brought back to the forefront. He would need to speak with her and decide for himself if she were friend or enemy.

"I will speak with this priestess and decide her punishment, which will be announced at our next council meeting," Kaito announced.

There was grumbling among the councilors but no real protests. It was good enough for now. With that, the council meeting was finished and Shin followed Kaito out.

"The oni is becoming a problem, we should watch out for him," Shin remarked.

"He is, be sure to keep an eye on him, won't you?" Kaito asked him.

Shin nodded his head in understanding.

"Will you go and speak with the prisoner?"

Thinking about it made his heart race. It wouldn't hurt to go in, just for a few minutes. Would it?

"I think I must. They were right, we cannot leave her locked up forever."

Shin quirked a brow at him. He knew him too well. But speaking to this woman, it wasn't as if he were betraying Suzume. It meant nothing.

Together they went to the stairway that led into the cells. A pair of guards were waiting at the entrance. Kaito nodded at both of them before he and Shin descended into the depths. The closer he got, the feel of Kazue's energy got stronger. He hadn't noticed it in the chaos of the battlefield, but unlike the other soul fragments, the water of Kazue's soul had a distinct feeling of Kazue. It was almost as if she had been reborn.

A barrier encased her cell, and she squatted at the back of it. They'd put her in shackles that suppressed her spiritual power. After seeing what she could do on the battlefield they weren't willing to take any risks. On the battlefield, she'd looked powerful and fierce, but now she looked small, shrunk, and so very young. She was perhaps a year or two younger than Suzume. In her stained clothes and her ebony hair falling in her face, he could see nothing about her that resembled the Kazue he had known. Even in tatters, Kazue had always held her head high.

As he approached her cell, her head perked up, there was a smudge of dirt on her cheek, and yet she was smiling. It was a bright and innocent smile as she stood up and approached the barrier, but the shackles held her back. "I was hoping you'd come."

Kaito crossed his arms over his chest. He must remember this wasn't Kazue, but a potential trap set by Hisato. "I came to ask you some questions."

"I'll answer anything you want!"

Her enthusiasm was seemingly genuine, but how could she be so eager locked in a cell and covered in dirt.

"Don't be mistaken, this doesn't mean I trust you," Kaito warned. It felt pertinent to make that much clear.

Her face fell, and her pouting expression was an echo of Kazue's. She always made that face when he would leave her. Back then, their time together had never felt like enough, duty was always calling him away. And no matter how long they spent together, it was never enough. As time went on, he started pouring more and more time into her, abandoning his duties to others. Standing back and looking at it now, perhaps she had been manipulating him the entire time, wrapping him around her finger until he could see nothing but her. Had Hisato coached this imposter trying to do the same? Filled her head with memories of a past that didn't belong to her? Well, he wouldn't fall for her lies again.

"Are you working for Hisato?" Kaito asked straight out, there was no point in beating around the bush.

"Yes, Hisato is the one who found me at the shrine where I was raised." She shifted from foot to foot, and her shackles clanked together.

She hadn't even attempted to deny it. Was she a simple fool, or was this some more subtle form of deception?

"I'm surprised by your honesty, and I suppose he was the one who ordered you to steal the staff and attack Suzume?" he asked.

She frowned. "She's an impostor who stole my staff and bewitched you. I had to stop her before she hurt you." She reached for him, but her shackles wouldn't allow her to get far.

"Is that what he told you?" he scoffed.

She canted her head to the side and fluttered her long lashes. "Everything I did was to fulfill our promise. It was one of my first memories, every night you were in my dreams. You flew to me as a dragon while I waited in the field of spider lilies..."

Her words evoked vivid memories. Kaito and Kazue lying together in a field of red spider lilies. The touch of her hair as she laid her head upon his chest. He shook himself. It was a trick, it had to be.

"You lie, you couldn't remember that."

She recoiled as if she had been struck. "I can see why you wouldn't trust me. I know what I did in my last life, how I trapped you. I wanted to leave that shrine, to find you and free you, but the head priestess, she kept me trapped, she wouldn't let me leave."

"Is that what Hisato taught you to say. Kazue made a fool of me, but you are nothing but a pale reflection of her."

She fell to her knees in a deep bow, and there were tears gathering on her lashes. "I know what I did in my past life can never be forgiven, but I hope you can find it in your heart to forgive me for what I did."

He stared down at her. And as much as he wanted to punish her in place of Kazue, who had betrayed him and for siding with Hisato, looking at her frail figure cowering before him, he could only feel pity for her.

"You sided with a dangerous entity, mere words won't be enough to convince me I can trust you," he replied.

"I was blinded by my desire to reunite with you. I can see that, the things he made me do..." Her voice cracked. "I'm not proud of it. But tell me what I can do to prove myself to you, and I will do it."

Either she was sincere, or she was a skilled manipulator to make his conviction waiver this way.

"Do you really think I am going to believe your lies?"

She stood up again. "But you have to believe me, I know what Hisato's plotting. He's been building a hybrid army."

"I know that much already, you'll have to do better than that."

She shook her head. "He's preparing an attack, he sent me to distract you. He has a force at a temple northeast of here gathering for an attack, if you can get to them first it will thwart his plans."

He narrowed his eyes as he studied her. It was possible this was all Hisato's plan, give him false information to lure him into a trap. But the thought of the strange incidents around the region, the way Hisato had been too quiet. He couldn't dismiss her words entirely.

"We shall see how much truth there is to your words."

He strode out before he did something else reckless. When he got to the top of the steps, Shin was waiting for him.

"What did you decide?" he asked.

"There's something I need to investigate. If I'm not back by nightfall, I want you to send our entire force to the northeast."

Shin nodded.

Before he could second guess the decision, Kaito transformed into a dragon and took to the sky. He flew in the direction that the water of Kazue's soul had indicated. Endless forest and the occasional fishing village were all he spotted for miles. He kept his senses spread out, prepared for an attack at any moment. After a few hours of flying, he sensed it, a variable hornets' nest of hybrids all gathered in one place.

The closer he got, the stronger the sensation became. Low

hanging clouds shielded the ground from view, but he could feel them, a slimy sensation that crawled over his skin.

Kaito dipped below the horizon, and there they were, just as the water of Kazue's soul had said. An army of hybrids. They were milling around like mindless animals. As far as he could tell, Hisato wasn't among them. They were like livestock in a pen, waiting to be unleashed. With the right force, they could sweep through them like a blade cutting silk.

There must be some trick, a trap hidden among this seeming force. He spent hours scanning the area looking for hidden power among them, some sign of a deeper strategy. But as far as he could tell, it was nothing. Kaito returned to the seaside palace, and reported to Shin and the others.

The councilors were understandably wary, but it was easy enough to convince them to bring a force large enough to handle the hybrids. They arrived where the hybrids were gathered and surrounded them. A barrier kept them penned in, but it was easily broken through.

The hybrids had not a chance, and they swept through Hisato's force, leaving nothing behind but a bloody battlefield. Kazue hadn't lied; she had, in fact, saved them from an attack from Hisato. Had this force caught them unawares, the casualty count would have been much higher. He had wanted to doubt her, but now he had to believe she was on their side.

Twenty-One

Rin, Hikaru, and the tengu prince arrived at the tengu mountain just as dusk was falling. This time as she approached, it was by air. He held both her and Hikaru close to him as they flew. His stamina was impressive, considering he'd been frozen solid in ice for centuries. From this vantage point, she could see the sprawling compound and the hundreds of tengu who lived within its walls. Once the alliance was confirmed, all of these soldiers would join The Dragon's forces, none of the others would dare to stand against him. It would mean a new era of peace, one where Hikaru and her wouldn't need to continue looking over their shoulders at every turn.

"It is good to be back at my old roost," said the tengu prince raising his voice to be heard over the rush of wind around them.

Tengu guards rose to the sky as they approached.

"It looks like they know we're coming," Rin shouted back.

The tengu approached in formation, weapons drawn.

"Oy, it's me! I've come home at last," the tengu prince shouted to the guards.

They surrounded them in masked faces, their black wings beat, creating a breeze that blew Rin's hair around her face and made it difficult to see.

The leader of the guards removed his mask, revealing himself to be Mori. "Brother, are my eyes deceiving me?"

"It's really me. Sorry, it took me so long to return."

The smile on Mori's face was as bright as the sun. "Come, let's go home."

He dove down for the ground.

"Hold on tight," the tengu prince told them, before following his brother down in a similar dive.

Rin clung to his side as the ground came closer and closer. Inches before they collided with the ground, the tengu prince pulled up, and they landed safely. As soon as they were on the ground, the tengu swarmed around the young prince, with Mori at the center. The two brothers embraced, and Rin thought she might have seen tears in the eyes of the elder tengu brother.

Hikaru put his arm around her shoulders, it was a touching scene. And she felt fortunate to be able to reunite the family.

Mori and the tengu prince broke apart, and he turned to Rin. "Thank you for bringing my brother back when no one else could."

Rin bowed her head, accepting his praise.

"Please, you must be exhausted from your flight, you have the tengu hospitality. Please rest and recover."

A couple of tengu stepped up to lead Rin and Hikaru to their room. It was twice the size of the room they'd been given on their first visit. And waiting for them were two steaming tubs of water where they could wash and take away the chill, that still lingered in her skin after facing the yuki onna. After sitting in the bathtub until the water ran cold, she dressed in a fine silk kimono, also provided by the tengu, and ate a sumptuous meal.

With her belly full to bursting, Rin rested her head on Hikaru's shoulder and let go of a contented sigh.

"Happy?" he asked as he stroked the hair from her face.

"I could get used to such a luxurious life," she said with another wistful sigh.

"Should we continue on as diplomats instead of returning to the shrine?" Hikaru teased.

She shook her head. "No, I've had my fill of politics. Once The Dragon's kingdom is restored, and Hisato defeated, I will be much happier living out the rest of our lives at the shrine."

Hikaru leaned down and planted a kiss on her lips.

"I feel the same."

They slept on a soft goose down futon, warm and contended. In the morning, they were served another meal, which she ate with gusto. Around midday, Mori came to escort them to their meeting with the Tengu Elder.

Rin's stomach was tied in knots. It was finally happening, she was going to gain the alliance of the tengu. The Tengu Elder lived in the innermost ring of the tengu compound, where only he and his immediate family dwelled. There were fewer tengu here, and they wore solemn expressions as Rin and Hikaru were brought to the audience hall.

The Tengu Elder was a wizened old yokai, one of the oldest she had ever met. His long white beard coiled on the tatami in front of him, and thick white brows framed his sharp black eyes over his large crooked nose. His black wings were folded behind him, but she imagined the wingspan when unfurled would be impressive. On each side, he was flanked by his seven sons, Mori and the youngest prince on his left and right.

"Rin and Hikaru, we thank you for returning our son to us," said the Tengu Elder in a booming voice.

Rin and Hikaru both bowed low. "It was the least we could do for one of The Dragon's oldest friends."

"Yes, Mori has told us of your desire to reform our alliances," the Tengu Elder leaned forward, his shrewd gaze fixed on Rin.

She wanted to squirm beneath his scrutiny, but resisted the impulse.

"It is our hope that we can resume our alliance of the past. The Dragon has returned and is gaining power, but the kingdom remains divided. With our combined strength, we could bring peace to Akatsuki."

"We tengu are proud, and we do not ask for favors lightly. Though I did not request that you rescue my son, a favor must be repaid. I will consider your request, for now, you are welcome to remain as honored guests of the tengu," the Elder declared with a tone of finality.

It had been perhaps a bit naïve to hope that these discussions would be resolved in one afternoon. But she wasn't ready to give up, not yet. They left the audience hall, and outside, a storm had come upon the palace suddenly. The sky was a cloud of white.

A shiver ran down her spine, she would be happy once they were back inside. As accommodating as the tengu had been, she could not see herself staying for long on this frigid mountain top. When they passed through the gates of the inner ring, to the second ring of the palace, she noticed tengu rushing about shouting to one another as a few took to the sky.

"What's going on?" Rin asked a passing tengu.

"The yuki onna, they've come for revenge, they're outside the gates right now," the tengu said before flying off into the sky.

Rin and Hikaru exchanged a look before bolting across the yard and to the outermost ring of the tengu palace. There was a ladder that led onto a rampart which overlooked the pass that led upward to the tengu compound.

A blizzard had obscured everything from view, and she had to squint into the gloom to see clearly. But there between the flurries of snowflakes, an army of figures were approaching. The yuki onna were on their way.

"We have to do something," Rin said to Hikaru.

He shook his head, "There're too many. We'll be frozen if we even try."

Hikaru was right, they were outnumbered, and she was just one Kitsune. But if they called on Kaito for help, then perhaps the combined force would be enough to save the tengu. They retreated from the wall and went back to the inner ring of the palace. She found Mori rushing out, a pair of guards following close on his heels.

"Mori!" She flagged him down.

He said a parting word to the tengu who took off into the air, before he strode over to them.

"Rin, my dear, I would be more at ease if you were indoors and out of danger."

"We want to help, I can send a message to The Dragon, to bring reinforcements."

Mori shook his head. "I appreciate all the help you've given us, but we cannot spare a man for the job. Don't worry, we'll chase them away in no time."

He strode away before she could argue. Maybe Mori was right, the tengu were legendary fighters. They could withstand this attack, couldn't they? The cold was getting worse, and she shivered. She really should head inside, but she knew she would only pace and wonder what was happening outside if she did.

"Let's go back to the wall and wait," Hikaru suggested.

She grabbed his hand and squeezed, at times it felt like he could read her mind. They headed back through the yard as groups of tengu took to the sky and flew into the storm to fight the yuki onna. She didn't have to worry; the tengu could handle this, they would get the alliance, and then they would return home.

As they stood on ramparts, Rin could see nothing much beyond the reach of her hand. They waited, minutes seemed to drag on into hours. The shouts of the tengu were dulled by the roar of the storm. Hikaru shivered in his coat, and they huddled for warmth. If this went on much longer, they would have to retreat indoors.

"It's been hours, and there's still nothing," she remarked.

Neither of them said what they were thinking. But the possibility of failure loomed large over them both.

"Help, is anyone there?" A cry came out from within the storm. The sound had almost been swallowed up by the storm itself.

Rin created a ball of fox fire and lifted it up into the air to guide the tengu back.

"We're here!" Rin shouted.

The beat of wings drew closer, until at last, the shape of a few dozen drew closer. Mori led them to the ramparts, carrying a man covered in frozen blood. The tengu landed, their wings were strung with icicles and their beards and hair covered in frost.

The guards on the ramparts rushed over to help carry away the wounded.

"Get them warm," Mori ordered the guards. He looked exhausted, as if he had been gone for days instead of just a few hours.

"What happened, did you see anything?" Rin asked him

"There's too many, there are more than I've ever seen before. They've created a wall of storm, it's near impossible to get through. We couldn't get close enough to attack." He ran a hand over his face. "We lost so many. We can't defeat them as things are."

A stone sunk in her stomach. "Should we evacuate the others?" she asked.

Mori shook his head. "They cannot breach our defenses. We're trapped inside."

"If you could get through their storm and get a message to Kaito, I know he would come to our aid."

"You're right, that might be our last chance…"

"But?" Rin asked.

"There's only one person who can fly fast enough to get past this storm, and that's my youngest brother."

He'd only recently returned, the Elder wouldn't let him go easily. "It's either he goes and relays the message, or we all die here, your father has to see reason," Rin said.

"You don't know my father."

They hurried to the main hall where the Elder had the young tengu prince sitting beside him. It seemed since he returned, he had not let him out of his sight.

Mori bowed before his father and Rin, and Hikaru followed suit.

"Elder, the yuki onna have us under siege, we must reach out to our allies for aid."

The Elder nodded. "I feared this would be the cost of having my son returned." He rested a hand on the young prince's knee. "You have my authority to send our fastest flier with the message."

The young prince stood. "None can fly faster than me, Elder, I will deliver the message."

The Elder gave him a stern look. "You will do no such thing. You are still weak, you cannot leave."

"Elder, my brother speaks the truth. The storm is too fierce; only he can possibly breakthrough."

"No." The Elder's voice shook the room with his fury. "I will not let him go. You must choose another, any but my boy."

"You will condemn us all to die if you do this," Rin said, alliance be damned, she wouldn't die here for one old man's foolishness.

"Rin," Mori said in a warning tone.

The Elder narrowed his eyes at her. "You forget your place, Kitsune."

"I risked my life to save your son, and if you had any honor, you would at least allow him the choice to decide if he will risk his life to protect his people."

The Tengu Elder looked at her for a very long moment, all the while, her stomach felt as if she had swallowed a live snake. It was a risk, and the Elder might very well toss her out into the storm to fend for herself against the yuki onna.

Then he turned to his son. "Is this really what you want to do?" His tone was softer than before, not a stubborn leader but a father who had just been reunited with his son.

"I must go," he said as he rested a hand on his father's shoulder. Before standing to address all those who'd gathered in the audience hall. "I will bring The Dragon back, and together we will defeat the yuki onna."

The tengu in the hall cheered as he marched out into the storm.

Rin, Hikaru, and Mori followed him. Before he took flight, he turned to his brother, and they embraced for a moment.

"Fly safe," said Mori as he took a step back.

The wind had picked up in intensity, and it ruffled the prince's feathers as he extended them outward. Hikaru grasped her hand as he gave them both a smile before launching into the air. In a few moments, his figure was swallowed up by the white storm. And with him went all her hope. She just prayed he'd get there safely and bring The Dragon back before it was too late.

Twenty-Two

Their cell was closing in on Akira. After centuries trapped in the shrine, guarding the staff, she thought she would be accustomed to enclosed spaces. But she'd grown used to the freedom Suzume had given them. When she had refused their apology, she condemned them to a place without a sunrise or sunset, just endless darkness, and the constant drip of seawater for all eternity.

"This is because we didn't tell Suzume in the first place, we deserve this," Tsuki said.

"If you would defend her after she's discarded us, you are a fool. She never really cared about us, that is why she threw us away so easily," Akira said.

Tsuki did not reply; what could he say? Looking back and regrets of paths not taken were pointless. If they couldn't rely on Suzume, then they could only count on themselves.

Footsteps approached from the stairs. Kazue, who was in the cell adjacent to them, did not even stir. Akira would not lower herself to appear curious. But she couldn't help but wonder who it was. Had Suzume changed her mind and come for them after all?

Kaito stepped out of the shadows of the stairway and approached Kazue's cell.

"He's back?" Tsuki remarked.

A few days prior, The Dragon and Kazue had a long conversation, and he had left looking more than a little rattled. But he had come back, had he fallen for Kazue's charms? It wouldn't surprise her; The Dragon had always seemed like the sentimental type to her.

Kazue approached the cell door and smiled as Kaito waved a clawed hand, and the barrier around her cell faded away. He wasn't letting her go, was he?

Akira stood and moved closer to the bars of her prison, so she could get a better view. Kaito removed a key from his sleeve and unlocked Kazue's cell. Before approaching her cautiously to take the manacles off.

"Your information was good, but that doesn't mean I trust you yet," he said.

She nodded her head eagerly, with all the innocence of a child. She hated to admit it, but Kazue was clever to play him this way. Like a fool, he was falling for her lies. She had no doubt whatever camp he had cleared, had been left there just to earn his trust.

"We should warn him," Tsuki said.

"And what good will it do us? The dissonance remains, if we speak out against her, she will destroy us."

She couldn't help but wonder what would be worse, wasting away in this cell for eternity or letting the oblivion of becoming something new, transformed by Kazue's spell.

It sent a chill down her spine. After seeing what she was capable of, the cold detachment of her actions, she pitied The Dragon more than anything. The pair of them left, and Akira and Tsuki were once more left alone in the dark with just one another for company.

Some time must have passed, it was hard to tell just how long had passed. But footsteps approached again. She didn't pretend indifference this time and instead waited at her bars for their visitor.

Kazue smiled at her, that twisted, deranged smile that made the hairs on the back of her neck stand on end.

"Aren't the two of you a pitiful sight," Kazue said as she strolled over to them.

"Did you come to crow over your triumph?" Akira replied, stepping back from the cell walls. Was she going to punish them for failing to capture Suzume for her? Was this the end at last.

"We could try and fight," Tsuki said.

She appreciated his naive optimism, but there was no more hope for them; they'd gambled and lost it all.

"I won't kill you, not if you're still willing to work for me."

A chill ran down her spine. A part of her had hoped being locked away, they would be safe from her.

"Would you rather stay in this cell?" Kazue canted her head to the side as she examined them.

"What could we possibly do for you locked in this cell?" Akira gestured around them.

"Getting you out is easy enough, I've won Kaito's trust now."

"Enough games. I won't hear anything you have to say unless you're willing to remove the dissonance you placed inside us."

"Akira. You cannot be thinking of trusting her, can you?"

"No, Akira is not so naive as to trust. But you both must see that you have only one choice."

"Maybe we'll choose to stay locked in this cell, what is it you want us to do?"

She could feel Tsuki's disapproval through their bond. But she ignored him.

"I need you to help me lure Suzume away from the palace. If you do that, not only will I free you of the dissonance, but I will separate you from one another."

"Big promises," Tsuki said aloud.

It was, and Akira's heart raced just to think of it. After so long trapped together, to think freedom might be this close. But she had been fooled before.

"How do we know you are strong enough when the others weren't?"

"You've seen what I am capable of, you know I am not like the others. So, do we have a deal?"

"I don't like it," Tsuki said.

"It doesn't matter what you think, it's either this or we remain trapped together forever, would you want that more."

There was a long silence, he was thinking and trying to keep his thoughts guarded from her.

"I can't say no, can I?"

To Kazue, Akira said, "We have a deal."

SUZUME RAN HER SHAKING HANDS OVER THE SAKURA BLOSSOM PATTERN of her kimono. It felt like a lifetime ago since she'd worn silk this fine. She sighed and adjusted the jade pin in her hair. Kaito had insisted she wear it tonight, another request she couldn't refuse. She used to love wearing pretty hairpins, and combs. She turned her head this way and that, it had been a lifetime, it seemed since she'd looked at herself in the mirror, the woman who stared back at her was a stranger. Shoulder length hair, tanned skin, and muscle definition in her shoulders and arms. She wasn't the delicate palace flower anymore. And she didn't want to be her, either.

The girl who would have been delighted by the expense of the dyed fabric, and the intricate details felt like a stranger to her. The obi and the constricting layers of fabric would only get in the way if she had to fight. And considering she was attending a celebration with the yokai, it might come down to a fight tonight. Why had she ever agreed to attend?

That's right because she couldn't say no to Kaito, not when he'd been so excited. It bothered her that he'd gone hunting for the hybrid camp alone, but things had been going so well lately, and she didn't want to fight. Then when he'd told her he was having a banquet to celebrate his victory, her head told her it was a bad idea, but her mouth had agreed. What was he doing to her? Wearing the silk he'd given her and the pin, she felt more like his doll that he could dress up and do with what he liked. She'd considered turning him down, rejecting these gifts and tonight's dinner, but if she did, would he give up on her. Kazue had returned, what was to stop him from tossing her aside and restarting their past relationship in a new life?

There was no avoiding it now. This banquet was going to happen whether she wanted to attend or not. If she were lucky, she would escape without a yokai revolt. Her staff was leaning against a nearby wall. There was no easy way to carry it in her current outfit. But she would feel safer if she brought it with her, on the other hand, it might also be seen as a threat. Kaito wanted her to be his empress, and the only way that was going to happen was if she earned the yokai's trust. She was going to have to leave her staff behind.

She headed out the door, but Tsuki blocked her way. Her head swiveled back to her staff. Could she make it before Tsuki? How had he gotten out of his cell?

"Did I scare you?" He chuckled as he rubbed the back of his neck.

They must have gotten free and were coming to steal the staff again. Suzume backed up toward her staff slowly. "What are you doing here?"

"Kaito let us go," he said with a smile.

"Why would he let you go after you turned against us, you almost killed me."

"But I didn't," he laughed.

Suzume scowled back at him. She fumbled behind her, reaching for her staff.

"Sorry, I shouldn't make jokes, should I? Kazue vouched for us, she explained our situation to him..."

Kazue had vouched for them. "Why would he listen to another prisoner, the person who you said turned you against us," she asked. Did they think she was an idiot? Her hand clenched around the hilt of her staff.

Tsuki blinked at her a few times. "Didn't he tell you? Kazue is free, she gave him information that led to destroying the hybrid camp."

No. He hadn't told her that. Why would he forget to tell her something so important? Unless he didn't want her to find out, unless he was afraid of her finding out they'd spent time together. Had she told him that she had all of Kazue's memories? Was Kaito being swayed by his old love? Her chest clenched, just thinking about it. No. She wouldn't let that happen. He declared her his empress to all the yokai. He wouldn't discard her now that a woman claiming to remember their past walked into the picture.

She pushed past Tsuki and hurried down the hall. Naoki followed after her, but she didn't wait to make sure he was shadowing her. She had to see Kaito, surely Tsuki was lying. The yokai had gathered together, and their raucous voices were raised up to the high ceilings, spilling out into the hall beyond. As she approached, she slowed her steps, took a deep breath, and brushed the folds from her kimono. Whatever the truth was, she needed to be in control of her image. She wouldn't let the yokai see her ruffled.

Suzume stepped into the room. Servants circulated about with bottles of sake. Suzume scanned the crowd searching for Kaito, and found him at the head of the room, his head tossed back in laughter as he sat beside Kazue. Her insides turned to water. She didn't want to believe her eyes; he really had let her out of her prison.

That didn't mean anything, maybe he had just forgotten to tell her. She strode through the crowd to get closer to him, he hadn't taken his eyes of Kazue. She leaned in closer to whisper something in his ear, and a smile curled his lips. Anger boiled in her gut.

Suzume approached them and stared down at Kaito, he was so absorbed in chatting with Kazue he didn't even bother to look up at her. Flames danced along her skin. If she weren't careful, she would lose control and burn the entire palace down.

"Looks like we have an unexpected guest," Suzume said through gritted teeth.

Kaito glanced up at her and then looked to Kazue. He stood up and came around the table to greet her, he reached to embrace her, but she backed away. The yokai were watching, and their angry stares only made her feel more nervous and angry. How dare he continue to flaunt her in front of them, putting her further in danger.

"You didn't tell me that you'd let her go," Suzume said, resisting the urge to glare at Kazue.

Kaito blinked at her as if he didn't understand her question. He glanced over at Kazue then back to her. "Didn't I? Everything moved so fast, I must have forgotten to tell you. Kazue's tip helped us find and capture the hybrids. Part of our celebration tonight is to thank her for her assistance."

Suzume balled her hand into a fist at her side. This dinner was for her? "Then don't let me get in the way of your party." She turned to walk away.

Kaito caught her by the wrist. "What's gotten into you?"

"Nothing," she bit out. "I just want you and Kazue's reincarnation to have a lovely evening together."

Kaito's face paled. He knew, and he'd purposefully kept it from her. And that hurt more. Secrets, lies, how long before she was the second woman left forever waiting for his return.

"Can we talk about this later?" Kaito asked in an angry whisper, his gaze darting to the yokai who were leaning forward to better hear their conversation.

"Don't worry, I won't ruin your celebration, I'm not in the mood to celebrate." She pulled the jade comb from her hair and tossed it down at his feet.

Turning on the balls of her feet, she stormed out of the room. Angry tears threatened the back of her lids. Suzume returned to her room and tore off the silks and ruffled her hair in anger. Damn him for making her feel this way. Never before had she let any man get under her skin, control what she did, or wore. And for what? For him to lie and sneak behind her back.

She roared in frustration and fell onto her knees on the ground. She leaned her head into her hands and sighed. But despite everything, she was angry at herself. For being jealous, for being so afraid of losing him. Over and over, he had assured her there was no one for him but her. Maybe she had let her jealousy get the better of her and spoken out of anger. Maybe he had a reasonable explanation of why he hadn't told her sooner about Kazue.

The party should be over soon. She would wait for him in his room, and apologize. When she stepped out, she heard his voice approaching. Perfect timing. But he wasn't alone, there was another voice, a woman's voice.

Kazue. Had he walked her back from the banquet? Perhaps it was just a kindness, the yokai were still dangerous after all, and she was new here. It was probably innocent. Suzume stuck to the shadows and watched as they entered the courtyard, and the pair of them stopped beneath the sakura tree. She couldn't hear what they were saying to one another, but Kaito's gaze was focused on her.

Whatever it was they were talking about, she didn't like it. She took a step toward them, prepared to break them apart just as Kazue leaned forward and kissed Kaito.

TWENTY-THREE

Kaito leaned over to pick up the jade comb he had gifted Suzume. How much more stubborn would she be? He gave her gifts, he put her on a place before all others in his kingdom, but it was never good enough. Why couldn't she trust him when he said that she was the only one in his eyes. Under any other circumstances, he might have found her jealousy charming. But when she tossed down his gift, she made a fool of him in front of his court. He should go chase after her, make her understand that what happened between him and Kazue was the past. He never meant to deceive her.

But if he went chasing after her, the yokai would see it as a weakness. Rumors would spread. The Great Dragon brought down by his human woman's temper. The Great Dragon bewitched by a priestess. They all knew he had been defeated by a human woman before. They were already quick to disobey, to test his authority. They were like hungry sharks circling, waiting for their chance to pull him down from his throne.

No. It was better to put on a show, pretend nothing was happening. Later he and Suzume would talk, after she'd had time to cool her temper.

"Bring another barrel of sake," Kaito said.

The proclamation was met with cheers as more barrels of sake were rolled out and cracked open for the yokai to enjoy.

Kaito took his own seat and guzzled his glass of sake. The pleasant burn ran down his throat. He would need more than one glass to take the edge off his frustrations tonight.

"Did I do something wrong?" Kazue asked as she touched him lightly.

He stared at that connection and pulled away.

Kazue watched him with those long lashes, framing large brown eyes. She was all sweetness and innocence. It reminded him of Kazue when he had first met her. A servant refilled his glass, and he drank it down quickly. These were dangerous thoughts. He didn't need these memories to chase him tonight. Not when he was so close to everything he ever wanted.

"Not at all, there was just a misunderstanding." He took another drink. The numbness was starting to spread, just enough to loosen him up a bit. "Don't worry, tonight is for celebration."

She held up her glass to him in a cheer before turning away to take a delicate sip.

Suzume was the one who was being unreasonable. He hadn't done anything wrong. Did he have to tell her every move he made? Where every piece of intelligence came from? Her jealousy was blowing things out of proportion. So what if Kazue had memories from his past. It was for that reason she should know he could never take her back. The scar remained even if Kazue's face changed. He could never trust her fully, nor open his heart the way he was able to with Suzume.

The celebration wore long into the night. Numerous times he told himself once he finished this glass, he would retire. But his glass never seemed to empty. Little by little, the yokai stumbled out as the sake, and the food began to run out. Beside him, Kazue's head was starting to droop as she leaned on her own hand.

For a human, she had drunk more than he was expecting.

"We should get you to bed," he said to her.

Her eyes half-lidded as she flapped her hand at him. "I'm fine, I can stay up a while longer." She slurred her words.

It was definitely time to get her back to her room. The yokai who were hanging around kept glancing in her direction. An intoxicated priestess would be an easy target. He grabbed her by the forearm and helped her stand. "No, I insist."

She swayed on her feet, giggling as she lost her balance. She leaned against him, pressing herself against his arm. Kaito pulled away to an appropriate distance, but she continued to beam at him.

He led her back to the inner rings of the palace, all the while, she laughed and brushed against him, and each time, he put distance between them. When they reached the inner courtyard of the palace, everything was still and quiet. The sakura tree had lost all of its blossoms and was once more dormant. Kazue broke away from him to stumble over to it. She rested her hand against the rough bark.

"Do you ever wish to go back?" she said. She looked at him over her shoulder while she leaned against the tree.

"Not particularly." There were too many bad memories in the past, it was better to keep looking forward than looking back on the things he couldn't change.

"What if you could do it all over again?" She stepped away from the tree toward him; she wasn't slurring or stumbling now.

Thinking about the past, there was much to regret. But if changing any of it meant he wouldn't meet Suzume, then he wouldn't change a thing.

Kazue was suddenly very close to him, her hand on his chest.

"What are—"

She leaned forward and cut off his question with a kiss. And at the same time, he pushed her away. He should have known, the way she kept brushing against him. He should have made it clear sooner.

"Is this what you've been hiding?" Suzume shouted.

He swiveled his head in her direction. She was standing outside her door, her face flushed with anger. No, this couldn't be happening.

"Suzume, I can explain." He took a step in her direction.

She shook her head and ran back into her room. He tried to chase after her, but Kazue grabbed him by the arm.

"Don't go. We promised."

"I'm sorry if I gave you the wrong impression, but I cannot uphold a promise I made to Kazue. My heart belongs to someone else."

There was a flicker of anger in her expression, only for the briefest moment before she shook her head.

She let him go and took a step back. "It was my mistake. I shouldn't have—" Her voice caught, and tears shimmered on her lashes.

He bolted for Suzume's door and pounded on it. "Suzume, let me explain."

"Go away," she screamed.

He slammed a fist against the door again. Damn it, why did she have to come out just at the wrong time. He should have followed her when she threw down the pin at dinner. Now she would only assume the worst of him.

"I'm sorry to interrupt—" Shin said.

"Leave, I don't care what it is," Kaito snarled without looking at Shin.

"Time is of the essence, I'm afraid," Shin replied.

Kaito swiveled toward him, and grabbed a hold of Shin's collar. "What is it, tell me quickly before I lose my patience further."

Shin didn't flinch but stared at him with a somber expression. "A tengu prince is here, he says it's an emergency that he speak with you."

Kaito released a ragged breath and then looked to Suzume's door. Knowing Suzume's temper, it would burn hot and long, even if he were to wait outside her door all night, she wouldn't come until she was ready. He couldn't neglect his duty as ruler of Akatsuki for a misunderstanding, not if it were a true emergency. But so help the bastard if it weren't one.

"Let's make it quick," he said. He would resolve the tengu matter and then return to Suzume.

The tengu prince was waiting for him in the map room. His black wings were drooping, and there were dark circles under his eyes. As Kaito entered, he rose but fell to his knee. It must be serious if he had flown so hard and fast that he was nearly about to collapse.

"My Dragon," he said, pressing a fist to his chest. "I've come to beg for your help, my people are under siege from the yuki onna."

Never in his long life had he heard of yuki onna organizing into a siege. But he'd seen many strange things since waking from his prison.

"What of my emissary, Rin?" Kaito said.

"It was her who asked me to seek your aid," the prince said.

Then that must be why it had taken Rin so long to return. All the other emissaries had returned from their missions but her. If the tengu were in need of aid, then he was more than willing to give it. By doing so, it would all but cement their alliance, and with the support of the tengu, he would once more be the strongest force in Akatsuki, no one would dare speak up against him. No one could tell him who he could choose to marry.

"Gather a force, we leave as soon as possible," Kaito said to Shin.

Shin bowed to Kaito and did his bidding. But preparing for war meant he couldn't go to Suzume and explain. There simply wasn't time. When this was all over, he would explain everything. For now, he had a siege to break.

SUZUME KEPT REPLAYING THAT KISS OVER AND OVER IN HER MIND. IT kept her awake and kept her pacing her room. She was going to wear a hole in the ground with all her pacing. Last time, he had waited outside for her until she was ready to talk. But what if this time he wasn't there. That creeping dread threatened to swallow her whole and kept her from checking, and kept her feet moving.

But the uncertainty was nearly as painful. She walked to the door and away from it dozens of times. But as the sun was coming up on the horizon, it was nearly time for practice with Souta. She couldn't stay locked away forever. She had to face the truth.

She took a deep breath and slid open the door. She poked her head outside and found an empty hall. He wasn't there. The reality came crashing down on her like a wave, threatening to pull her out to sea to drown her in her own self-pity. But she refused to let it. She wouldn't give in to her emotions. She didn't need Kaito before, and she didn't need him now.

She shoved those feelings aside, buried them deep in her heart to be examined at a later date or maybe not at all. She grabbed her staff and headed to the training grounds. She would pummel a dummy for a few hours, work out her frustration, and then she would move on. It was good he wasn't here, cause she might burst into flames if she unleashed her anger upon him.

Naoki waited for her silently. For a moment, she considered asking him if Kaito had waited outside her door before giving up. But she held herself back. She marched through the halls to the training yard. The halls of the palace were more scarce than usual today, and for that, she was grateful. If she happened to run into someone on her way there, then she might have burst into flames and burned them to nothing but cinders for daring to cross her path.

Souta was in the training yard when she arrived, a frown on his face as he stared out onto the horizon.

"Good morning," she said, forcing a bright tone. She wouldn't let anyone see her pain, it was better to keep these things hidden. No one could hurt her if she didn't show them her weaknesses.

Souta looked at her with a quirked brow. "Have you not heard the news?" he asked.

"What news?" Suzume replied.

"The Dragon and a group of yokai soldiers are headed off to the tengu fight."

He'd left, without resolving their fight. Without saying good-bye, as if she meant nothing at all to him. She inhaled sharply and then blew it out her nose. It didn't matter. He could do as he wished.

Suzume shrugged. "Good for them, shall we get started with practice?"

Souta watched her for a moment, and she felt as if he could read her, as if her feelings were written there on her forehead. If he asked her what happened, she would crack open like an egg. She would fall into an emotional puddle. But he also wasn't the type to pry, and when he gave a small shake of his head, she knew she was safe from further questioning. And she stuffed her feelings down further.

"Kazue will be joining us today, we need to start working on our resonance as a group," Souta said.

Her face flushed. She wasn't sure she could face her, not yet. She hoped to avoid her for a while longer. But seeing her smug, gloating over her win, she might lose control. But she couldn't protest. She had to put on a brave face and pretend that everything was fine.

"Sounds great," she said, her smile must have looked more like a grimace.

"Oh good, she's here." Souta nodded toward the entry to the training ground. Kazue walked over, her head held high as if she were ruler of this place already. Now that Kaito had Kazue back, would he make her his empress instead?

No. Don't think about it. Forget it all.

"Since we're all together, shall we get started then?" Souta asked.

Suzume's lips were pressed together. If she opened her mouth, she was just as likely to breathe fire and launch herself at Kazue.

They started out practice with meditation to better help them link up their spiritual powers to one another. But Suzume's mind kept wandering. Over and over, she replayed the kiss. He never really loved her; to him, maybe it was all just a game. And fool that she was, she played right into his hand. Sparks burst along her skin, popping off her like embers in a fire.

"Suzume, focus," Souta scolded as he patted an ember which had landed on his sleeve.

"I am trying," Suzume snapped, and flames burst from her fingertips.

She stood up. This was no use. At this rate, she was going to lose all control. She needed more time and space.

She stomped off the training ground, her skin twitching with energy as her angry thoughts swirled into themselves. This was all Kaito's fault. Why had he decided to play her this way? Why deceive her into thinking she could be worthy of love.

TWENTY-FOUR

The palanquin rocked back and forth, and Ryuu had to brace himself on the wall to avoid tipping over. Across from him, the emperor's expression was serene with his hands folded in his lap, even as his head bobbed back and forth. Ryuu was not surprised when he'd been summoned early that morning to accompany the emperor on his trip to an undisclosed location. They'd made small talk at the onset of the journey. Ryuu had purposefully avoided asking where they were going at dawn's first light. After talking to a few courtiers, and hearing reports from his neko spy, he'd heard the emperor did not tolerate questions like he used to. Allegedly, he would explode in a rage when questioned.

Ryuu saw no hint of that now. The emperor seemed no more a threat than he'd ever been. In the long line of emperors who'd followed after Ryuu, the current emperor was the most unassuming. He ruled in a time of peace among humans, he had made no advancements and until recently seemed to lack any ambition. He listened to his advisers in all matters and generally did not challenge the status quo.

It was difficult to believe the rumors looking at him now. If it weren't for his fervent desire to destroy all yokai, that is. His court would see his desire to fight the yokai as eccentric, but the council should have convinced him to put a stop to it. And yet, he persisted. Rumor had it he had dismissed several prominent council members who'd spoken against him. What had changed, was it Izume's influence, Hisato's?

Ryuu pulled back the curtain on the palanquin window and surveyed the passing landscape. When he'd first seen the White Palace, he had chosen it for its beautiful location nestled between rolling hills and verdant forests. Even five hundred years later, it still took his breath away. Though much of the forest and hills had been carved out for rice paddies and small roadside villages. They were about a half day's journey from the palace now, where could the emperor possibly be taking him?

They were leaving farmlands again, and headed into the more remote forest regions. The deeper into the forest they went, the more a creeping sensation crawled over his skin. This energy, it was familiar to him, but he couldn't quite place it. Their procession came to a halt at the bottom of steep stone stairs with a torii arch over it. The emperor had brought him to a temple?

"Ah, we're here." The emperor's eyes lit up with excitement.

Ryuu stepped out first before the servants laid out a carpet for the emperor to walk upon.

The scent of old blood polluted the fresh mountain air. The hairs on the back of his neck stood on end. This place might have been a temple at one point, but whatever the emperor was doing, it had corrupted this sacred place.

The emperor climbed the steps as his servants rolled out a carpet before him, so that his feet never touched the stone. Ryuu followed, a growing dread settling in his stomach. He knew what this unfamiliar energy was now. It was hybrids. The monstrosities created by forcing together a human with yokai energy.

At the top of the stairs, the emperor stopped and folded his hands behind his back.

The scent of decay slapped him hard against the face. Twisted and deformed priests and priestesses shuffled about the grounds, with blank, unintelligent gazes. The spell that transformed them, had stripped them of all their humanity.

"Are they not magnificent?" the emperor remarked.

Ryuu's skin twitched just being near them. There was this feeling of being watched, but looking over his shoulder, there was no one there.

"What are your plans for them?" Ryuu asked, though he feared the answer.

The emperor turned to face him. "They are my perfect army, the ones who will help us rid this land of yokai."

A hybrid howled and charged toward them. Ryuu drew Tetsuyama, but it was in vain. The hybrid collided with an invisible shimmering barrier and was propelled backward. Ryuu stared in disgust as the hybrids turned toward the barrier reaching out toward them, grasping with their gnarled and bloody hands. This was the army the emperor was gathering to fight the yokai? It was an abomination. But seeing that fanatic gleam in the emperor's eye, he knew he would hear nothing against them, he had to tread carefully.

"Can they be controlled?" Ryuu asked.

"The priestess has full control over them. She took a force and is preparing a surprise attack on The Dragon as we speak."

"You trust this priestess who is creating these things for you?"

"Izume has vouched for her personally, she paid for her training."

Then it was just as he expected, Izume had been the sponsor who'd paid for the Water of Kazue's soul. And now she was heading straight for the dragon and Suzume.

"These things seem mindless, I worry they will kill indiscriminately, there is a town not far from The Dragon's palace..."

"How do you know where The Dragon's palace is?" the emperor asked.

He'd inadvertently revealed too much.

"I've been reading up on reports to better serve you, emperor." Ryuu bowed his head.

The emperor narrowed his eyes as he studied him. Would he see through his deception? He did not want to have to harm the emperor and lose his foothold at the palace. It would create an even bigger mess.

The emperor looked back to the hybrids. "Sacrifices must be made to protect our people, Ryuu. I thought you would understand that. You built this kingdom, and it was you who put the crown on my head."

"And my first duty will forever remain to protecting Akatsuki." Even if that meant waging a war to remove a mad man from his throne.

"Things are changing, the old ways are dying, and a new age is dawning. It would be best if we didn't cling to our old beliefs. Don't you think?"

"You are correct, emperor."

Ryuu had underestimated the emperor's quiet ambitions. If his power was left unchecked, he would burn through the entire country, destroying everything in his wake. He could leave now and go warn Suzume of the attack, maybe even remove her from dangers. But it wouldn't save the countless innocents who would get caught in the fray.

He must remove the emperor from his throne, and only he could do that bloodlessly.

By the time they left the temple, Ryuu's thoughts were storming. The trip back to the White Palace was punctuated by long awkward silences. And Ryuu was glad to be free of the suffocating atmosphere in the carriage. He had called the neko through their bond, and he was waiting for him when he returned.

"What is it now?" the neko said, stretching his arms over his head and fanning out his claws. He was supposed to be finding out what was happening to the missing priests, but he suspected he'd been out lazing about the temple instead. It didn't matter now, Ryuu knew where the priests were going. To think the emperor was kidnapping his own subjects... it was inhumane.

"I need you to take a message to Suzume."

"I was afraid you were going to say that." The neko yawned.

"Tell her that the emperor is gathering an army, and she needs to have Kaito prepare for the attack of the hybrids."

The neko's cat eyes grew wide. "Those things are coming for The Dragon, and you want me to head straight there?"

"Would you rather I force you?" Ryuu asked. He pulled on the bond, just a warning.

Forcing the neko to do his bidding exerted more energy and caused injury and pain to him. He didn't like to do it, but if he had to, he would.

The neko bowed, "I am at your bidding, master." There was a hint of bitterness to his tone.

"And if the worst is to happen, I want you to get Suzume out of there."

The neko bobbed his head before disappearing in a flash of smoke. Sending the neko made him uneasy, but there was too much work left to do. Ryuu went to his desk and prepared messages to go out by more human means. It was decades since he had called on his allies among the courtiers. But if he wanted the emperor removed from power without a war, he had to call in a few favors.

A HEAVY SNOWFALL OBSCURED THE MOUNTAIN TOP, AND THE FOREST before Kaito was swathed in white. This was no natural storm, he could feel it in the wind. He'd run across yuki onna in the past, but never before had he heard of them organizing or forming a siege. When the tengu prince told him, he didn't want to believe it. But a storm this fierce couldn't have been created by a single yuki onna.

"The scouts have returned with reports," Shin said.

Kaito turned away from the mountain to hear the report from Shin and his mate, Akane. There was a dusting of snow on top of both their heads.

"How bad is it?" he asked them.

"Not good, we're outnumbered three to one," Shin replied.

He'd broken sieges before, but never through a storm and never against such an unpredictable force as the yuki onna. They were solitary hunters, who normally lived in isolation. It reminded him of the kijo. What could bring them together to fight? Attacking them as he would an organized army, they'd be over-whelmed straight away, even if the numbers were in their favor.

"What are their weaknesses?" Akane asked.

"Fire." Kaito tapped his fingers on his forearm, his thoughts drifted back to Suzume. She was likely still angry with him. Her flames would have been effective against the yuki onna, but he didn't like putting her in danger's way either.

"We could lead with the flame yokai," Shin suggested.

"The yuki onna have the upper ground, they'd see them before they were close enough to attack." Kaito paced back and forth.

"What brought them all together this way?" Akane mused.

Kaito's head shot up, that was right yuki onna were solitary and territorial. But a leader could have brought them together, made them into a concentrated force. "And that leader would be the key to undoing their forces. If we eliminate them, then the yuki onna would be in chaos."

"You make it sound so simple, but the leader would be at the heart of the camp surrounded by yuki onna," Akane said.

"I'll go," Shin said.

Kaito put his hand on his friend's shoulder. He was talking about a suicide mission, Shin was more valuable to him as a general, than to risk his life on this mission. He wouldn't risk his best friend's life, he would go in alone and assassinate the leader.

"I need you here to lead the troops," Kaito said.

"Do you really think I'm going to let you go in there alone?" Shin asked.

As usual, Shin had seen straight through him. And he also knew that stubborn look on his face, this argument would drag long into the night if he let it. There was no choice.

"We'll go together, then," Kaito replied with a dramatic sigh.

Shin slapped him on the back. "I had a feeling you'd say something like that."

"Why do you insist on throwing yourself into danger?" Akane said with a shake of her head.

Shin pulled Akane into his arms as she squirmed away from him, casting embarrassed glances in Kaito's direction. Kaito turned his back on them to give them a private moment.

"I won't be gone long, keep order until we return."

It was good to see Shin settled again and so content. But it only further reminded him of Suzume and the state they'd left things. Hopefully, by the time they returned, her anger would have cooled. They would tie things up quickly and then return home. Once the siege was broken, everything would return to how it should be.

TWENTY-FIVE

There was something very satisfying about flinging fireball after fireball at the dummies. Each burst of flame from her fingertips released some of the bubbling rage that churned her gut. And as the fire consumed the hay stuffing and the fabric encasing, she could even imagine Kaito's unfaithful face in place of the painted leering face on the dummy. Control.

The sun had set while she ceaselessly shot balls of fire. Souta had left hours ago, after trying fruitlessly to get her to talk about what was bothering her. With no one in the practice yard but Naoki, who hung back by the entrance, she didn't run the risk of hurting anyone if she were to lose control. And better yet, she could let out all her anger and frustration without witnesses, apart from Naoki, who hardly spoke as it was.

Suzume leaned forward, grasping her knees as she caught her breath. She'd nearly used up all her spiritual energy. Warm orange light flickered over her. Almost all her anger spent, she felt nothing but a deep empty ache. Not since she had left the White Palace had she felt this alone. Tsuki and Akira had betrayed her, and now Kaito had abandoned her. The only thing keeping her at the sea palace was knowing that venturing out alone meant being attacked by wild yokai.

Footsteps approached from behind, and she spun around a ball of fire in her hands.

Kazue reached her hands up in the air. Her eyes were wide with fear. It was tempting to launch a fireball toward her and scar that pretty face of hers. But what was the point, Kaito would probably still have chosen her even if she were ugly.

"What do you want?" Suzume snapped and lowered her flaming hand before she gave in to her impulse after all.

"I wanted to apologize for what happened the other day."

Suzume scoffed. "Don't bother." She launched her fireball at the dummy, and it struck it straight in the head. Flames caught on the hay, and smoke drifted off it.

"That night I had a little too much sake, I wasn't thinking clearly."

Her energy was flagging, but she couldn't face her, she didn't want to witness the lies. What did it matter if she were drunk, it had still happened. Kazue wanted to start over again with Kaito, who was she to get between them. Her fireballs were much weaker now, as her energy was low. But she kept up at it to avoid looking Kazue in the eye and confirming it was really over between her and Kaito, before it had ever really started.

"I hope you can forgive me for that," Kazue said.

Suzume turned to face her, hands on hips. "Are you really sorry? Or are you here just to gloat?"

Kazue put on a show of being innocent, and pretending that she wanted to be Suzume's friend, but she could see right through her. She knew plenty of girls just like her back at the White Palace. Who pretended they were your friend. They would always smile as they stabbed you in the back.

"It was never my intention to upset you," she said, her eyelashes lowered as she stared at the ground.

"Leave me be," Suzume said and bumped her shoulders into Kazue's as she strode past to go grab a staff. Maybe striking a dummy would take off the edge off.

"This isn't easy for me either," Kazue said.

Suzume ignored her and took her staff, whacking it hard against the dummy. She thrust, and swung it up and around in a sweep.

But instead of catching the hint, Kazue came over and continued. "For my entire life, I believed I was Kazue's reincarnation. That I was destined to find and free The Dragon. I thought he and I were meant to be together."

"You're not making me hate you any less if that's your intention," Suzume said as she jabbed the end of her staff into the ground.

Why couldn't she leave her alone? She'd already stolen Kaito from her, how much more did she want?

She wrung her hands together and looked anywhere but at Suzume. "It wasn't easy for me to see him looking at you, the way he had looked at me— I mean Kazue in my past life. I thought we could start over, but there was someone else in his heart."

The small flame of hope inside her leaped hearing that. But she wasn't ready to believe it. Kazue could very well be lying to her.

"And who's that?" Suzume asked.

"He told me there's no one else in his heart but you."

Suzume's stomach flopped. Had he really said that? But if that were true, why had he left without explanation. She couldn't let her guard down. If she let him back in, he would only hurt her once more. What was more suspicious was why Kazue telling her this? If she were in love with Kaito like she said, wouldn't she be glad they were fighting?

"Why are you telling me this? You could have kept it a secret and let Kaito and I fall apart."

"I realize this might sound strange, but your friendship is more important to me," Kazue said.

Suzume turned again, raising a brow. She had to be joking. "You want to be my friend?" she drawled.

Did Kazue think she was a complete fool? She was willing to humor her before, but now she knew she had to be lying.

"Well, you see, I've never met someone like me. The priestesses I was raised with never understood me. They feared my power, and it made me an outsider. And from the moment I first saw you on the beach, I felt this connection to you, it was as if I were drawn to you by fate." She reached out to touch Suzume's hand.

Suzume pulled away and crossed her arms over her chest. Kazue might have saved her life on the beach when she fought the hybrids, but that didn't mean she could trust her.

"I don't need a friend, or to hear your sob story, if you'll excuse me." She took a few steps away from her.

"But you need me to defeat Hisato," Kazue said. Her voice was less simpering and more direct.

Suzume turned back toward her and met her gaze. It wasn't shy and innocent any longer. For a moment, her mask had slipped, and Suzume felt she was seeing the real Kazue beneath the innocent priestess.

"Which is why I haven't burned you to a crisp, yet," Suzume said.

"You wouldn't dare, because it would hurt you too," Kazue said.

A chill raced down her spine. What game was she playing here? Was she threatening her? Whatever her intentions, Suzume would need to keep an eye on her. Kaito might have let her go and trusted her, but there was something unsettling about Kazue, and she was determined to get to the bottom of it.

THE WIND HOWLED IN KAITO'S EARS LIKE THE MOURNFUL CRY OF THE dying. Shin and he had kept to the relative safety of the thick forest. But as they got closer to the heart of the yuki onna camp, the colder it was and the harder the storm tried to push them back. The yuki onna had built their encampment between snowdrifts, creating small icy huts. They swarmed over their landscape, their sharp, deadly beauty drew the eye, even from a distance. It was part of the danger of a yuki onna, their allure brought in their targets.

A human who happened to stumble across their path would have been drawn in and drained of his spiritual energy before even realizing what happened. Their collective power concentrated on one area made them that much more powerful, and even on guard, he felt himself drifting closer and closer like a moth to a flame.

"There are too many of them, how are we going to get close enough to attack?" Shin asked. His wolf tail was twitching, and his gaze was fixated on the yuki onna. He was feeling it too.

If he sent his army in, they would be torn to shreds in moments, and they would smile while it happened.

"We move quickly, keep your head down, and don't look at them," Kaito ordered.

Shin's lips were drawn in a thin line as he nodded.

Under the cover of a storm they crept closer to them. They hid behind a snowdrift, and Kaito peeked around the edge. A faint song drifted on the wind, he strained to hear the notes and make out the words, but it eluded him. A part of him wanted to follow that sound and the woman who was singing it.

Kaito shook himself. That was what the yuki onna wanted. To draw them out. Kaito ripped off an edge of his sleeve and shoved the fabric in his ears, before offering the same to Shin. If they could muffle the song, they would be safe from the yuki onna.

They darted out from behind the snowdrift, moving closer to the center of their camp. There was a structure made of ice. The energy was strongest there, it must be where their leader was. A pair of yuki onna stood outside, presumably guarding their leader.

Clouds of vapor escaped from Kaito's lips each time he breathed. Frost was starting to collect on his sleeves. He wasn't imagining it, it was getting colder. Ice was not a problem for him, but Shin's teeth were chattering.

"Come on, the leader must be in there," Kaito whispered.

Shin nodded and then bolted for the building. But as he did, the song he'd heard before got much stronger, it froze him in his tracks, and he turned, craning to find the source. Kaito clapped his hands over his ears and rushed toward the back of the building. A single icy window let light into the interior.

"It is done as you asked, my queen," said a yuki onna from within.

"Good, send word to Ai, and let her know we almost have the tengu in our grasp."

"Yes, my queen."

Ai. She was behind the yuki onna. It had been a mistake to let her go free. She must have been the one stirring up problems in his kingdom, drawing his attention away with the kijo. Well, once he destroyed the yuki onna leader, he and the tengu would have their revenge.

"Ready?" Kaito turned to signal Shin, but he wasn't beside him.

The song must have caught him. Kaito growled in frustration and backtracked his steps. Shin was wandering through the yuki onna encampment approaching a group of yuki onna who thankfully had their backs to them as they sang in the storm, which trapped the tengu in their compound.

Kaito grabbed Shin by the arm and yanked him backward.

"Let me go, I want to go to them," Shin said, his eyes glazed over in a trance.

"Not today, lover boy." Kaito hauled him over his shoulder just as a yuki onna turned and spotted them.

She hissed and alerted her sisters, and the whole pack of them rushed toward them. Kaito threw out his arm, sending up a wall of ice to slow their progress. He weaved through snowdrifts heading for the forest as the yuki onna were screeching behind his barrier. So much for a surprise attack. If anything, they'd be even more alert than before.

Once he was among the trees, far enough down the mountain that he was certain they hadn't been followed, Kaito set Shin back on his own two feet.

Shin rubbed his head, and his gaze was still unfocused.

"How you feeling, lover boy?"

"Like I drank an entire barrel of sake. Those yuki onna send a powerful punch."

"You're not kidding, they almost had you there." He clapped Shin on the shoulder. "Lucky for you, I rescued you in time."

"What about the leader, did you find anything?"

"Just that the yuki onna have given themselves a queen whose allied with Ai."

"Ai, the daughter of the Lord of the Sea? What does she have to do with this?"

"I don't know, but I plan to find out. For now, we need to retreat and make plans. Sneaking in isn't an option anymore, I'm afraid."

They returned to their camp. Time was of the essence. It wouldn't take long before the yuki onna came for them and sought revenge. They had to strike and quick, while they still had some element of surprise.

"The queen is their weak point, but she's heavily guarded. I can try and go back in again," Kaito said as he paced around his tent they'd set up in their camp.

"They'll be prepared for another attempt. It won't work," Shin said.

"Besides, you might fall under their spell this time," Akane commented. She had her chin cradled in her hand, and her brow was furrowed.

"We can't wait around. We need to move quickly."

"A woman could get past them, and a woman could sneak in and kill the yuki onna queen," Akane said.

"No. Don't even think about it," Shin said, grasping her hands. "I won't let you walk off into danger."

He understood the sentiment, how many times had he seen that same look in Suzume's eyes. But Akane was right, she wouldn't be affected by their song as they were. But even as strong as she was, she couldn't take down all the yuki onna alone.

"I appreciate your bravery, but this isn't something you could do alone," Kaito said to her.

Shin gave him a look of relief.

"Not me, Rin. I would need to get to the tengu palace and ask Rin first, of course. But you said they are weak to fire. Her fox fire could help us defeat the queen."

"Akane, this is insanity."

Kaito scratched his chin. It was risky, but it was the only hope they had.

"She's right, my friend. It's the best shot we have."

Shin's expression was conflicted as he looked into Akane's eyes, and then he nodded his head in agreement.

Twenty-Six

Suzume's arm trembled as she raised her chopsticks to her mouth, and her food fell back on her plate. In retrospect, pummeling the dummy until late at night might have been a bad idea. She pushed her plate away, it wasn't as if she had a stomach to eat it anyway. With the dawn of a new day, it meant facing Souta and Kazue during practice. Staying in bed wasn't an option, she was too restless to sit still. And like it or not, she had to learn how to resonate with Kazue if they were going to face Hisato together. With a heavy sigh, Suzume got up and dressed to go to practice.

Naoki was waiting outside her room to escort her as usual. With him at her shoulder, the yokai didn't bother her. And it was a good thing too, she couldn't guarantee she wouldn't burn anyone who crossed her path today. Souta and Kazue were waiting for her in the practice yard. Souta threw his head back in uproarious laughter. She wasn't sure she'd ever seen Souta laugh like that. It only made her bad mood worse. Why did everyone find Kazue so charming? Was no one suspicious of her but Suzume?

"Oh, you're here?" Kazue said as she tossed her hair over her shoulder with a bright smile.

"Oh, you're here?" Suzume mocked her under her breath.

"What was that?" Kazue asked.

"You're joining us again for practice?" Suzume said, forcing a smile, though even pretending to be friendly with Kazue, made her want to gag.

Kazue was all sweetness in front of Souta. But how did she expose her? She wouldn't reveal her true face easily, not now that she knew Suzume was onto her.

Souta cleared his throat. "Now that we are all here, why don't we get practice started."

"I hope we're sparring, I volunteer to go first," Suzume said, looking at Kazue. There was no way she could hold onto her innocent facade in the middle of a fight. Plus, there was the added benefit of knocking Kazue into the sand a few times.

"No, we need to work on our resonance. We're not going to be able to defeat Hisato if we cannot sync all of our energy," Souta said.

"Sounds wonderful!" Kazue clapped her hands together.

Suzume rolled her eyes. Just her luck. Resonance felt too intimate to do with someone like Kazue. She would have to open up and share her energy with someone she didn't trust.

"Isn't it a little soon to be resonating, we hardly know one another," Suzume replied.

"There's no time to waste, Hisato is gathering his armies as we speak. The longer we wait, the more people will get hurt," Kazue said with a poignant look at Suzume.

In other words, Suzume looked selfish and cold-hearted if she didn't try and resonate with them. She could make a stand and refuse, and likely come out looking like the bad guy. Or she could grit her teeth and get this over with. They did need to learn how to work together, and even if she didn't like her or trust her, she still needed her.

"Fine. Let's get to it then."

Suzume took her place in the sparring ring and closed her eyes to gather her energy. She could do this; she'd done it many times with Souta and Hikaru. All she needed to do was let the energy flow and seek out the connection of Kazue's soul between them all. The sun was warm on her skin, and it stoked the fires of her energy. Breathe in and out, in and out, let the sun's heat sink in and breathe it out to share with her partners.

Reaching for Souta, she imagined her energy like an invisible hand outstretched to clasp hers. Making a connection with him was easy, she sensed the strong caress of a summer breeze that she related to him. His energy entwined with hers; it fanned the flames, making them burn hotter and higher. Together their strength and energy were more than the sum of their individual parts. The part of her that was Kazue vibrated with excitement, eager to be reconnected.

If Hikaru were here, she would have connected with him next, letting the stability of earth ground the chaotic energy of her fire. But he wasn't here, and when her invisible hand reached out, it was shocked by the cold depths of the water element. She recoiled, retreating immediately. Unlike the other elements, which strengthened her, their connection suppressed her power, and she felt as if her power was being smothered.

"Hold the connection," Souta instructed.

She didn't want to reach out to Kazue again, but she reached her. Kazue's energy poured into her and made Suzume's chest tight. It overwhelmed her own power, destroying it as it threatened to conquer her from within. It felt as if the water was being forced down her throat, drowning her on land. Panic rose up in her, she wanted to pull apart, but Kazue only tightened her grip upon her. The energy between the three of them arched bouncing between them and sparking out of control.

Suzume pulled her connection closed and fell to her knees, grasping her throat, which moments before had felt like it was closing. The sudden closing of her spiritual barriers sent a burst of energy through the connection and to the other two through the remnants of the bond. It knocked them off their feet

"What happened?" Kazue asked, rubbing her head with bright red hands from the burns Suzume had inflicted on her.

"You almost drowned me, is what happened!" Suzume snapped.

Kazue pressed her hand to her chest. "I did? How, you're dry?"

Suzume touched her dry clothes and hair. "It wasn't with water; you sent too much of your energy into me. I'm fire, you could have smothered all of my spiritual energy."

"Souta, was the energy I sent too strong?" Kazue asked him.

Souta had a red mark on his cheek where she had burned him as well. "Everything was fine for me until Suzume's flame burst out of her."

"Are you saying I'm lying?" Suzume asked, hands on hips.

"I'm just saying that this is our first time attempting resonance, there're bound to be mistakes," Souta said calmly.

But she could read between the lines. When they practiced, she was always the slowest to connect, the last to master her powers, and the most likely to lose control. Did Kazue know that and try to twist the facts against her?

"She did this on purpose, to make me look bad." Suzume pointed at Kazue.

"I'm sorry for whatever it is you think I did." Kazue sniffled and rubbed away her fake tears.

"Unfounded accusations aren't necessary. I know we are all on edge lately, but we should try to get along," Souta said.

"How can you trust her? For all we know, she is working with Hisato."

"I swear, I am not. I know it looks bad because I took your staff, but he lied to me and told me that you stole it from him." Kazue buried her head in her hands to disguise the fact that she wasn't really crying.

"Suzume, I think you're being too cruel. Why don't you apologize to Kazue?" Souta said as he put an arm around Kazue's shoulder.

Surely Souta should know better, a man who'd live as long as him, and he couldn't see through a few fake tears and a story too convenient to be believed.

"You don't really believe this, do you?" she asked him.

"There cannot be division between us four. Arguing is exactly what Hisato wants. I think that you are letting your personal feelings cloud your judgment," Souta said, meeting her gaze.

"What are you saying, that I'm jealous?"

He didn't respond, and she didn't need him to. It was clear he had chosen his side in this argument. Normally Souta was neutral and impartial. But even he had turned against her. Was there no one in this place who hadn't fallen under Kazue's spell?

"If that's how you feel, I'll just go." She strode away before she did something else she might regret.

It had been naive of her to think she could learn to work with Kazue. Even if she weren't working for Hisato, she was too insufferable with her fake smiles and forced tears. Suzume returned to her room, where she tossed aside her staff and flopped down on her bed. Why was she torturing herself by staying here? How could she hope to defeat Hisato if she couldn't resonate with the other soul pieces? And when Kaito came back and confirmed he had chosen Kazue over her, she'd just rather not be there. It would be safer to run away, at least their distrust couldn't hurt her if she didn't have to face it.

Suzume groaned and rolled over and then froze. A shadow was looming just outside the door that led onto her balcony. Very slowly, she reached for her staff. Whoever it was didn't seem to notice her as she crept closer from behind, her staff clenched in her hand. She eased the door open all the way and brought the staff down on the head of the person outside.

Tsuki stepped out of the shadows and rubbed his head. "What was that for?"

"What are you doing in my room?" she countered and held her staff tighter.

"I saw something creeping around outside and came to investigate," he said as naturally as if he had never betrayed her.

Unfortunately for him, her memory wasn't as short as his apparently was. She pointed her staff at him. "Do you really think I'm going to believe that excuse? What are you doing skulking around my room, really?"

Tsuki held up his hand to silence her. "Hear that?"

Was she a joke to him. "Like I'm falling—" Tsuki covered her mouth.

She struggled against him for a moment, until she heard it, footsteps above her. He hadn't been lying, someone was on her roof.

Tsuki removed his hand and then pressed a finger to his lips. He crept onto the balcony with Suzume right behind him, holding her staff tight. Tsuki jumped up, catching the edge of the roof and climbing up and over. She craned her neck to try and see but couldn't see anything beyond the eaves.

"You're not getting away," Tsuki shouted.

There was a brief scuffle and what sounded like a hissing cat. A few seconds later, Tsuki jumped down from the roof with a squirming cat in his arms.

"Here's your culprit." He dropped it onto the ground.

As it hit the ground, it transformed from cat to humanoid with cat-like ears and a scar across his face. She'd met this particular neko before. It was Ryuu's familiar.

"He's no threat." She sheathed her staff on her back.

"Then what was he doing creeping around?" Tsuki asked with a frown.

She was about to remind him that not long ago, Tsuki was the one who had attacked her and tried to break into her room. But held her tongue instead. She'd had enough arguments today, and besides, he had a point.

"He's right, why not come through the front door?"

"You never know who's watching," the neko said, brushing invisible dust off his haori.

Those words sent a cold chill down her spine. Did the neko know something she didn't? She glanced at Tsuki and Akira.

"I'm in no danger from the neko. You can leave now," Suzume said to Tsuki.

Tsuki looked disappointed, but she still couldn't trust them. If Ryuu had sent the neko, he must have a message to tell her, and she wouldn't risk whatever it was getting back to Hisato. That is if Akira and Tsuki were still working for him.

Once Tsuki left, Suzume turned to the neko. "What did you have to tell me?"

"My master sent me to tell you that the emperor is sending a hybrid army to attack the palace."

"What! We need to prepare, send a message to Kaito," Suzume said and raced to the door.

"It's too late for that. He won't get here in time. The only choice left is to get you out of here."

He grabbed her by the wrist as if he would drag her out. She shook free. Why was he trying so hard to get her out of the palace?

"Hold on. Kaito already defeated the hybrid camp."

"I don't know what Kaito has done, but it didn't stop them. Come look." He gestured to the balcony.

Suzume followed him out there. And if she squinted into the distance, she saw hundreds of black dots closing in.

"Do you not value your own life? I've seen these hybrids, they don't discern who or what they're attacking. The Dragon's force doesn't stand a chance."

An army of hybrids. That was where Hisato had been all this time, creating an army. Even if she could resonate with Kazue and Souta, they wouldn't be enough. They all would be destroyed.

"Now, let's go before they get any closer," the neko said, heading for the door.

Since she'd discovered her power, she had fought in countless battles, and before this moment, she had never genuinely feared for her own life. Kaito wasn't here, she couldn't count on anyone to have her back. She could either run and save her own life or face the coming attack and possibly die...

Twenty-Seven

The blizzard had blown large drifts that reached the tops of the ramparts. The ground was slick with ice, and Rin had to be mindful of each step she took as she paced back and forth. Had the tengu prince arrived safely, was Kaito on his way to help them? She couldn't see much other than the flurry of snow and the sleet-gray sky overhead. Standing vigil here wouldn't make Kaito come any faster, but she hated sitting still and just waiting.

"Rin come inside," Hikaru shouted from the entrance to the guard's room.

"Just a few more minutes," she called back.

Hikaru would have stood by her side if the cold hadn't driven him inside. Even the tengu who lived their entire lives on this mountain top, had been driven inside by it. Rin had kept herself warm by cloaking herself in fox fire, but even that couldn't keep out the biting wind. She would need to go inside soon or risk losing a few digits or her nose, which had started to ache from the plummeting temperatures.

The tengu were starting to lose hope, she could feel it. As each day passed and the storm was stronger without any sign of stopping, their chances of rescue grew slimmer, as did the reality that the tengu prince might never have made it off the mountain. Rin sighed. Maybe she should head inside, start thinking of a new plan to get them off the mountain.

From the corner of her eye, she saw something moving in the snow. She might have imagined it. Rin squinted into the storm. A white wolf trudged through the snow, their head down. Was that, Shin? Then the tengu prince had been successful after all.

Rin bolted for the guard room. She threw the door open, and a flurry of snow entered with her. "Open the gate, The Dragon has sent a messenger."

The tengu huddled in the room looked to Mori, who was leaning against the far wall.

"Are you certain it's an ally? It could be a trick," Mori said, frowning toward the door.

She'd been so excited, she hadn't even considered the possibility. But if it was Shin and they kept the gate closed to him, he would freeze to death.

"I'm sure," Rin said.

Mori nodded. "Open the gates."

The tengu hopped to do as Mori had commanded, and Rin followed them out into the courtyard, preparing to greet Shin. Banks of snow had built up around the entrance, and it took four tengu to pry the doors open enough for the wolf to come bounding in. Their fur was covered in ice crystals.

"Are you alright, not hurt?" Rin asked, looking him up and down.

Akane transformed into her humanoid form and grasped her arms around her body, shivering. "Fine, but a bit cold. Is there somewhere we can go in and talk?"

If Akane were here, did that mean Shin was injured? What about Kaito? Her mind was racing as she led Akane into the guard room. A blanket was found, and they wrapped her up and offered her a steaming cup, which she drank from.

Rin paced behind her. "Is everyone alright, The Dragon, Shin, the tengu prince?" Rin asked.

Akane blew on the steam of her mug, her teeth were still chattering, but the blue was beginning to fade from her lips. "All fine. They would have come themselves, but the pull of the yuki onna was too strong for them."

Rin's tense shoulders relaxed. So she had worried for nothing. "Why did you come here in the blizzard if everyone is safe?" Rin asked.

"We're outnumbered. Kaito and Shin tried sneaking in to take out their leader, but were unsuccessful. Kaito says the yuki onna are weak to fire, and so I came to get you."

Rin's chest suddenly felt tight. But she could see the logic behind it, the yuki onna were weak against fire. She could disguise herself to get close, and she wasn't as susceptible to their allure. With the queen destroyed, the yuki onna would no longer have anything to rally behind. It was the perfect plan.

And yet she hesitated. She'd just barely made it out alive the last time she'd run into the yuki onna. Could she escape a second attempt unscathed, this time without Hikaru to back her up and to destroy their queen? She was more powerful than any other yuki onna Rin had ever seen. Hikaru reached for her hand and squeezed it. He would support her no matter what the choice.

For the future they dreamed up, for the peace of Akatsuki, she would have to try.

"I'll start preparing, we should not delay to attack," Rin said.

"Are you sure about this?" Mori asked.

Rin swallowed past a lump in her throat. No second-guessing.

"Yes. But if I don't return in a couple hours, I want you to promise me you'll protect Hikaru."

"Rin—"

"You have to stay alive, for the sake of Akatsuki, the piece of Kazue's soul inside you must stay safe." She cupped his cheek.

Hikaru pulled her into his embrace. She never wanted to let him go. But time was running out.

"Be careful," he said before they stepped apart.

"I'll be back soon," she said with more confidence than she felt as she stepped out into the storm.

SUZUME WAS PARALYZED BY INDECISION. RUN AND SAVE HERSELF OR stay and risk her own life for yokai that hurt her. It should have been an obvious choice. But what if this were exactly what

Hisato wanted. He expected her to run at the first sign of danger. And she was tired of running, tired of looking over her shoulder for that blade to fall on her neck. He had sent Kazue here for a reason, she might have deceived the rest of the palace, but she could see it clearly now. The kiss, all of it had been meant to distract her, to drive a wedge between her and Kaito. All leading to this moment, where she would be on her own, and easy prey for Hisato to capture her at last.

"Did you not see that army? We have to get out of here while we still can." The neko gestured to the balcony.

"I'm not going," Suzume said. "I'm going to stay here and defend the palace."

"You're a damn fool if you think I'm going to sacrifice my hide for your foolishness." The neko rushed toward her, and she swung her staff to block him. He grabbed onto the staff and tried to wrest it from her hands.

"I'm not going anywhere, and you can tell Ryuu that from me," Suzume said.

"And do you think he's just going to accept that? You don't know my master." He shoved, and she lost her footing on the tatami.

The neko was stronger than her; in a show of brute force, he would win. He would carry her far from the battle. All because Ryuu wanted to keep her safe. But she wasn't the princess in need of being protected anymore. She was her own person, and she had her own power. Suzume summoned the flames, which flickered over her staff. The neko yowled and let go of the staff stumbling backward as he stared at his burned hands.

"Fine. I'm not going to force you to come—enjoy fighting those monsters," the neko said.

Then with a puff of smoke, he was gone. There wasn't a moment to lose, she rushed for the door just as Naoki and Tsuki came through.

"We heard a struggle," Tsuki said.

"Don't worry, I've got it handled," Suzume said. "We have bigger problems, the hybrids are coming, and they're planning on attacking the palace. We have to warn the yokai and prepare for the attack."

Naoki turned and ran off to go and do as she told him, only Tsuki lingered behind.

"What can we do?" She wanted to cling to her anger at their betrayal, but there was no time for hurt feelings. "Help me gather up the yokai," she said.

He nodded his head and hurried off to do as he was told. As for her, she had to find Souta and warn him about Kazue. Suzume flew through the halls of the yokai palace, her heart thundering in her ears. Any yokai she passed, she shouted to tell them to gather in the audience hall, she didn't wait to see if they listened or looked at her like a crazy woman.

When she got to the training yard, it was empty. Kazue and Souta weren't there. Could they have returned to their rooms in the inner halls of the palace? She turned to go back and look for them, Naoki caught up with her.

"The yokai are gathering and asking questions," Naoki said.

She wished Kaito was here. He would know what to do, she was no general. She'd never led anyone in her life. But then she remembered what Kaito had said, he had chosen her as his empress for a reason. These yokai might hate her now, but if she married Kaito, one day, she would rule over them. Instead of cowering before them, she had to learn how to lead.

"Find Souta and tell him that Kazue cannot be trusted," Suzume told Naoki.

She rushed to the audience hall. The yokai had all gathered and were muttering among themselves. She pushed her way through the crowd, making her way to the front. The concerned murmur grew to a fever pitch, and sparks danced along her palms. Suzume took a few calming breaths. She could do this.

"Hybrids are on their way to attack the palace," Suzume shouted.

The yokai fell silent; at least she had her attention now.

"We need to prepare for the attack."

The shouting started up again.

"We won't listen to a human."

"Where is the dragon?"

They were closing in around her, forcing their way toward her.

"Listen, we need to stay united. The hybrids don't care—"

Someone grabbed her ankle and dragged her toward the edge of the dais. Suzume shot a ball of fire just over his head. He let go, but it was like lighting a tinder, the yokai who were holding back before, were swarming her. Suzume grabbed her staff and swung it around her trying to keep them back. But it was no use. She was arrogant to think they'd listen to a mere human woman's orders.

The circle around her was closing in when a sword slashed through the yokai in front of her. They started to scatter as Tsuki pushed his way to the front of the crowd, blocking Suzume from harm.

"You alright?" Tsuki asked.

Suzume nodded at him. He had come to her rescue, when he could have easily run away in the chaos.

Akira took control of the body her and Tsuki shared.

"The hybrids are already on the beach. It is a matter of minutes before they will be storming our doors. You will either fight with us, or take your chances with escape. But no one will harm the priestess without going through us first."

The body of the dead yokai laid at her feet, it wasn't exactly enough to inspire trust. But at least they weren't trying to tear her apart.

A howl echoed through the palace. The hybrids were upon them. The yokai looked around, realizing the danger they were in, and then they scattered.

"We need to get you out of here," Akira said.

"Are you suggesting we just abandon the palace?" Suzume asked.

"It's already lost, we cannot hope to defend it against an army just ourselves," Akira said.

She didn't like the idea of running away, it felt like cowardice, but Akira was right, staying at this point was suicide. She'd tried to convince the yokai to fight, and now she'd made her choice.

"We have to find Naoki and Souta," Suzume told them.

"Naoki and Souta have already left, he told us to come to find you," Akira said.

A boom echoed through the building as it shook. The hybrids were getting closer. They would have to reconvene once they were outside the palace. She just hoped they all survived until then.

TWENTY-EIGHT

The wind howled in her ears and pushed against Rin, making her progress slow. It was as if the storm were telling her to turn around. The landscape was nothing but a sheet of white, even if she were to turn back she wasn't she could find her way. As she stumbled blindly forward, trees appeared in the gloom. Ice clung to her lashes as if she might freeze to death before she ever reached the yuki onna.

Using the tree to block the unrelenting wind, she huddled behind it and lit her fox fire, trying to warm her frozen digits and face. She spread out her senses and searched out the yuki onna. They weren't much further; she was going to make it. Getting into the yuki onna camp was only half the battle; at least when she'd snuck into the yuki onna palace, she had Hikaru for back up. This time it was just her.

Rin rubbed her frigid hands together, no use delaying further. She pulled out a leaf from her sleeve. This disguise would need to be perfect. Last time the yuki onna had discovered her by her breath. To prevent that, she would need a second layer of disguise apart from her appearance that on casual examination would make her appear to have all the energy and characteristics of a yuki onna. But the cost of such a powerful disguise was her energy. Once she got close to the yuki onna queen, she would only have enough energy for one shot at killing her. Rin inhaled and then exhaled. She could do this. She focused her fox fire onto the leaf, pouring as much as she dared into it and then affixed it to her forehead. A warm tingle spread across her body, the disguise was complete.

Just maintaining it cost her, and she would have to be quick. With a renewed sense of purpose, she headed for the yuki onna camp. The storm began to dissipate as she passed through the borders of their camp. The surrounding snowdrifts made for the perfect cover, and Rin darted from one to another, creeping closer. Even in disguise, she imagined there would be questions as to why she was stepping out of the forest.

She was nearly to the heart of the camp. After checking to make sure there were no yuki onna nearby, she stood up from behind the snowdrift and strode through the camp purposefully. The yuki onna who she passed paid her no mind. And Rin let go of a breath she'd been holding. At least her disguise was working. The yuki onna queen's location was obvious, a snowy structure had been built for her. And it was larger than all the others, as if declaring someone important dwelled within. Rin appreciated her arrogance because it made her task that much easier.

A pair of guards chatted as they framed the door. Neither of them was paying attention to their surroundings. Getting past them shouldn't be too hard, she hoped. Rin's hands trembled, and she balled them into fists. Rin strode up confidently. Maybe she would get lucky, and they'd let her walk right past them without question.

They threw out their arms to stop her.

"Where do you think you're going?" the first yuki onna asked.

Rin scowled, pretending to be inconvenienced. "I have an urgent report to give the queen. Do not delay me, unless you wish to bring her wrath upon you."

The guards looked at one another with quizzical expressions. Please let this work.

"What news?" the second yuki onna asked. She scanned Rin up and down, could she see through her disguise?

Rin's heart thundered in her chest, she hoped it wasn't audible to them.

"We've discovered a spy in the camp. He's working for the dragon. We need to know how to proceed with the information we've obtained from them," It was a gamble; if either of them looked at her too closely, then she could be exposing herself.

"They caught them then. Good. Was the okami as delicious as he looked?" said the second guard, she licked her lips.

"Oh yes," Rin said, forcing a devious smile that she had seen on other yuki onna.

They nodded in approval before stepping aside to let her in. Rin swallowed past the lump in her throat and stepped inside. The Queen had her back to her, her gaze fixed on the map in front of her.

"What is it?" she asked without looking up at Rin. This was perfect, with the queen distracted, she could strike before she knew what was happening.

"We've captured the spy, my queen," Rin said inching closer to her. She had only one chance, and she didn't want to miss her shot.

"Good, and did they reveal any of their plans?" The queen shifted the maps on her table.

"They did." Rin could reach out and touch her; she raised her hand, the fox flames burning bright in her palm.

The Queen turned, her brows raised, and then transformed quickly. Rin reached for her, slamming her foxfire into her chest. The yuki onna queen screamed as the flames caught and spread across her body. Rin attempted to back away and let her burn, but she grasped her by the neck. The yuki onna opened her jaw, revealing rows of sharp jagged teeth. Rin struggled to free herself, clamping a flaming hand on her arm, but she wouldn't loosen her grip.

"I'll suck the marrow from your bones—" the yuki onna queen hissed before she leaned down to clamp on Rin's neck.

With both hands engulfed in fox fire, Rin grasped the sides of the yuki onna's head. The fire spread hot and fast, but the queen wouldn't let go. The queen was drawing out Rin's energy, weakening her even as the flames burned and bubbled her skin. They were trapped in a game of tug of war, as Rin's flames weakened the queen, her absorbing Rin's energy renewed her depleting stores.

The world around her was a swirl of blood and flames as she wrestled against the yuki onna queen. The edges of her vision were going dark. Her flame had consumed all of the yuki onna's body now, and her fingers on Rin's neck loosened. Rin collapsed onto the ground as the yuki onna queen melted into a puddle. All that remained of her was a soaked kimono. She'd done it, but now she had to give Kaito the signal. Rin stood, and her legs buckled beneath her. She shook her head and tried to call her fire, but all she could manage were a few meager sparks.

The guards were rushing in. She had to give the signal, or all of this would be for nothing. Gathering the last of her strength, she focused it on her fox fire. She unleashed it upward, it burst through the ice roof of the queen's tent and flashed against the sky. She prayed it would be enough.

Kaito watched the sky as Shin paced behind him nervously. Akane had to have gotten through to the tengu. He refused to believe anything else. Hours had passed, and there was no news. The army was on high alert, all they waited for was the signal that the yuki onna queen was dead.

"It's been a while, hasn't it?" Shin asked, his pacing had worn a pathway into the snow.

Night was closing in, and it was getting even harder to see in the storm. Would Rin's fox fire be strong enough to be seen given the weather? If they missed it, Rin might be captured or worse. He hated putting his friends in danger like this. If the signal didn't come through soon, he would rush in himself. Blue flashed against the white of the snow fall. It was faint, but that had to be it.

"She's done it!" Shin tilted his head back and howled.

"Attack," Kaito shouted to his soldiers.

They roared as they rushed forward into the storm. Even as they approached, the storm was getting weaker. The yuki onna must have realized that their leader had fallen and were abandoning their posts already. As his soldiers crested the snowdrifts on the fringes of the camp, the yuki onna rose up out of the snow. Their song both beautiful and terrifying.

The two forces clashed together. They were outnumbered, and the yuki onna's power was too strong. The soldiers slowed in their steps, captivated by the yuki onna's song before they fell upon them.

"Block your ears," Kaito shouted.

His voice was swallowed up by their song. Some of them heard Kaito and followed him as he cut his way through. The yuki onna's song floated on the wind, and Kaito felt the pull of its lure. But through pure force of will, he kept moving forward, slashing at the yuki onna who crossed his path. His soldiers fell around him, drained of their spiritual energy, and left discarded in the snow. There was no time to mourn.

Rin's pained howl ripped through the air, the storm was all but gone now, and he took his dragon form and flew up into the sky. Rin stood in the center of a ring of yuki onna. Blood ran from a wound at her neck and soaked her haori. Kaito dived down next to her, and the yuki onna jumped backward as he landed in a spray of snow.

"Just in time," Rin said, her eyes were heavy, and he could sense she'd lost too much spiritual energy.

He assumed the yuki onna would scatter once their leader was gone, but it seemed half the camp had surrounded them. He hacked at them with his sword, but for every one that fell, two more were there to take their places.

Down the hill from him, Shin in his white wolf form was tearing through yuki onna, inching closer and closer to them. Once he got to them, they could crush the yuki onna between them. Rin slumped forward in the snow, the cold and exhaustion finally getting the better of her. Kaito knelt down and helped her to stand, her head was lolling to the side.

"Leave me, go and protect..." Her eyes fluttered closed.

Kaito circled in place, holding Rin tight. The yuki onna closed in, their song ringing in his ears. Beyond the yuki onna swarming, he saw Shin slowing to a stop as five yuki onna sang to him. They'd lost. The yuki onna grabbed at him, tugging at his clothes, and he couldn't stop them. His body was no longer his to control, he'd given over to their control. Maybe dying wasn't so bad if it were at the hands of beautiful yuki onna.

A horn blasted overhead, and it shook him from the spell. Kaito looked up as a sea of black wings swooped down from above. The tengu had arrived to give them reinforcements. Seeing the tengu army descending on them from above, many of the yuki onna turned and fled. Kaito wasn't the only one who'd broken free of the spell, Shin came barreling toward him, having knocked out the yuki onna who tried to subdue him. Between the two of them, they knocked out the remaining yuki onna. And the tengu cleaned up the rest.

Many had escaped, but a few had been taken prisoner and were being led to the tengu compound, their fate to be decided by the Tengu Elder.

Kaito carried Rin to the tengu compound. As soon as he was through the gate, Hikaru was rushing over to them, Hikaru took her into his arms, caressing her cheek.

"She'll be fine with rest," Kaito said to him.

Rin's eyes fluttered open, and she reached out to touch Hikaru's face. "We did it." Rin smiled wanly.

It was such an intimate gesture, he couldn't help but feel he was invading on something private. Kaito turned away from the pair, across the courtyard, Akane threw herself into Shin's arms. He twirled her around as he kissed her. He couldn't help but feel envious of the joyful reunions, and it led his thoughts back to Suzume. He'd been so focused on breaking the siege, he had not even stopped to say goodbye or explain what had happened between him and Kazue. The victory of battle faded as he thought about the things that hadn't been said. He never should have left that way or even given her any room to doubt.

"We are indebted to you for your help today," Mori said, he bowed his head.

"You would have done the same for me, old friend." They embraced.

Before his fall, Mori had been one of his most trusted advisers, and he hoped they could resume their alliance soon. But right now, there was only one reunion he wanted.

"Come, we shall drink and talk of the future of our two kingdoms," Mori gestured for him to join him in the inner ring of the palace.

"Soon, my friend. But there's something I need to do first. "

Kaito transformed and took off to the sky. He had a long overdue apology to give Suzume.

Twenty-Nine

Another blast shook the walls, and pieces of the ceiling came crumbling down. Suzume threw up her arms to shield herself from the falling debris as she ran; yokai were running in all directions. Panic on the air made her skin prickle. But the yokai were too concerned with saving themselves to pay any attention to her and Tsuki trying to flee. He led her to a stone stairway that she'd never seen before.

"This way," he said. The sun was starting to set, and it turned the sky crimson and orange. Against the dying light of day, she could see the hybrids gathering on the opposite shore. If only there was some way they could stop them, but what could she do on her own?

The pathway hugged the side of the rocks that the palace was built upon. And it was slippery from waves that crashed over them periodically. It was a mistake to look over the edge and see the white foam that sprayed over the jagged rocks at the bottom. Suzume clutched the slick rocks, her legs trembling.

"We're almost there." Tsuki held out his hand to her.

She'd been in such a panic thinking that the palace was under attack, she'd just been moving forward blindly. But things were starting to fall into place. Tsuki and Akira had told her that Kazue forced them to work for her, she hadn't wanted to listen because she was so angry at what she had seen as their betrayal. But maybe she'd been wrong about them after all. They had come to save her when they just as easily could have escaped with their own lives or used the chaos to turn on her.

She grasped Tsuki's hand, and he guided her the rest of the way down the steps. At the bottom was a small sailboat that bobbed on the waves.

"Where's Naoki, I thought he'd be here with Souta?" Suzume asked.

"They escaped a different way, the boat won't hold us all," Akira said using Tsuki's face.

Suzume glanced back to the palace. Maybe they should go back, just to be sure they'd gotten away safely. A flaming ball arched across the sky and landed on the roof of a nearby building. It spread quickly, and the screams of panicked yokai filled the air. Even if she went back to check, there was no guarantee she would get out alive. She had to just trust Naoki could save Souta.

Suzume got into the boat, which swayed with each step. She threw out her arms to balance her. There was a single seat on the prow and room for someone to man the sails. Suzume curled up into a ball and sat down as Tsuki took control of the sail. The rope tying them to the dock was undone, and after a little maneuver, they were out onto open waters. Tsuki unfurled the sail and they glided away from the palace.

On the water she felt vulnerable, and exposed. The shore was lined with hybrids and war machines. Torches glowed against the growing night. Surely they would see them and sink them. She couldn't swim, and even if they could get to a shore, neither one was safe. As she looked back at the sea palace, it was ablaze. All of Kaito's hard work to rebuild what he had lost was going up in smoke.

They sailed past the palace and far enough from the coastline that they couldn't be seen. Suzume wasn't sure how much time had passed by the time they came to shore in a small cove. The sounds of the fighting had faded away. As they disembarked on the pebble cove beach. Suzume's skin prickled. She drew her staff.

"Do you feel that?" Suzume asked.

Tsuki had his blade drawn as well. "Yeah."

"This was supposed to be the meeting point, right?"

"It is, but it's possible they were followed." Tsuki took the lead up a worn dirt path from the cove to a cliff overlooking them.

Souta shouted, and Suzume picked up her pace. A group of yokai had Souta surrounded. He sliced toward them with his wind shoving them back. But it only slowed them for a moment. They needed to resonate, she tried to reach out and create the connection with him, but as she did, a pair of hybrids turned on her and came roaring toward her. She had to abandon making the connection, as she instead swung her staff at the head of the hybrid. Her staff struck solid flesh, and it kept on coming. She backed up but found only a cliffside. She braced for impact, but before the mangled fist of the hybrid could strike her, it was severed from its arm.

It waved its bloody stump at her, spraying her in blood. Suzume jutted the butt of her staff against its gut, and it doubled over. Tsuki sunk his blade into the back of the monster, and it slumped over on the ground next to another hybrid Tsuki had killed.

"That was close," she panted.

"You can say that again." He smiled at her.

It felt like old times again. But there wasn't time for reminiscing. The hybrids had escaped and taken Souta along with them. Suzume ran into the forest, but there wasn't a sign of them anywhere. It was as if they'd evaporated into thin air.

She spun around in a circle clutching her staff. This had to be Hisato, he'd taken Souta through a portal. But where did he take him?

Tsuki jogged over to her. "Did you find them?"

She shook her head. "They took them. But where is Naoki, he was supposed to be guarding Souta."

Tsuki scanned the forest. "I don't sense his spiritual energy nearby. Maybe they got separated?"

Or worse. She didn't want to even consider it. Naoki had always seemed so invincible. She couldn't imagine him falling so easy to a few hybrids.

"Maybe we should wait for him and then make a plan to find Souta."

"If Hisato has him, we're running out of time," Akira said, taking control of their body. "He was using Kazue to make these hybrids, and he'll want to use Souta for the same. The longer we wait, the more people will be in danger."

Suzume frowned. She had a point. She'd seen what had been done to that village, and the destruction that the hybrids had brought to the seaside palace. There was no more time to hesitate.

"But how do we find him?"

"I think I know where he might be, they wouldn't have gone too far. They're likely at the temple you saved us from."

It was their best shot, maybe their only one, and she would have to take it.

GUILT WAS GNAWING AWAY AT TSUKI. WHEN HE HAD AGREED TO HELP Kazue, he'd only been thinking about how Suzume had turned on them. But as they led her like an animal to slaughter to Kazue, he was beginning to have second doubts. As much as he wanted to be separated from Akira, was this price really worth it?

"We can't second guess ourselves now. This is life and death now," Akira said.

"A life for two lives, is that what you're saying? What about Father and Souta who we abandoned in the seaside palace," Tsuki countered.

"What did he ever do for us? While Mother slowly wasted away on that mountain top, where was he?"

That was always her argument, wasn't it? Even once they'd reconnected with their only living family, the resentment remained. Their mother, Sayuri, goddess of the moon, had fallen in love with a man beneath her station. Her guard, Naoki. When her husband, the Lord of the Sun, found out, she was banished to a mountain temple where her light slowly faded. She gave birth to them in secret, and on that mountain they remained, until Mother's health took a turn for the worse, and they were forced to search out alternative energy sources just to keep her alive. Their greed grew too great, and that was how Kazue was able to trap them. They'd been desperate enough to take a risk, and now they were making that same mistake all over again, only this time it was their lives on the line.

How many more people would die, how many more lives would be ruined because of them.

"Once we are free, you will feel differently," Akira said.

Tsuki didn't bother to respond, he wouldn't argue with her, the damage was already done. They'd done as Kazue asked, and lured Suzume back to the temple. He couldn't save her, not without risking his own life. And as noble as he wanted to be, his desire to live was stronger than his distaste for his task.

The temple wasn't much further; they would be there before the moon was high in the sky. Soon it would all be over, and then they could restart their lives.

Suzume fell back to walk beside them and cleared her throat, "I didn't get to say anything earlier, but thank you for your help back there. Actually, I've never really thanked you for all the help you've given me since we first met. I was wrong to assume you would betray me, I'm sorry."

His eyes were wide as he blinked at her. Was this another one of Kazue's tricks. Cause surely Suzume hadn't just thanked and apologized to them...

"You don't need to thank me," Akira said smoothly.

"She really shouldn't since we're about to betray her," Tsuki remarked.

"I do. We're friends, and I should have trusted you when you told me why you did what you did." She met their gaze. It was painfully sincere.

He couldn't do this. They couldn't turn on her.

"Don't," Akira reminded him.

"When this all is over, I'll make sure I separate the both of you no matter what," she said.

His stomach twisted. He had to warn her, but Akira held him back, suppressing his ability to talk. This was wrong. There had to be another option, they could all run away together, find a way to fight Kazue together.

"You're very kind to say that," Akira put a hand on Suzume's shoulder and squeezed. "Looks like we're here."

The temple glowed in the moonlight, even from a distance, Tsuki could feel Kazue's energy.

"This is it," Suzume said. "I can feel Kazue's energy. It's calling to me."

She took a step toward the temple as in a trance. He had to stop her.

"Su—" Tsuki tried to call out to him, but his words were strangled in his throat.

Suzume hadn't seemed to hear him anyway, she kept walking toward the temple. The pieces of Kazue's soul were calling out to one another. He felt it humming in his own veins through the dissonance Kazue had corrupted them with.

"You will not ruin this for us," Akira said.

He couldn't stand by and let this happen, no he refused to let this happen. Tsuki fought against Akira's control, and she struggled to keep hold of it. They were caught in a tug of war between their dueling sides. The energy between them was fluctuating, and their form shifted chaotically.

"Suzume, run!" Tsuki shouted.

She turned, her gaze clearing. He'd broken the spell. But like a fool, she wasn't running from them but toward them.

The darkness was creeping in around the edges, Kazue's power inside them was growing.

"You fools. You were nearly free," Kazue said, her voice echoing inside his mind.

Her song rose up inside his skull, it tore him apart from the inside out. Piece by piece until there was nothing. The lines blurred between them, and there was no longer Tsuki or Akira, there was just them.

THIRTY

When Suzume got close to the temple, she felt an ache deep in her soul. The part of her that was Kazue cried out, reaching to be united. She'd felt this before when she'd first met other pieces of Kazue's soul. But it was so much more urgent and desperate. This hunger, this aching loneliness that threatened at times to consume her. The unvoiced cry of her soul promised her if she would only reunite Kazue's soul, the pain would go away, and Suzume would be reborn, without pain, without uncertainty, and power beyond her imagining.

Her feet moved of their own volition. Everything else fell away but the temple and finding the source of this soul-deep call. She reached out her hand as if she could grasp the incorporeal voice that called to her without words.

"Suzume, run!" Tsuki's voice jolted her from her trance.

She turned around, he had fallen to his knees, his skin was bubbling and contorting. Their features were a cross between the two, it was a stranger's face who stared at her with black pupiless eyes. The same gaze they'd had the night they'd stolen the staff from her. She drew her staff and rushed toward them, she had to stop the transformation somehow. Flames flickered along her staff as she swung for them.

They caught the edge of her staff and smirked.

"You are too late. They're gone," their voice echoed as if two people spoke at once.

Suzume yanked the staff free and backed away, she didn't have a spell to separate them, and she wouldn't hurt her friends. Tsuki had tried to warn, her but he was too late. They stalked closer to her. She had only one choice; she had to seal them.

"I'm sorry I didn't want to have to do this." Suzume gathered her power, the song was on the tip of her tongue. She'd only ever learned the spell in theory. Ryuu had made her practice it over and over until she could recite it in her sleep. But practice wasn't the same as practical application.

It gathered in her like a firestorm until she was nearly bursting with it. She unleashed the power, and it struck them in the chest. Chains made of fire unraveled from the ball of flame wrapping around them and pinning their arms to their sides. They wrestled against the binding, as Suzume tried to hold the notes of the song, her voice was wavering, and they tugged on the bonds. They were going to break free of it.

She strained to hold on, but it was no use. She would have to let go and make a run for it, head for the forest and regroup, maybe look for Naoki and make a new plan. They snapped through the first chain. She held her breath and let go before bolting for the forest. Their feet were pounding on the ground behind her. Suzume tried running faster. But she'd never been able to beat

Tsuki in a race. They grasped her by the arm, nearly yanking it from her socket as she tumbled to the ground.

She kicked and slammed a flaming hand against his chest. It didn't slow them down, they pinned her arms to her sides and carried her from the forest and toward the temple. There was no breaking free of their grip. It would be better to conserve her energy as she made a new plan. Despite that, flames flickered along her body. Panic rushed through her veins.

They brought her into the temple grounds, and that sensation swept through her again. It was like being swept under the waves of the ocean, but instead of panicking, trying to gasp for breath, she wanted to let it carry her away to a place that had no worries, and no pain. No, she had to fight it whatever this feeling was that wanted to consume her, she couldn't let it.

The temple had a simple shrine, the doors of it open. Souta knelt before the alter his white hair was scraggly and falling into his face. He raised his head as they brought her closer. He had a black eye and a split lip.

"No. She got you too."

They dropped her on the ground beside him, and she crawled closer to him.

"What happened to you?" Suzume asked, her eyes scanning over his wounds.

"Kazue, she controls the hybrids. You were right—" He trailed off, his eyes were blown wide.

Suzume looked over her shoulder to see Kazue standing in the doorway, her eyes glimmered blue.

"No, finish what you were saying." She gestured for Souta to continue.

"I knew you were up to something." Suzume pointed her flaming staff at Kazue.

"Yes, it was just like Hisato told me, you're painfully easy to read, Suzume. So easy to manipulate. It didn't take much to drive you and Kaito apart. Just like the first Kazue." She laughed and shook her head.

"You're not going to get away with this," Suzume said as she took a step closer to her.

The fire was raging inside her now, eager to be unleashed. If she weren't careful, Kazue's flame would consume her, and she would lose herself to the fire.

Kazue tossed her head back as she laughed. "You cannot harm me without hurting yourself."

Suzume flung a ball of fire at Kazue's head, which she dodged.

"Maybe I'm willing to hurt myself to take you down."

Kazue smiled, it was too-wide and crazed, and reminded her of Hisato. "Haven't you realized it yet, Suzume. There is no end to this except with death?"

"You're not going to scare me with that, fight me." She rushed toward Kazue, swinging the staff and bringing it down.

Kazue rolled out of the way and shot a stream of water at her from the jug of water she had at her hip. It extinguished her fire and wreathed Suzume's head in smoke. She didn't need her fire to fight and instead spun and struck at her with the staff. Kazue blocked her attacks, stepping away inch by inch.

"You can feel it, Kazue's soul wants to be reunited," Kazue said.

Suzume ignored her taunts and flung another fireball her way. Kazue blocked it with her water again, before shooting another stream at her. It hit her upside her head and set her off balance, but only for a moment. The fire inside her was starting to grow, the sensation of Kazue's power threatened to overwhelm her, she had to hold back or let it consume her.

"Kazue never meant for us to be united. The longer you spend together, the more you will lose yourself, become a part of her and lose yourself," Kazue said, gesturing to Souta behind her.

Suzume was panting for breath. Holding back her energy was using up more of it than it would to expend it. "What are you suggesting? That we let Hisato transform all of Akatsuki into those monstrosities?" Suzume threw out her arms.

"No. Those are just the beginning, with enough power, we will be able to reform, to make new bodies which will never age, never grow tired. We will fulfill Kazue's dream for all of Akatsuki. Can you not see it? It is beautiful." Her eyes were filled with a manic glow.

"I'll never join you," Suzume said as she rushed toward her, aiming a ball of flame straight for her heart.

The ball fizzled against a wall of water that wrapped around her head and shoved water down her throat. Suzume grasped at her throat as she struggled to breathe. Kazue stalked closer.

"I don't need you Suzume, I just need what belongs to me. Kazue's heart."

She reached for Suzume's chest, and Suzume screamed. It felt as if she were pulling her apart from the inside. Her back arched as everything became nothing but white-hot pain.

Smoke turned the sky to ashen. Kaito didn't want to believe his eyes. Heart in his throat, Kaito landed among the rubble, what remained of his palace. Everything was destroyed, the bodies of the fallen hybrids and yokai lay like broken dolls around him. Suzume. Where was Suzume?

His chest constricted. No. She couldn't be.

He turned over bodies, tossed aside rubble searching for her. Panic rose up in him like the tide. How could this have happened, he had defeated the hybrid camp. Unless Kazue had lied to him. What a fool he'd been. While he was blinded by nostalgia, she had deceived him completely, driven a wedge between him and Suzume...

A groan came from beneath a nearby beam. Kaito rushed to the sound. Naoki had been pinned beneath a wooden beam and rubble. His skin was caked in dust and blood. He shifted the rubble around to lift the beam and helped Naoki out.

"Where is Suzume?" Kaito growled as soon as he was on his feet.

"Not here. I lost her in the chaos, but Tsuki and Akira were with her..."

He had to find her. He refused to believe she had died. It couldn't happen. They searched the wreckage together, discovered a few more survivors, but still no sign of Suzume. The inner ring of the palace was nothing more than a smoldering pile of embers. He made his way through it, spreading out his sense, desperate for the barest hint of life. As he picked his way through the rubble, he caught a glimpse of an ash-covered item.

Kaito pulled it out of the ashes. It was the jade comb he had given Suzume. He clenched it tight enough to break the skin. He left the wreckage of the palace behind and found Naoki, where he had gathered the survivors together.

"Anything?" Kaito asked, half dreading the answer.

"Nothing but this yokai thinks he saw something." Naoki nodded toward the itachi, who was covered in grime.

"What did you see?" Kaito asked.

"I saw the priestess get in a small sailboat with that shifter, they looked like they were headed northwest along the coast. But I could be wrong, it was chaos then." He rubbed his head with a paw.

It wasn't much of a lead. But it filled him with hope. If she had gotten out of the palace alive, then perhaps she had landed somewhere safely. Kaito transformed into a dragon and took to the sky. He would find her, even if he had to turn the entire island upside down to do so.

Thirty-One

Suzume's entire body burned. It felt as if Kazue was raking her body over with hot coals. She had become nothing but pain and a growing fire so strong she feared it would burst from her and incinerate her entire body. Kazue didn't want to just kill her, she wanted to tear her soul apart. She would never reincarnate her soul; she would simply cease to be. Despite her fear of oblivion, she welcomed the escape of death, anything to be freed of this pain.

A whoosh filled her ears, and the pain eased. The crushing pressure in her chest was gone. Suzume opened her eyes to the starless sky, soaked and trembling. Wind whipped around her and stung her eyes. Even the twitch of her finger ached. Souta stood arms outstretched; a wall of wind separated them from Kazue.

"I cannot hold this for long; she drained me of nearly all of my spiritual energy," he said, a vein popped on his forehead, and his neck was strained with the effort.

Suzume stood up on trembling legs. Souta looked ready to collapse, and she felt as weak as a newborn fawn. What could she do against Kazue, she was too powerful. Kazue's water broke through the wall of wind, and sprays of droplets splashed on her skin. It was only a matter of time before she broke through and finished ripping her heart from her chest.

"Suzume, you need to resonate with me," Souta shouted.

The rush of water thundered in her ears. Kazue was gathering a tsunami size wave, that was building and cresting over their heads. They should run, save their own lives.

"We need to run, come on." She grabbed onto Souta's arm, trying to tug them away.

"We cannot escape her. The only choice is for you to take hold of Kazue's power within you as we resonate."

She couldn't; the last time she had taken hold of Kazue's power, she had nearly killed Kaito in the process. And how much more could Souta possibly give without harming himself? She wouldn't risk harming him. She couldn't do it.

Souta's knees buckled, and he fell to the ground. The wind was dying down, a downpour dumped upon them. Kazue's wave loomed over them; it would crash upon them any moment.

"Suzume, you have to, or we both die."

The water came thundering toward them. She said she was done running away, but here she was still too afraid of the power within her. Suzume closed her eyes and reached Kazue's flame within her. Her heartbeat was a flickering flame that grew into a blaze. She was made of a wildfire that's only goal was to destroy. Her reason was slipping away; Kazue's fire would burn away the girl who was Suzume and let her be reborn in flame.

A blast of Souta's wind energy filled her, stabilizing the fire, balancing out the destruction within her. This power was hers, and she would use it to destroy Kazue.

The wave fell upon them, and Suzume threw out her arms, creating a shimmering barrier. The water rushed over the barrier, and for a few moments, they were underwater. Suzume had never felt more alive, more powerful in her life. She had captured the flame; it no longer burned along her skin but hummed in her veins.

The wave receded and revealed Kazue standing on the other side of her barrier, there was a bemused expression on her face.

"You're wasting your time with all of this," Kazue said with a shake of her head.

"I'm not going to let you win, even if it kills me," Suzume countered.

The flames burst from her, reaching out of the barrier and shot at Kazue, wrapping her up in fire. Kazue screamed as the flames caught on her hair and clothes. With a wave of her hand, she extinguished the flames with her water. But Suzume was already outside her barrier, staff twirling before her in an arc of fire.

Kazue backed away as she shot funnels of water at Suzume, which she dodged. She was closing the gap between them and pushing Kazue's back against the wall. One more strike, and this would all be over.

A blow struck Suzume from behind, and pain seared through her arm. The puppet of Tsuki and Akira swung their sword at her head, and she ducked to avoid losing it.

Suzume backed up to get the two opponents in her sights. She didn't want to hurt Tsuki and Akira, she knew they were inside this thing somewhere. But she couldn't fight them both at once.

"You really are a fool, Suzume. You have the power in you to destroy them, and yet you hesitate." Kazue laughed.

"Unlike you, I care about my friends," Suzume said.

Kazue threw her head back and laughed even harder. "Is that what you think, what about Souta? Aren't you curious why you can control Kazue's flame now?"

Suzume chanced a quick glance back toward Souta, he was lying motionless on the ground. He had expended too much energy and exhausted himself, hadn't he?

"Let me tell you something, Suzume. You can never defeat Hisato, not unless you're willing to sacrifice. Not unless you're willing to kill everyone who shares Kazue's soul with you and take that power for yourself."

Suzume shook her head. No, it wasn't possible. She was lying to her; she had to be. They'd learned to resonate together. The power could be shared.

"I don't believe you," Suzume snarled back as she raised a ball of flame and flung it at Kazue.

Kazue knocked it aside, not with water but with a black shield. Ebony smoke curled around her hand. Kazue had taken on Hisato's dark energy, that was what had made her stronger.

"You had a chance to take his power, to spare them all. But your greed will be your downfall." She held out her hand, and a midnight blade materialized there.

She rushed toward Suzume, slashing at her. The tip of the blade caught her cheek, and where it cut, it burned spreading outward. Suzume surged for her, gathering as much of her energy into a single strike as she could. Kazue attempted to dodge, but she caught her with her flames, and wrapped them around her.

Kazue screamed as the fire caught her once more, but Tsuki and Akira were rushing for her again. Suzume blocked them with the staff, looking into the bottomless, black eyes of those who had been her friends.

"I know you're still in there, I know you don't want to do this."

"You don't know us at all." They shoved her backward.

She lost her footing, and Kazue, free of Suzume's flames again, pinned her between the two of them.

"I'm sorry for this," Suzume said to Tsuki and Akita as she unleashed the flames; it exploded from her, sending the two of them flying backward and singeing the ground around her.

She had felt Kazue's pain numbly before; this time, it rippled through her as a painful echo encompassing her entire body. And she kept moving forward, despite the burns that were blistering and burning her. Tsuki and Akira got to their feet once more, their clothes smoking and blisters on their face from their burns.

Kazue was on all fours, her skin red and burned. She looked at Suzume through a sunken hollow gaze. "This is not the end."

"Yes, it is!" Suzume charged once more.

Just as she was about to reach her, Akira and Tsuki picked Kazue up, cradling her in their arms as one would a child. One of

Hisato's portals opened behind them, and they carried Kazue through it. Suzume reached, trying to follow, but it closed up before she could get through.

Suzume's knees gave out beneath her, and she fell to the ground. She grasped a handful of dirt and clenched it into her fist. She had been so close this time. Kazue's taunts continued to ring in her ears. Embracing her inner flame had made her stronger, but it still hurt to attack Kazue. And when she faced Hisato next, he would have Kazue on his side. How could they defeat him without the united force of all the soul pieces? Would she, Hikaru, and Souta be enough?

Souta. Suzume scrambled to her feet and rushed over to where Souta was lying. His expression was relaxed, as if he had fallen asleep. His chest wasn't rising and falling. He wasn't moving.

No. She hadn't.

With a shaking hand, she reached for him. His skin was still warm. "Souta, wake up."

She shook him lightly, and his head lolled back and forth. Nothing about him stirred.

Suzume stood and stumbled away. He couldn't be dead. She had killed him. Her throat was tight as she took a shaking breath. Souta couldn't be dead. They'd resonated so many times before. Why now?

Hands grasped her from behind, and she spun to see Kaito.

"Thank the eight you're alive." Kaito enveloped her into his embrace.

She tangled her hands in his shirt. Never before had she been more grateful to see him. She wanted to wake up in his futon and find this was all a bad dream. Tears were pouring down her face, she couldn't stop them from falling.

"Are you hurt, where?" Kaito asked.

"Souta he's—" She choked on the words, she couldn't admit what she had done. Would he hate her for it?

Kaito looked to Souta's motionless body.

"Don't worry, we'll catch Kazue. I should have listened to you. I should have—"

"No. It wasn't Kazue." She inhaled shakily. No more running away. She had to face what she had done. "I killed Souta."

THIRTY-TWO

Ryuu arrived at the minister of religion's home just after twilight. It was an expansive home surrounded by gardens with fruit trees, ponds bursting with koi and manicured shrubs. Standing in the garden, waiting for the servant to announce his arrival, he felt as if he had been transported back in time. Decades ago, he had all but removed himself from the politics of court life. Though he maintained connections with the most powerful families. None of them knew his real identity and therefore only saw him as a high ranking priest, with connections. It opened doors to him, but he would need more than a few open doors to remove the emperor from his throne.

The servant came down the steps from the house. "My master is ready to greet you," he said.

He led Ryuu up the stairs and into the main part of the house. The sliding paper screen doors were closed, and long shadows of the minister of religions other guests could be seen through them. When Ryuu had first reached out to the minister of religion requesting a gathering, he had expected a few other powerful ministers. Judging from the number of voices coming from that room, he had invited half the council to dinner. Ryuu supposed it shouldn't have surprised him that so many influential men at court wanted to see the emperor removed from power. An insane ruler was bad for the entirety of Akatsuki, and they must only see what the emperor was doing as madness.

The servant opened the door, and Ryuu entered. The ministers were gathered around drinking sake and chatting pleasantly. Ryuu's gaze skimmed over them and fixed on Izume, who was plucking at the strings of a Shamisen. Izume wouldn't look at him. Her eyes were directed downward, the picture of a demure woman. She was good at making herself unassuming, many men had fallen for her fake innocence. But what he wanted to know was what she was doing here? The ministers he had contacted had been carefully curated because they were not in her web.

The minister of religion stood and bowed to greet him. "Thank you for coming, we've been eagerly awaiting your arrival."

Ryuu tore his gaze away from Izume and bowed to the minister of religion.

The minister of religion gestured for Ryuu to sit beside him. As he went to his seat, he bobbed his head to greet the other ministers and high ranking government officials who'd joined them for dinner. They all watched him with hungry gazes. At court, everyone was looking to advance their place, the right connection could catapult your career. Ryuu's quick rise to power in the white temple had led to speculation as to how he had done it. He'd heard all sorts of rumors, that he had saved the life of a minister, that he was the bastard son of the now-deceased emperor. Because they thought they could gain something from him, they desired him. But if they knew he wasn't entirely human, they would be quick to turn on him. He'd made that mistake enough times to never make it again.

It disgusted him to think about handing over the crown prince to their jackals. But he couldn't allow the emperor to continue on this mad quest against the yokai either. It would only destroy Akatsuki from within and leave them vulnerable to the mainland, whose power only grew with each passing decade.

Izume played a soft tune. A few glanced in her direction, though none seemed willing to acknowledge the emperor's favored concubine was in their midst. Servants presented glazed fish, minced venison and sautéed vegetables, miso soup, and steaming bowls of rice. He had no appetite, but he picked up his chopsticks and pretended to eat just the same. Conversation flowed around him as he resisted the urge to look at Izume. She must know what he had come here for and was trying to stay one step ahead of him. Or she was simply here to taunt him in the same way she had flaunted her control of the emperor over him.

"I have a question for you," said the minister of education as he twirled his long white beard between his fingers. "What does the temple have to say about the auspicious stars in the sky?"

Despite tonight's intentions, the ministers were too careful to ask questions straight out. Say the wrong thing to the wrong ear, and they'd be executed for treason. The White Temple had power, and soldiers that Ryuu commanded. If he were to give his support to removing the emperor, it would give these ministers the confidence to put their own voices toward the emperor's early retirement.

"We are seeing a new star burning in the sky. A new age is imminent, I believe."

There were pleased smiles all around as they shared glasses of sake. He looked up, and Izume was looking at him, her expression was difficult to discern. Normally he could read her like a book, but tonight it was as if she were wearing a mask.

"The empress and crown prince have been gone for quite some time, perhaps it is time they returned to the palace," Ryuu said to the minister of religion as he refilled his glass.

The minister of religion shifted in his seat, folding and unfolding his arms. "The empress must stay away for her health, and the crown prince is a filial son who wishes to stay with his mother."

Ryuu frowned. He thought they were in agreement? Why the hesitation. The empress's family was rich and powerful, many high ranking officials were her brothers, uncles and other extended family members.

"The emperor seems weighed down by worries as of late. With such a great burden upon him, I thought it would be time for the Crown Prince to take on some of his father's responsibilities," Ryuu said.

The men around the table avoided his gaze. The music stopped, and Izume rose to stand. All those gathered turned to look at her. There was such a regal carriage to her stance that no one could escape the allure of her charms.

"It is true the emperor's thoughts are often troubled as of late." She sighed heavily, her eyes downcast. "I have thought the same as Ryuu, that if only the emperor could lay down some of his burdens... But he worries about who will be fit to rule in his place. The crown prince, while a filial son, is tender of heart and not suited for these troubling times. "

The ministers all nodded their heads.

"Yes, he was always more studious than a swordsman," said the minister of education.

Ryuu narrowed his eyes and watched Izume. What game was she playing here?

"If the crown prince is not suited for the role, perhaps one of the emperor's younger sons should rule," suggested the minister of religion.

There were murmurs of agreement.

"The crown prince may not be a warrior, but more than anything, we need a leader who will lead us with wisdom. What are generals if not the sword of the kingdom?"

"Is it truly enough, when the mainland builds ships and conquers more and more of their neighboring countries, forcing them to pay them taxes?" Izume countered.

"The crown prince has been groomed for his position his entire life. If we were to put any of the other princes on the throne at such a delicate time, we would be even more vulnerable," Ryuu countered.

The minister of religion cleared his throat, and Ryuu frowned at him.

"What about your son, Izume," said the minister of education. "He has always excelled in his studies of past emperors, and political reasoning."

"And he is skilled with a blade," added the minister of religion.

"My son?" Izume's hand fluttered up to her lips in mock surprise. "I'm not sure..."

"If you were to try and put the prince on the throne, you would risk civil war. The crown prince has many who support him," Ryuu said with a meaningful look to Izume. She might have outmaneuvered him in winning the ministers to her side, but he would not let her take the throne as well.

Izume laughed. "I would never dream of such a thing. It is the emperor's choice who will take the throne following him after all."

She thought she had the emperor wrapped around her finger. That simply exiling the empress and her sons was enough to secure her son's throne. But this would only be the beginning. He'd seen how this played out too many times before. Power corrupted, and power in the hands of a young man who'd just barely become a man, was too dangerous to be risked. But he could also recognize when he had lost a battle.

When dinner was finished, Ryuu excused himself and headed through the garden. It was his mistake to underestimate Izume's abilities. Now that she was favored by the emperor, she would only become stronger. It would lead to her ruin, partnering with Hisato, risking civil war for her own ambitions. He couldn't stand to watch her self-destruction anymore.

"Leaving already?" Izume's seductive tone caressed his ear.

He spun around, putting the appropriate amount of space between them. She was overconfident to approach him in public this way.

"The emperor's favor is making you bold, don't you fear the rumors?" he asked.

Hurt flashed across her face, for the blink of an eye. If he hadn't known her as well as he did, he might not have even noticed. Her mask was so quickly replaced.

"Would you believe me if I told you I don't care what they say about us?"

"I know you too well to believe that. What do you want?"

She took a step closer to him, and the wind carried the scent of her perfume to him. It was always his favorite, and when she left his bed, the saddest moment was when that scent faded. Because that's how it always was with them, she wanted him when it suited her, and then left him when he was no longer convenient.

"You broke your promise to me."

Was this some sort of trick, what promise had he broken?

"I don't know what you're talking about."

Drunken laughter came from the house. One of the ministers must be leaving. She looked over her shoulder, was she nervous about being caught after all?

"You swore to protect Suzume, but you left her alone, and she nearly died," she said, there was genuine fear in her eyes.

Panic clenched his chest, had the neko not gotten to Suzume in time. Had she been hurt? Or was this another one of Izume's lies, a way to get him out of the palace and out of her way to the throne.

"You better not be lying to me," he said.

She slapped him hard against the face. It was unexpected. She had never struck him before.

"Think what you like, but know this, I would do anything for my children. If you cannot keep your promise, tell me now, and I will find someone who can." She was breathing heavily, her gaze burning in a way he'd never seen before.

This wasn't her usual deception. Suzume must really have been in danger. He thought Souta could protect her in his absence, he thought that he was doing something for the greater good.

"Where is she?" asked Ryuu.

She searched his face, and for a moment, he saw a glimpse of the woman he had loved before. "She's with the dragon, they were seen heading to the tengu mountain where his allies are gathered."

A billion questions were burning in his mind. How did Izume know that? What had happened to Suzume? But those questions would have to wait.

He turned to leave, and she grasped his arm. "Swear to me you will keep her safe."

"I never broke my promise to you."

They held for a moment, trapped in time to the people they had been before the lies and betrayal tore them apart. The voices of the party guests were getting closer, and Izume let him go and disappeared into the dark garden.

He could chase after her, demand answers. But knowing Izume, it wouldn't make any difference anyway. She revealed only what she wished.

THIRTY-THREE

Kaito burned Souta's body. It would have been better if they'd had a ceremony, said some words. But he didn't know what to say. After Suzume confessed to killing Souta, she hadn't spoken a word. Her vacant eyes just stared out at the ocean. So he had taken care of the body. He touched her shoulder to let her know it was time to go, and her skin was feverish, and her eyes were glassy. He flew her back to the tengu palace. There was no other safe place for them now. The seaside palace was gone. His subjects scattered.

Even passing through flurries of snow, Suzume sweated enough to soak her clothes. This wasn't a normal fever, and he didn't know how to help her. He touched down in the tengu palace and was greeted straight away by Mori and his guards.

"She's not well, do you have a healer? Anyone who can see to her?" Kaito asked him.

"A human? Our healers wouldn't know the first thing to do." Mori shook his head.

"Then give me a room at least," Kaito said, biting back his impatience.

Human bodies were so fragile, and he'd never felt more powerless than in this moment. As he held Suzume tight, he felt the power that thrummed through her. He wasn't sure how she had killed Souta, but he knew whatever had happened in that battle had left her changed.

Mori showed him to a private suite of rooms where he laid Suzume on a futon. She wasn't responsive, groaning as she rolled around, muttering under her breath. He left the windows open to let the winter air graze against her skin. But what if she froze to death? Kaito paced back and forth, uncertain of what to do.

There was a knock at the door, and he rushed to answer it. Perhaps they'd found a healer after all. He opened it to find Hikaru.

"I heard Suzume was ill?" he said.

Kaito showed him to her bedside. Hikaru knelt beside her, touched her forehead, and recoiled. "She's burning up."

"It's only getting worse, what should we do?" he asked.

"We'll have to keep her as cold as possible and hope the fever breaks on its own."

They gathered up snow, which they bundled in some fabric and put it around her. As soon as it touched her skin, it melted, puddling on the futon. The blankets had to be stripped and started over again. After hours of work, her fever started to go down, and her breathing returned to normal, but she still hadn't woken.

"What now?" Kaito asked.

"We wait and hope for the best," Hikaru said somberly.

Rin woke to her entire body aching. Hikaru lay slumped over at her side, clutching her hand in his. When she stirred, he sat up and rubbed the sleep from his eyes.

"You're awake? How are you feeling? Do you want me to get you something to eat?"

Her stomach growled in response, and Hikaru laughed. She was ravenous, as if she hadn't eaten in decades.

"Something to eat would be nice." Rin laughed.

"Wait right here." He kissed her on the forehead before he disappeared through a door that connected to the sitting area. As she looked around her, familiars became more familiar, she was in the tengu compound, in the guest rooms. She reached for her neck, a small bump remained where the yuki onna's teeth had sunk into her flesh.

If Kaito hadn't come when he did, she wouldn't be here. And seeing as she was alive and in the tengu palace, they seemed to have won against the yuki onna. The tengu alliance was all but secured now. It was a relief. As soon as she was strong enough, she hoped they could return to the seaside palace.

Hikaru returned with a tray of food and set it beside her. Rin grasped for it, inhaling it all in what felt like a few bites and was still hungry. It would take more than a few mouthfuls to replenish all the energy she'd had stolen from her by the yuki onna. But after eating, she was feeling stronger than before. She wanted to talk with Kaito and start working toward the alliance with the tengu.

"Where is Kaito, I want to talk to him about the alliance," Rin said.

Hikaru's brows furrowed. She knew that look, he wasn't telling her something. "I don't know if that's possible."

"Why not?" Rin asked.

Hikaru tugged at a thread on his sleeve. It must be really serious for him to be fidgeting this much.

"Hikaru, what are you not telling me?"

He sighed heavily and met her gaze. "Souta is dead."

"What? How?" She jumped to her feet and swayed; she was still too weak. Hikaru leaped up and gave her a shoulder to lean on.

"Don't get up. Mori said it will take time until you're at your full strength."

She felt as if her brain were filled with cotton, this couldn't be true. Souta dead? He had a piece of Kazue's soul inside him, how were they going to defeat Hisato without him.

Hikaru guided her to sit and took her hand in his. "While we were on the mountain. They found the last piece of Kazue's soul, but she brought a hybrid army to the seaside palace and destroyed it. Suzume and Souta fought her, but he didn't make it out alive."

She felt dizzy. This couldn't be happening. It had to be a bad dream, after all the things they'd fought for to gain peace among the yokai, to get stronger to defeat Hisato. It was as if someone had come and cleared the board. It was like starting all over from nothing. And what scared her more was if Souta could die, what about Hikaru? She'd lost him once, and it nearly broke her. She couldn't risk losing him again.

"Let's run away," she said.

"We can't, what about defeating Hisato—"

"Souta is dead. The water of Kazue's soul has sided with Hisato, how can we possibly hope to defeat him?" Her hands trembled as she took Hikaru's in hers. He stroked them lovingly.

"I lost you once, I can't do it again," Rin said as tears rolled down her cheek. He pulled her into his embrace, holding her tight.

"I'm not going anywhere, you don't need to worry." She clung to him as if letting go meant she would lose him. And a part of her feared that's exactly what would happen.

AFTER PASSING THROUGH THE TENGU GUARD'S SCRUTINY, RYUU WAS finally allowed into the tengu compound. A message had to be sent up to Kaito, and he feared that the dragon would turn him away. Instead, as he entered the tengu compound, The Dragon came to greet him.

"I'm glad you're here," Kaito said to him.

Ryuu blinked a few times in surprise. Never would he have thought that The Dragon would be happy to see him. There was no time for sentiments.

"Where is Suzume?" Ryuu asked.

The Dragon's face looked drawn, and though yokai were not able to get dark circles under their eyes, his expression was shadowed.

"She's not well," he said.

"Take me to her," Ryuu said with his heart in his throat. He never should have left her behind, and the moment he'd heard about the hybrid attack, he should have returned himself to protect her. When he saw the neko next, he would punish him for his failure to do as he was ordered.

The Dragon brought him to Suzume's room. She lay on her rumpled futon, a sheen of sweat on her forehead. As he got closer, he could feel the wrongness of her energy. It wasn't just flame but wind and fire. No. That fool, he hadn't...

With a trembling hand, Ryuu knelt beside her and pressed his hand to her fevered brow. The energy inside her was chaotic, battling the foreign wind energy as a body fought disease. Souta had fallen similarly ill when he'd first taken on the wind of Kazue's soul. It was the body's way of rejecting a foreign soul. But if Souta's soul piece was inside her, that meant he was gone from this plane.

He'd only been thinking of Suzume's safety; he had never considered the risk to his oldest and closest friend. Ryuu clenched his hand into a fist. He'd been so blinded by his desire to uncover Izume's plot, he'd lost sight of those who were most important to him.

"Can you do anything?" Kaito asked him.

Ryuu turned toward him. A selfish part of him wanted to tell him to leave her to him, blame him for his losses. But there was no one to blame but himself. Even if he wanted to take Suzume and hide her away from the world, The Dragon would upturn it all to reach her. He could see it in his gaze.

"She's taken on Souta's wind energy, and her body is fighting to find resonance within itself," Ryuu said and stood.

Kaito looked incredibly tired, his shoulders sagged. "I need to speak with the Tengu Elder, will you stay by her side?"

It had shocked him; never before did he think Kaito would entrust Suzume to him.

"Why me?"

Kaito eyed him for a few moments. "Because I know you alone will protect her with your life."

His words surprised him, and warmed him more than he thought they would. It was a simple sentiment, but one that spoke volumes. Perhaps there was a chance they could find common ground between them. Though it was early days, this was enough for now.

Thirty-Four

Kaito didn't want to leave Suzume's side, but her condition continued unchanged. And he knew Ryuu would take care of her. The seaside palace might have fallen, but he was still ruler of Akatsuki. And the soldiers who had followed him here to break the siege and who remained at his side, needed him. Now more than ever, securing an alliance with the tengu was crucial.

He went to the audience hall, where the tengu were gathered. The Tengu Elder sat at the head of the room. Mori beside him. Both of their expressions were blank, as he would have expected from the tengu, they never gave anything away.

Kaito bowed low before the Tengu Elder. There was no room for pride here.

"We welcome you Dragon, and thank you for your role in protecting the tengu mountain from the yuki onna," the Elder said.

"Forgive me for not greeting you sooner, an urgent matter came about that I could not delay a moment for," Kaito replied. It was fortunate he had. If he hadn't left when he did, Suzume might have collapsed alone from her fever, or worse.

The Tengu Elder pursed his lips. "Does this urgent business have anything to do with the human woman you brought here?"

"It did, Elder. She is my intended bride."

Murmurs of surprise rippled through the tengu. The Elder shifted in his seat, his black wings twitching behind him.

"Surely this is a joke. A yokai and a human to wed?" the Elder remarked. If he really thought it was a joke, he didn't look very amused to Kaito.

"I came here today to agree upon terms of an alliance," Kaito said, he already knew there would be obstacles against his marrying Suzume. But that didn't concern the Tengu Elder.

"We have never agreed to an alliance, Dragon," the Tengu Elder said, as he threaded his fingers in front of him.

"You would deny me even after my emissary rescued your son, and my army spared all your people from the yuki onna attack?" Kaito's voice was rising, and he had to take a few controlled breaths to stop himself from losing his temper.

"Do you know what is whispered among the yokai about you? They are calling you pretender. Even here removed as we have become, we have heard of the human woman who uses you like her puppet. And now, what do you have but a ragged band of yokai whose allegiances may very well change with the next breeze." The Elder shook his head, and his long white beard swayed back and forth.

Kaito ground his teeth together to prevent himself from saying something that would only make things worse. He exhaled through his nose. When he'd first built his army in preparation to take over Akatsuki, he'd come against similar opposition. People that doubted his strength and his ability to rule.

"You know me, you saw me when I first rose to power. You, Elder, were one of the first to swear your clan to support me. What has changed that you won't put your faith in me again?"

"The world has changed while you slept, Dragon. I have lived a long life and saw many things. I appreciate what you've done for our people, but I have no desire for war. I only want my people to live in peace."

Kaito clenched and unclenched his fist. "The Elder I knew repaid debts in kind. I find it hard to believe you would spit upon everything we've done for you."

"You are mistaken, I may not give you the war you crave. But I will give you and your men who fought for us shelter, and you will be treated as honored guests among the tengu. But I can promise you no more than that."

His loyal soldiers had risked their lives and died for the tengu, and he would have him accept the scraps with a smile. His pride told him to refuse, but then he thought of Suzume sick with the fever, and soldiers who would need to be housed and fed. The palace was gone; there was nowhere else for them to go. He forced himself to bow before stalking out of the audience hall.

Suzume had been sleeping for days. The energy inside her was still chaotic, the clash of Souta's wind energy continued to fan the flames inside her. A sheen of sweat glistened on her brow. He'd removed the sleeping spell from her, but the fever that raged through her body, if not resolved, might destroy her.

Suzume's dreams had been haunted by strange images. People she had never met, but seeing them, she felt as if she had known them her entire life. A White Palace that was both familiar and foreign. And over and over, Ryuu. He wore different clothes, and at times, a different face, but she knew it was him. As the fever abated, she realized that the things she saw were Souta's memories. They were the last lingering traces of a very long life. A part of her never wanted to wake because when she did, he would really be gone, and she would have to face the reality that she had killed him.

When she finally escaped her fever dreams, she was bundled under a blanket in a room that was unfamiliar to her. She had woken in enough strange places that she wasn't even surprised anymore. The window was open onto a snowy garden. Flakes drifted downward and collected on the windowsill.

She felt strange in her own skin. Souta's wind energy whispered through her in harmony with her flame. It felt wrong. How could she live when Souta had died? She climbed up from her futon and walked over to the window, she pressed her hand against the cold glass.

The flames warmed her frigid digits without effort. It was cruel to be given this much power. She'd fully harnessed Kazue's power, but the cost was much too high.

"I'm glad to see you're awake," Ryuu said.

She couldn't look at him, Souta was his friend, and she had killed him.

"You've been unconscious for several days. You should eat to regain your strength."

"Don't bother." Her voice cracked, and her lips were dry.

He put a hand on her shoulder, and she shook it away. She didn't deserve his sympathy or care, not when she was living with Souta's stolen energy coursing through her veins. She never should have tried to take Kazue's flame. Kazue was right, the only way to become stronger was to destroy everyone around her.

"Kaito told me you think you killed Souta, but that isn't true," Ryuu said.

"How could you know, you weren't there." Her voice wobbled.

"I know Souta, if he had to choose between your life and his, he would have chosen yours."

She spun around to face Ryuu.

"Why me, why did I deserve to live and he didn't?" The tears kept falling down her face, she couldn't stop them, and she swiped them away with the back of her hand.

Ryuu sighed. "Souta lived a very long life, hundreds of years longer than any human should because I tried to stop death. I know he had no regrets."

Suzume collapsed to her knees. It didn't feel right, any of it. But she wouldn't squander Souta's sacrifice. His physical form was gone, but as his energy lived inside her, she would hold onto it, and she would use it to destroy Hisato and Kazue, no matter what.

EVEN THOUGH THERE HADN'T BEEN A FUNERAL HELD FOR SOUTA, Suzume wanted her own private one to say goodbye and thank you to him. Bundled in layers, she had left the tengu compound with Kaito. He'd been busy with the soldiers and negotiating with the tengu for their shelter and making plans to rebuild his kingdom, but he agreed to join her without protest. They found a spot that overlooked a valley.

It was a cloudless day, and the snow reflected the sunlight in beams of rainbows. Standing at the edge of the ledge, the wind rustled through her hair. He would have loved it here. The snowcapped mountains dotting the landscape and the horizon that stretched all the way to the sea. A lump formed in her throat. She'd promised herself she wasn't going to cry today.

In such a short time, she'd lost so much. Akira and Tsuki had been corrupted and joined Hisato, Souta was gone and so was the seaside palace. Kaito embraced her from behind, holding her close to his chest. She leaned back into him. They'd lost much, but she'd gained even more.

"I never knew it was going to be this hard," Suzume said.

"Nothing worth fighting for ever is," Kaito replied, squeezing her tighter.

"If I had trusted you, if we hadn't argued—"

"Don't blame yourself. I should have seen through her."

"We were both fools," Suzume said and grabbed his arms to pull him tighter around her.

"We were." He nuzzled against her neck.

Her heart raced, and the wind blew harder. It picked up snow from the ground and tossed it around her in a spiral. A tingle raced over her skin, the wind powers were new, and it would take time to get used to them. But even now, she felt more in control of them than she had when she first discovered her flame power.

Despite that, the future had never felt more uncertain. Would she and Hikaru be strong enough to defeat Kazue and Hisato themselves? Had Kazue been telling the truth when she said that to defeat Hisato, others would die in the process?

"Something on your mind?" Kaito asked.

"I'm scared for the future," she admitted. It felt even more real speaking it out loud.

Kaito turned her around to face him, and spoke to her with both hands on her shoulders.

"No matter where you go, I will be with you. And whatever obstacles you face, I will be with you."

"Are you making a promise?" She laughed. His expression was more solemn than usual.

He captured her lips in a kiss, and when they broke apart, she was a little breathless. "It is my vow to you. I am yours, Suzume. Forever and always."

Don't miss the series finale: The Immortal Vow now available for pre-order. Reserve your copy here. Want to be notified when the

book is released? Join my readers group to get an exclusive short story, SORCERER.

AND THEN THE WHILE YOU WAIT, CHECK OUT MORE FROM THE WORLD of Akatsuki, and find out how Rin and Hikaru met in Kitsune. Get it here or read on for an excerpt from the book!

Acknowledgments

As I write this acknowledgment, I am overwhelmed by gratitude. The seeds that would bloom into the Dragon Saga germinated in high school. Though the final version looks nothing like the story I first envisioned, the earliest themes of elemental magic and a love that stretches across eons and tale of epic proportions remained. This book started out on Wattpad, where it gathered a small cult following of persistent, dedicated readers who spurned me to complete the first draft, which took me two years to write.

This series has been a decade in the making and I must heap praise upon my husband, Drew, whose always supported me as I've struggled with it giving me quiet encouragement and excitement over every story related triumph and comfort in the dark parts of the creative process. I also would be lost without my sounding board and best friend, Nicole, who is and will always be my biggest cheerleader.

This gorgeous edition you're holding in your hands wouldn't be possible without the support of my Kickstarter backers. I never thought I could see my words bound in such a beautiful fashion. Thank you a million times for helping me make my dreams a reality.

Also by Nicolette Andrews

<u>Moonlight Dragon</u>

Empress Ascending (Newsletter Exclusive)

Dragon's Deception

Dragon's Temptation

<u>Thornwood Series</u>

Fairy Ring (Free)

Pricked by Thorns (Free)

Heart of Thorns

Tangled in Thorns

Blood and Thorns

<u>World of Akatsuki</u>

The Dragon Saga

The Priestess and the Dragon (Free)

The Sea Stone

The Song of the Wind

The Fractured Soul

The Immortal Vow

Tales of Akatsuki

Kitsune: A Little Mermaid Retelling (Free)

Yuki: A Snow White Retelling

Okami: A Little Red Riding Hood Retelling

<u>**Diviner's World**</u>

Duchess (Free)

Sorcerer (Free)

Diviner's Prophecy

Diviner's Curse

Diviner's Fate

Princess

<u>**Witch of the Lake Series**</u>

Feast of the Mother

Fate of the Demon

Fall of the Reaper

ABOUT THE AUTHOR

Nicolette is a native San Diegan with a passion for the world of make believe. From a young age, Nicolette was telling stories whether it be writing plays for her friends to act out or making a series of children's books that her mother still likes drag out to embarrass her with in front of company. She still lives in her imagination but in reality she resides in San Diego with her husband, children and a couple cats. She loves reading, attempting arts and crafts, and cooking.

You can visit her at her website: www.nicoletteandrews.com or at these places:

facebook.com/nicandfantasy

x.com/nicandfantasy

instagram.com/nicolette_andrews

amazon.com/author/nicoletteandrews

bookbub.com/authors/nicolette-andrews

goodreads.com/nicolette_andrews

pinterest.com/Nicandfantasy